APACHE AMBUSH

"Trouble," Trey said as he drew the Remington from its boot. "Looks like we've got company."

Juan came to the creek bank with his Sharps and a cartridge pouch and peered into the darkness. "Do you see anything, señor?"

"There they are," Trey whispered.

Juan lifted his head. *"Madre,"* he said hoarsely. "Apaches! There are so many!"

A cry echoed from the slope. One warrior raised his rifle and kicked his pony to a lope. More cries sounded back and forth along the line of Indians as they heeled their mounts into a run.

"Take your time," Trey said. "Only thing that matters is how many of 'em you kill."

The multicolored ponies were now racing down on them at full speed. Trey selected a warrior for his first shot, and when the Apache's chest was in his gunsights he feathered the trigger.

The .50/.70 slammed into his shoulder with an ear-splitting roar.

SANTA FE SHOWDOWN

FREDERIC BEAN

ZEBRA BOOKS
KENSINGTON PUBLISHING CORP.

ZEBRA BOOKS

are published by

Kensington Publishing Corp.
475 Park Avenue South
New York, NY 10016

First Printing: February, 1993

Printed in the United States of America

Chapter One

Elbows resting on the bar, he idled over a nickle glass of beer. Once, he glanced down the bar to watch a man in a split-tail frock coat toss back a shot of sweet-smelling whiskey. He knew good whiskey intimately, though it had been a few years since he'd tasted the best, rolling it across his tongue before he sent it to his gullet. In his present condition he'd barely been able to afford the horseshoe nails to reset the iron on his roan. A handful of coins rested at the bottom of his pocket, the sum total of his wealth. Things hadn't always been this way.

There had been a time when Colonel William Treyble Marsh afforded the best of most everything— the best whiskeys, the finest blooded horses, expensive clothes from top haberdasheries, the prettiest women. That time was long past, swept away by four bloody years of war and the defeat of the Confederacy.

He looked briefly at his reflection in the mirror behind the bar. A haggard face stared back at him, pale gray eyes that told of unspeakable pain, a chiseled face, hardened by worry and doubt and sorrow. It was not the same face he'd seen reflected years earlier, before the war had robbed him of everything except his dignity. He held resolutely to that dignity which had been a part of his training in

5

Richmond before the war. The military institute in Virginia had taught him many things, not the least of which was the military bearing he still wore unconsciously, for it was a part of him now. It would be a part of Trey Marsh until he went to his grave, a circumstance that seemed more imminent, given his recent disposition.

He sipped carefully at the lukewarm beer, savoring its taste when he allowed it to travel down his throat. Countless miles lay ahead of him, miles where there would be no distilled spirits to soothe the agony within his soul. New Mexico Territory was empty land . . . a few adobe pueblos scattered through the mountains until he made Santa Fe. He would share the company of an indifferent blue roan gelding over the miles, an animal with which he conducted conversations now and then, one-sided though they were. Being alone never bothered Trey, for he had learned to rely on no one else when the heat of battle threatened him from all sides. He no longer felt the need for anyone else, now that Marybeth and their son were in their graves back in Galveston.

The man down the bar ordered another whiskey. Trey ran his tongue across his lips, remembering the nectar of good barley, the scent of its vapors. "Damn the luck," he muttered under his breath as he brought the mug of beer to his mouth.

A sound distracted Trey, the scrape of a boot on the boardwalk outside the saloon. Out of old habit he glanced in the mirror to see who was coming through the batwing doors behind him. Instinctively his right hand moved to the edge of the bar to be near the butt of his .44. No one needed to remind Colonel Trey Marsh to watch his flanks, or his backside.

A drummer pushed through the batwings, wiping dust from his suitcoat and trousers, then his derby hat. Trey knew at once that the overfed peddler posed him no threat, for he could read other men like some

6

men read a newspaper. Trey's attention returned to the mug of beer.

"Whiskey," the drummer cried as he approached the bar.

The muscles in Trey's cheeks tightened. It seemed everyone in Tascosa could afford the price of whiskey. Of late Trey had begun long-winded discourse with the blue roan about the uneven distribution of wealth. Across the empty miles from Childress to Tascosa he'd complained about it to the uncaring animal. West of Childress the horse had loosened a shoe, further compounding Trey's financial dilemma, the new nails required worsening the drain on his dwindling resources. Thus he drank a nickle beer while the blacksmith went about his task across from the saloon, knowing the roan needed new irons for the ride to Santa Fe, yet without the money to buy them.

A bartender spilled whiskey into the drummer's glass. A silver coin rattled on the bar, tossed carelessly from the drummer's hand. Sweet vapors reached Trey's nostrils.

"Could I interest you in a game of cards?" The man in the split-tail coat appraised the drummer with a look, offering a grin as his question was asked. Trey watched the gambler's reflection in the mirror. He understood his kind all too well. His grin would be as false as the game he played.

Another swallow of beer crossed Trey's lips. Above the rim of his mug he saw the bulge of a gun inside the gambler's coat.

"What's your game, sir?" the gambler asked when the drummer gave no reply.

"Buttons and fasteners," the drummer answered, bringing the brimming shot glass to his mouth. "I'm not a gambling man."

The gambler's grin faded. He turned back to his drink. "This town ain't fit for a gentleman's

7

pursuits. No sporting men hereabouts and no ladies to share a man's company. Bartender, tell me how much I owe you; then I'll give you the chance to double your money with a single cut of a deck of cards."

The bartender's face darkened. "Hard money, mister," he growled as he corked the bottle in front of the gambler. "You owe me a dollar and four bits. Put the money on the bar and go cut your crooked deck someplace else."

Trey watched the gambler adopt a look of indignation. "I merely offered you a sporting opportunity to double your take, my friend."

The bartender shook his head. "We ain't friends. Now count your money out."

The drummer downed his drink and turned for the doors. The gambler watched him depart before he turned back to the bartender. "Your unfriendly nature has just cost you another customer. Two, in fact, for I was about to buy the button peddler and myself a drink. Your manner is offensive. I'll take my business farther west, to Santa Fe. Here's your lousy dollar, mister. And a good day to you and your empty saloon."

The gambler tossed a silver dollar on the bar and tipped his hat before he wheeled toward the doors.

"You still owe me four bits," the bartender growled. Trey watched the man's hand reach for a shotgun on a shelf below the polished mahogany counter.

The gambler halted midway across the floor. He turned and spread his palms. "Can't you count, my good man? I drank only a pair of drinks in your establishment. At four bits apiece, the total is one dollar."

A short-barreled shotgun appeared in the barkeep's hands. "You emptied three glasses, you pay for three drinks."

8

The gambler glanced sideways at Trey. "You saw the whole thing, stranger. Tell this fool that I ordered just two whiskeys."

Trey turned slowly, pale eyes on the gambler. "You drank three," he said evenly, a hoarse whisper.

The gambler stiffened. "I see you're in cahoots with the barman. By the cut of your worn denims and general downtrodden appearance I'm sure you'll ask for a free drink in exchange for your testimony as soon as I'm gone."

Slowly, casually, Trey let his right hand drop from the bar without taking his eyes from the gambler. "I'll give you some advice," Trey said softly, never changing his flat expression. "If you like that fancy coat the way it is, without any holes in it, then this will be the last time you accuse me of giving anyone false testimony."

The gambler's eyes flickered to Trey's Colt .44, and the nearness of Trey's curled fingers to the gun butt. He swallowed. "I merely asked that you give the barman a truthful accounting of my drinks."

"I did," Trey answered, "and the question damn near got you killed."

The tone of Trey's reply awakened a new understanding of his mistake in the gambler's brain. Now Trey saw fear in the gambler's eyes as he realized the nature of the man he'd involved in the game he tried to play. "Then, three drinks it is," he said. Some of the color left his face as he reached in a pocket for a coin and then brought it quickly to the bar.

The gambler turned to leave. The barman fisted his coin and returned the shotgun to its shelf. Yet something gave the gambler pause . . . he turned to Trey. "It would appear I owe you an apology," he said quietly, walking toward Trey as he spoke. He offered a handshake. "I'm Woodrow Stiles."

Trey ignored the gambler's hand. "I honestly don't care who you are," Trey answered. "I've already learned one thing about you ... that you're an obnoxious son of a bitch. I make it a practice never to shake hands with pimps and card cheats and four-flushers, so you can put that hand away. I won't take it."

A flush crept into the gambler's cheeks. His hand dropped to his side. "I wanted to apologize," he said.

Trey nodded. "You've done it. Now get the hell away from me before I change my mind and decide to put a bullet hole in that fancy Saint Louis coat."

At last the gambler understood he was on dangerous ground. He shook his head and turned for the doors. Trey listened to the sounds of the man's boots as he turned back to his mug of beer.

When the gambler was gone the bartender came toward Trey, and Trey saw a grin on the barman's face. "You've earned yourself a beer on the house," he said, reaching for a clean mug behind the counter.

Trey drained the last of his beer, then pushed away from the bar and started for the batwings.

"Hey, stranger," the barman cried. "I said I'd give you one on the house."

Trey paused just before he shouldered through the swinging doors. "I told the truth. It costs you nothing," he said softly. Trey went out, rattling his spur rowels on the boardwalk before the barman could form a reply.

A gust of hot wind swept down the street as Trey crossed to the blacksmith's shop. His roan stood hipshot, swishing flies in the shade of a thatched ramada beside the smithy's forge.

The blacksmith looked up at Trey's approach. Beads of sweat ran down his muscular arms, forming tiny damp circles in the dust around his boots. "That iron's mighty thin, stranger. I set the right foreleg shoe the best I could. Appears you've put some miles on your roan. Damn good animal ... a little thin, maybe. Any fool can see he's bred to run."

Trey dug in his pocket. A small handful of silver glinted in the sunlight. He counted out the coins for the smithy.

"Hope you ain't got far to ride," the smithy remarked, rattling Trey's money in a calloused palm. "Like I said, that iron is damn thin."

"Santa Fe," Trey replied, examining the roan's right forefoot. The shoe was properly applied, the nails turned through the wall of the hoof before touching the quick.

The blacksmith shook his head. "That's mighty rough country, stranger. In case you ain't heard, there's plenty of Apache troubles out that way, and some folks claim there's a range war brewing down around Lincoln. Some of the big outfits are hirin' paid shootists to protect their herds. Damnedest bunch of hard cases I ever saw have been comin' through Tascosa, headed that way. A man could get himself robbed on the trail to Santa Fe if he ain't careful."

"I'll keep my eyes open," Trey replied quietly, his mind on other things. If the roan lost another shoe in rocky country, he would be walking to Santa Fe.

The blacksmith chuckled dryly. "If a feller can judge a man by his looks, I don't figure you'll have much trouble, stranger. Some gents have a way about 'em . . . I reckon it's the way they walk. Maybe it's the way you've got that gun tied low on your leg. Just thought I'd make mention of it, so you'd ride careful."

"I'm obliged," Trey said, pulling the cinch on his worn, high-backed saddle. The roan grunted unhappily, switching its tail when it felt the girth tighten. Trey loosened the reins from the hitch-rail and stepped in a stirrup. He felt the blacksmith's eyes on him as he swung a leg over the cantle.

"Hold on a minute, stranger," the smithy said. He rummaged in the bottom of a tool box and brought

11

forth a handful of new horseshoe nails. "Put these in your saddlebags. I'd say you're a feller who's down on his luck just now. Should that gelding rattle another shoe loose in the mountains, you'll be in a fix. If you ain't got a hammer, you can drive 'em in with a rock."

Trey eyed the handful of nails. It went against his grain to accept charity from anyone. "I'll get by," he said softly. "I appreciate the offer anyways."

Trey gathered his reins to ride away from the blacksmith's shop, but the smithy grabbed the cheek of the roan's bridle with his empty hand. "No sense in bein' so hardheaded about it, cowboy. I ain't offerin' them to you in the first place. Feel sorry for a good-blooded horse, is all. Them's damn rough mountains you're about to cross. Don't make sense to cripple a good animal just 'cause a man's got too much pride."

Had another man with a different purpose grabbed the bridle of Trey's horse, Trey would have most certainly killed him. He looked down at the smithy, clamping his jaw to keep harsh words inside his mouth until his temper cooled. Taking the nails would be the sensible thing. Of late, however, Trey's actions didn't always make a hell of a lot of sense.

"I can't pay," Trey said quietly. The words stung him like the lash of a whip. Cleveland Marsh had taught his sons to pay their own way or do without.

"Never asked for no money, did I?" the smithy replied. "The nails are for the horse. He'd take 'em if he could say the words, if he know'd what them mountains was like. If you was ridin' a crowbait, I'd send you on your way, but it's a damn shame to see a proud man ruin a blooded animal. Take the goddamn nails, stranger."

Trey sighed and bent out of the saddle to take the nails. He could feel the color rising in his cheeks. "On account of the horse," he muttered, shoving the nails angrily in his saddlebags.

"Best of luck to you, cowboy." The smithy grinned, letting go of the roan's bridle.

Trey sighted along the western horizon. "Luck's a funny thing, mister. Lady Luck smiles on some folks and shits on some others. It don't appear there's any way to change her mind on it. I'm obliged for the nails."

He touched a spur to the roan and trotted away from the blacksmith's shop, reining west toward a late afternoon sun. A gust of hot wind blew in his face as he sent the gelding into a short lope away from Tascosa.

A mile from town he turned back in the saddle; old habits kept Trey constantly on the lookout for trouble. His eyes slitted when he saw a horseman following him from a distance. He knew by the cut of the man's clothing that it was the gambler.

Trey slowed the roan to a long, ground-eating trot; then he spoke to the horse. "Looks like I'm gonna have to kill a man, ol' hoss. That fancy-suited bastard is behind us, and I figure he'll get too close by and by. I ain't in the mood for company."

Chapter Two

He smiled inwardly as the roan lengthened its strides, listening to the solid sound of fitted iron on the gelding's hooves. On the ride to Tascosa the clatter of a loose shoe had robbed him of the simple pleasure he found crossing open country. Riding a good horse through unfenced land provided the only peace he'd known since he rode away from the weed-choked graves in Galveston. It was there, inside a rusted wrought-iron fence encircling the graveyard, that he'd shed his last tears. Though only two headstones marked the final resting place for his wife and infant son, a part of Trey Marsh had gone to rest beside them. In the years since, he'd come to understand what had happened to him that day as he knelt beside the graves, weeping bitter tears: that indefinable thing called his soul left him to be with Marybeth and little Billy. What remained was nothing more than a shell of a man who cared for nothing and no one else, a man sentenced to drift from place to place on a desperate mission to find the only thing left for him, a place to die. Riding open spaces, always on the move, gave him a sense of purpose. Perhaps in the next town, or just over the next rise, he would meet his fate, thus putting an end to his meaningless existence.

On a hilltop he turned again to watch the rider. For now, the gambler was keeping his distance. Considering the mood Trey found himself in, the gambler's caution was the only thing keeping the man alive. At nightfall the gambler would seek out Trey's campfire, as men of his ilk were wont to do, desiring company to share idle banter. Trey had already given the gambler one warning to stay clear of his path. There would be no such accommodation the next time. And there would be another time, for Trey understood the nature of men . . . he had commanded them, men of every shape and size and disposition. Men like the gambler fed on weaker men to ply their dishonest trade. Alone, they became whimpering cowards, the first to run away from a fight.

Trey spurred the roan off the rise, following the wagon ruts that would take him to Fort Sumner, then Santa Rosa and Santa Fe. A crude map of the territory rested in his saddlebags, guiding him westward. Somewhere, he would stop long enough to find day work, a necessary thing to refill his empty pockets. Then he would be on the move again, renewing his quest to find a man who was faster with a gun. He had no conscious wish to destroy himself; back in Galveston he'd had to come to terms with a terrible truth, that he lacked the courage to end his own life with the pistol now resting against his leg. Thus he found himself a man without choices, a man looking for a place to die and another man with a gun who possessed the skill to accomplish the feat against him.

The land in front of him yawned endlessly to the horizon, miles of gently rolling prairie studded with clumps of slender mesquites. Dry bunchgrass whispered in changing gusts of wind. Little puffs of caliche dust arose from the gelding's heels as it trotted along the ruts. Trey read the sign upon the

16

barren stretches of earth. There had been no recent wagon traffic and only an occasional horse since the last rain. The blacksmith's warning about the hostile land west of Tascosa had not been Trey's first. Travelers told stories about sudden, bloody Apache attacks, and gangs of highwaymen who preyed on unarmed wagons. Trey wondered about his ammunition supply, should he face a conflict. The cartridge loops on his gunbelt carried a full load. Half a box of .50/.70 rimfires rattled in his saddlebags, enough to fuel a short fight with the Remington Rolling Block carbine booted beside his saddle. The rifle was for hunting; wild game had been most of his fare since he quit the ranch job at Waco. He had a handful of coffee beans and a short sack of flour and some twists of brittle jerky for when the game grew scarce. All in all he was in better shape than usual. There'd been times when his belly had rubbed against his backbone and his saddlebags had contained no remedy.

The sun lowered near the horizon, forcing Trey's attention to the task of finding water. Dry streambeds crossed the road in places. There were no telltale cottonwoods anywhere in sight where he might dig out a tiny seep spring. The canteen resting against the pommel of his saddle would keep him alive, but what of the horse? Trey stood in his stirrups to scan the horizon.

Moving westward into the purpling dusk, he watched the flight of doves in the distance. Birds flew toward water before going to roost at night; thus Trey studied the doves' flight path. North of the wagon road the doves disappeared beyond a grassy knoll. Trey reined the roan toward the hill and struck a lope.

A tiny pool of collected rainwater sat in a rocky hollow in a sheltering of stunted cottonwoods. He rode toward it, slowing his horse to examine the

17

shadows beneath the trees. Caution had become a part of his nature, to expect the unexpected, and as a result he never approached unfamiliar places without exercising great care. The shadows below the trees were empty shadows. He allowed the roan to hold a trot to the edge of the pool to quench its thirst.

In the failing light Trey examined his surroundings. The water hole would be a dangerous place to make camp, for as easily as he'd found it, so would roving Apaches and other travelers who knew the land. When the roan lifted its muzzle from the pool Trey swung down to splash water on his face; then he cupped a few mouthfuls, sampling the pool for gypsum before swallowing.

As dark came full to the prairie he rode away from the trees to find a campsite. He knew the gambler was out there somewhere, awaiting the beacon of Trey's fire. "I'll kill him, hoss," he muttered as the roan trotted to the top of a rise. "You ain't the best company I ever had, but you're all I'm gonna tolerate."

A clump of windblown mesquites offered a minimum of shelter from prying eyes in a draw between two knobs. Trey rode for the trees at a walk, his hand resting on the butt of his gun just in case the trees held unexpected guests. He found the grove empty and swung down from his saddle in the shadows. First he fitted the roan's hobbles; then he stripped his gear from the horse's back and set about gathering an armload of firewood.

He built a circle of stones to shield the flames as best he could. When the fire crackled to life he made a sparing pot of coffee from his canteen and put the tiny pot beside the flames.

The roan grazed hungrily on a slope below the trees as Trey pulled the heavy Remington from its saddleboot to scout the hills around his camp. Moving on soundless feet, he crept from the grove and made a sweep toward higher ground, leaving his

18

spurs to hang from the horn of his saddle, useless until he boarded the roan again. A gentle night wind swept the prairie grasses, creating the illusion of waves, a vague, unwanted reminder of his home on Galveston island. He had tried to put the sights and sounds of the sea far behind him, always riding farther inland to escape ghostly memories of a happier past. The years had dropped away slowly, painfully at first, until he now thought about his beginnings less often. It was as if the good times had happened to someone else a long, long time ago.

Trained eyes found movement on the prairie. A lone horseman came toward him at a walk, still more than a half mile in the distance, outlined on a hillside by pale starlight. "The dumb sonofabitch is gonna ride right up and get himself killed," Trey groused, his anger coming to a boil in accompaniment to his coffee.

He squatted in the shadow of a spiked cholla plant to watch the gambler approach the cottonwoods a quarter mile below Trey's camp. The gambler rode recklessly to the pool. "Just one old, crippled Apache and the fool would already be dead." Trey sighed, shaking his head.

Minutes later a fire came to life in the cottonwoods. "The crazy fool is gonna make it easy for me," Trey whispered. "He'll get himself killed and save me the trouble. Might as well have hung a sign telling every renegade within five miles that he's ripe for the taking. Pleasant dreams, gambler. They're liable to be your last."

He walked back to his fire and poured coffee with a gloved hand. Chewing a twist of salty jerky, he stretched out on his bedroll and gazed up at the stars. "Wish I had myself just a pinch of good whiskey to sweeten the cup," he complained. Later, he smothered his fire with dirt and pulled his .44 before he rested his head against his saddle, covering his face

19

with the sweat-stained cavalry hat, a last token of his service to the Confederacy. He slept.

The roan snorted once. Then there was the snap of a twig underfoot. Trey's fingers tightened around his pistol grip, yet he lay still, peering out from beneath his hat brim. "To my right," he thought quickly. "I wonder if it's that stupid gambler."

Off to his left he heard the whisper of another footfall. "Two of them," he told himself, coiling his muscles for a sudden spring to the shelter of a nearby tree trunk. "At least it ain't the gambler. Wonder how many more of 'em there are?"

More than any other objective, he knew he must not allow anyone to steal his horse. Afoot on the road to Santa Fe, he would die of starvation and thirst. Dying wasn't something Trey feared, but he meant to have some say-so on how the job got done.

Slowly, he pulled his knees under him and inched into the trees. Suddenly the roan snorted again, and he heard the gelding struggle against its hobbles. In the same instant Trey was running toward the edge of the grove.

A shadowy figure was trying to chase down the hobbled horse on foot; the roan hopped a few yards ahead of the man, slowed by its bound forelegs. Trey gave the horse thief no warning; he simply aimed and fired.

The shadow spun crazily. A shrill cry of pain echoed in the night stillness as the .44 slug tore through flesh and bone. The man landed disjointedly, arms and legs askew; yet Trey saw only a glimpse of his first target's fall, for he now crouched with his gun aimed toward the other side of the trees where he'd heard the second footfall.

A bright muzzle flash illuminated the darkness, outlining a crouching man at the edge of the clearing. A spent slug snapped a tree limb above Trey's head as he triggered off an answering blast from his .44.

A strangled groan gave evidence of Trey's marksmanship; then twigs snapped as a heavy body fell. Another muffled gunshot sounded as the man fell on his pistol, muscles obeying reflexive commands that closed a trigger finger as his life ebbed away.

Trey moved quickly to another position in the trees, staying low as he ran, listening for telltale sounds of other bushwhackers. A wet cough came from the first man to fall, telling Trey that his bullet had found a lung on its way through. Motionless now, Trey waited patiently for his enemies to make the next move.

Minutes later Trey stood up. Only two men had made the try for his horse; he was sure of it now. He walked through the trees to view the body of the second man he'd shot. A bearded cowboy lay on his back at the edge of the clearing, staring sightlessly at the night sky. Trey's nostrils wrinkled at the coppery scent of blood.

Next he walked down the hill to his first target. A young cowboy lay on his side, struggling for breath, the sound bubbling wetly in his chest. Trey knelt beside him. "You'd never have made much of a horse thief anyway, son," he said quietly. "You made too damn much noise. When a man enters a new profession, he'd better spend some time making a study of how it's supposed to be done."

Pain-ridden eyes fell on Trey as he spoke. The boy looked to be eighteen, about the same age as roughly half the number of raw recruits under Trey's command at First Bull Run. Too many times to count, Trey had knelt beside pink-cheeked boys as they neared death on a battlefield. There were no words that would comfort them, and never any morphine to fight the pain.

The cowboy took a final, shuddering breath and went still, his eyes glazed over. Trey fingered the eyelids shut and stood up, for a new and troublesome sound reached his ears: a running horse was galloping up the draw. Trey guessed it would be the gambler, drawn to the sound of the gunshots.

"If he's real polite, I won't kill him." Trey sighed. "He showed the good sense to camp a respectable distance from me . . . I'll give him that much."

The gambler's sorrel raced up the draw, charging foolishly into a fracas that could easily have been an ambush. "He's dumb," Trey muttered, "but he's got more guts than I gave him credit for."

The gambler saw Trey and slowed his horse. "I heard shots," he shouted as the sorrel slid to a stop. A nickle-plated pistol reflected starlight in the gambler's hand, a card-cheat's gun, a small caliber. The gambler was either brave or just plain stupid to ride out in the open like he was, Trey decided, and truthfully he did not care which description fit.

"A couple of fools tried to steal my horse," Trey said.

"Where's the other one?" the gambler asked, out of breath, searching the darkness.

"Dead, same as this one."

"I thought I'd come lend a hand. I've been behind you all the way from Tascosa, so I figured it was you having the trouble."

Trey holstered his .44. The pair of horse thieves would have horses hidden somewhere, and saddles, maybe food and camping gear. Their pistols would fetch a price at the next trading post he ran across. A turning of the fates had brought Trey a windfall. The dead men's horses and gear would see him through to Santa Fe. He turned to the gambler. "A piece of advice, Mr. Stiles. If you aim to ride through hostile territory, you'd better get yourself a gun. That peashooter is liable to make somebody mad when it

22

raises a welt."

The gambler adopted a lofty expression. "For your information, I've killed a man or two with this pistol."

Trey grunted and shook his head. "Maybe if you swing it hard enough to club a man to death with it. It's none of my affair, gambler. Suit yourself on it. It's your funeral."

The gambler returned the pistol to an inside pocket of his coat. "To tell the simple truth, I find I'm temporarily short of funds. I'd planned to enlarge my purse in Tascosa, thus to outfit myself for the trip to Santa Fe. I discovered Tascosa was not a sporting town, leaving me with no selection. I'll have to live by my wits until my fortunes turn."

Trey was tired of the banter. "Just stay out of my way or your fortunes will take a permanent turn for the worse, Stiles."

The gambler nodded. "I was hoping we might share each other's company. It's a long way to Santa Fe, if that's the direction you're going."

"My direction is none of your affair, and I choose the company I keep. Stay wide of my trail or you'll regret it. I never warn a man twice, but I'm making an exception this time because I find I'm in a gentler mood. Killing helps take the edge off my nerves."

Trey saw the gambler swallow.

"Suit yourself, stranger," the gambler replied, swinging his horse. "It's a lonely road to Santa Fe, and I do have a good stock of provisions. Should you change your mind, you'll be welcome at my campfire. I brought along a jug of whiskey . . . not the best, mind you, due to my circumstances, but it'll help take the chill out of the night air.

The gambler rode off down the draw. Trey licked his lips as he thought about the taste of whiskey, until he decided the price would be too high, having to tolerate bad company.

Chapter Three

At dawn he indulged himself with salt pork taken from the horse thieves' saddlebags. He'd found a coarse-boned bay gelding and a ewe-necked sorrel mare tied in a clump of trees beyond the next rise. Both animals were near starvation, and the mare walked with a decided limp. The pair wouldn't fetch much of a price at the next town, and the saddles they bore were a patchwork of mends and worn leather. Trey considered the pile of gear and the two crowbait horses while he chewed fried meat and drank coffee. The guns the outlaws packed weren't much either: the boy carried an old .36 Navy Colt, and the bearded gent still clutched a .44 with a loose cylinder, worn beyond repair. The unlucky thieves had had the misfortune to try their luck against the wrong man, and now their bodies lay in the morning sun, swarming with hungry blowflies. And there they would remain, for Trey had no intentions of taking the time to bury them. They were not honorable men, and only men of honor deserved a final rest below the ground.

Trey smothered his fire and went about saddling the roan; then he saddled the bay and the sorrel and tied the spare gear behind the saddles. When the horses were tied head-and-tail, he swung up and led the animals away from the mesquites, crossing a barren ridge to angle back to the wagon road. The little mare had trouble keeping up on her injured foreleg, thus Trey was forced to keep the roan at a walk as he rode through the dewy grasses of early morning.

Later in the day, as Trey followed the empty wagon ruts, the land began to change. In the distance he could see deepening canyons; and beyond, the sharp rise of rocky peaks. "It's gonna get a little rougher, hoss," he muttered, watching the roan's ears turn back when he spoke. The horse was an obedient listener. It never interrupted him, and it offered no argument when Trey voiced an opinion on this or that. The gelding's indifference often irritated Trey. Just once, he wished the horse would whicker its agreement for one of Trey's ideas.

As Trey expected, the gambler followed, keeping a safe distance, little more than a speck on the eastern horizon. At times Stiles would close the gap between them, but when Trey halted on a piece of high ground to turn back in the saddle, the gambler seemed to understand. He fell back until Trey was almost out of sight.

At noon Trey found a running stream at the bottom of a shallow ravine. He watered the horses and busied himself with a shave and a cursory washing of his face and arms; then he changed into a clean bib-front shirt and rode out of the ravine feeling better. Now and then he thought about the jug of whiskey the gambler carried, wondering if he could tolerate the man's wagging tongue long enough to imbibe with him. Then Trey would put such thoughts aside, for if he once allowed the gambler to join him, he would have the man's company all the way to Santa Fe, and Trey found the idea too unpleasant to be worth the few swallows of corn squeeze.

26

At mid-afternoon Trey saw the dust of a wagon boiling from a distant turn in the road. Then two spans of mules plodded into view pulling a freighter. Soon the rattle of harness chains echoed from the hills, along with the occasional crack of a teamster's whip.

Half an hour later he drew rein alongside the wagon. A grizzled driver spat a stream of tobacco juice into the dust as the mules settled to a stop.

"How's the road west?" Trey asked, eyeing a double-barrel shotgun beside the driver.

"Seen some 'Paches this side of Santa Rosa," the bearded teamster replied casually. "Weren't but five. They shadowed me for a few miles, 'til they seen the wagon was empty. If'n I was you, I'd keep an eye on them extra horses. Stinkin' 'Paches will steal a man's horses a'fore he can blink, 'cept them two you're leadin' ain't much to look at. Maybe them Injuns won't bother with such sorry-lookin' horseflesh."

Trey shook his head. "It's clear all the way to Tascosa," Trey offered. "Maybe a mile farther on you'll run across a gent who fashions himself a gambler, but he's harmless enough. I wouldn't let him have the first cut of the deck, if I were you."

The teamster chuckled and spat again. "If a man tries to cheat me at cards, I generally cut his throat." As the man spoke he drew a gleaming Bowie knife from a sheath inside his boot. "I figure I'm doin' folks a favor. Ain't nothin' more worthless on the face of this earth than a bastard who cheats at cards."

Trey touched his hat brim with a lazy salute. "We share the same disposition toward card players. Thanks for the word about those Apaches."

Trey spurred past the wagon as the driver's whip cracked over the rumps of the mules. The sounds of creaking axles and rattling chains moved away. Soon the wagon was out of sight, and Trey was alone again, listening to the horses' hooves on the wagon

27

ruts. He decided to watch for a clean shot at a wild turkey hen, for he'd found turkey prints in the soft mud beside the stream. His belly now demanded food, and his palate wanted no more of the tough salt pork he'd eaten at breakfast. Pulling the rifle from its boot, he made sure of a chambered cartridge and then rested the gun across the pommel. His mouth watered as he envisioned a roasting turkey above flickering flames.

Toward dusk he rode down a gentle slope seeking water on lower ground. A snakelike draw twisted southwest, and in the distance he saw stands of trees along the bottom of the draw. Within those trees could rest the roosting places for the wild turkeys he sought, and the draw would most certainly contain water. Trey's belly juices rumbled when he thought about a roasted drumstick and tender turkey breast.

Following the ravine at a slower gait, he drew near the first stand of shinoaks cautiously, ready with the Remington for the chance to down his supper. He found the limbs empty, and rode on.

Deeper into the dry wash, he found a brackish pool of water in a bend of the streambed, where he allowed the horses their fill. Coon and possum tracks criss-crossed the mud around the edges of the pool. There would be no turkey dinner to silence his rumbling stomach.

Trey rode toward a clump of shinoak farther down the wash and selected his campsite. When the horses were hobbled on good grass, he gathered firewood and sheltered the flames with stones. Soon coffee bubbled in the smoke-blackened pot. Darkness came swiftly to the prairie around him. He settled back against his saddle to chew jerky.

The click of a horseshoe against rock startled him awake. He'd been dozing beside the glowing embers of his fire, foolishly marking his camp for inquiring eyes from the dark. Trey pulled his Colt and rolled away from the circle of firelight, aiming toward the sound of an approaching horse in the rocky streambed.

"Ahoy there, stranger!" came the gambler's shout. "I'd like a word with you. I saw your fire, and it seems I've run out of matches. Can you spare a sulfur stick or two?"

The gambler had wisely halted his horse a safe distance down the draw. Trey lowered his gun and let out an impatient sigh. "Ride in, Mr. Stiles," he replied.

The gambler rode to the fire and swung down. In his right fist he held the drawstring on a burlap sling containing a masonry whiskey jug. Soon the gambler found Trey in the shadows and held forth the jug of spirits. "I'll offer a trade," he said cheerfully, wearing a grin. "A drink or two for a sulfur match. You'll have the best end of our bargain."

Trey approached the dwindling fire. The gambler quickly saw the gun in Trey's hand.

"No need for the armament," the gambler protested.

"I'm not in the mood for company, Mr. Stiles. I'll give you the matches and take a cup of your whiskey. Then you'll ride clear of my fire. Understood?"

The gambler nodded and offered Trey the jug. "Your meaning is quite clear, sir. I wouldn't have ridden over had it not been for the matches. There's a chill in the air."

Trey holstered his .44 and took the jug, which was wonderfully heavy, almost full, whetting Trey's appetite for a considerable share. He tossed out the remains in his coffee cup and poured generously, to the rim. The gambler's eyes widened slightly.

"You've got quite a thirst, sir, and I'm sharing my spirits with you without even knowing your name."

Trey grunted and took a sip of the whiskey. A delicious burn accompanied the bitter fluid down

29

Trey's throat. "Rotgut," Trey complained, making a face.

"I've already explained . . . I'm short of funds."

Trey pointed to his saddlebags near the fire. "The matches are over there. Take no more than two. My name is Trey Marsh."

The gambler shook his head and knelt over Trey's saddlebags. "From my previous ill-fated introduction, you already know that my name is Woodrow Stiles. My friends call me Woody."

Trey watched the gambler's hand fumble for the matches. "A crooked gambler has no friends," Trey said quietly.

The gambler frowned. "You've misjudged me, Mr. Marsh. I run an honest game."

"I doubt it," Trey replied.

The gambler took two matches from an oilskin pouch. Trey corked the whiskey, careful not to spill a precious drop over the rim of his coffee cup. He handed the gambler the drawstring.

"I'm grateful for the matches," the gambler said. He pulled the cork and hoisted his jug in a toast. "Here's to a safe journey to Santa Fe, Mr. Marsh."

Reluctantly, Trey joined the toast and drank from his cup.

"Rotten whiskey," the gambler hissed, lowering the jug from his mouth. "It's a sad state of affairs when men of good breeding have to share the dregs of the distiller's art. This is hardly more than sludge from the bottom of a poor man's still. It is, however, all I have at the present. Perhaps in the next town, things will change."

Trey eyed the gambler. "What makes you so sure that we're both men of good breeding, Mr. Stiles? Back at Tascosa, I seem to remember a remark you made about my downtrodden appearance and the cut of my worn denims. What has changed your mind?"

The gambler grinned. "Simple observation, Mr.

Marsh. It is quite obvious now that you were once a military man. An officer. It's the way you carry yourself, sir. I'm a man of many talents, not the least of which is making judgments about people. I'd say you were a Confederate officer, Mr. Marsh. A captain, or even a major."

Trey understood the gambler's game. "I don't suppose the fact that I'm wearing a Confederate cavalryman's hat helped you arrive at your conclusions. And I held the rank of colonel, Mr. Stiles. I served under General John Bell Hood with the First Texas Brigade, if it matters. Now we've finished with our introductions, and you have your matches. Get back on that horse and ride clear of my fire. You've worn my patience mighty thin."

The gambler turned for his sorrel. "I had hoped for more, Colonel Marsh," he said over his shoulder, fastening the whiskey to his saddle. "It's a long ride to Santa Fe, through empty land filled with hostiles. I hoped we might share each other's company through the mountains."

Trey shook his head as the gambler mounted. "You had it figured wrong. And calling me Colonel won't help change my mind. I don't want your company."

"As you wish, Colonel. I won't trouble you again, although it seems a waste. I would enjoy hearing your stories about the war. It would help to pass some time."

Trey's jaw tightened. "You figured wrong again, gambler."

Stiles paused as he reined his horse away from the campfire.

"How's that, Colonel?"

Trey let out a whispering sigh. "Figuring I'd waste my time telling you stories about brave men putting their lives on the line for the Confederate cause. Fighting and dying for a cause is something a card

31

cheat would never understand."

Suddenly the gambler wheeled his horse toward Trey, and there was a hard look on his face as he spoke. "Once again you've misjudged me, Colonel Marsh," he snapped. "I served my country as bravely as any man who fought in your command. Were you ever at Andersonville during the war, sir?"

The gambler's question caught Trey off guard. The Andersonville Confederate Prison was a death camp for Yankee soldiers. "I saw Andersonville half a dozen times," Trey replied softly, puzzled by the question.

The gambler straightened in the saddle. "I was there, Colonel, as a prisoner of your Confederacy. For two long years the cause you believed in tried to starve me to death with a handful of parched corn and a cup of water as my daily ration. However, as you can see, I survived your mindless cruelty. I existed on moldy corn swarming with weevils. I survived, living by my wits! I had only a deck of cards and my instincts, surrounded by almost thirty thousand men who sometimes ate each other when the food ran out. Your lofty cause made no provisions for starving men, Colonel Marsh! Men died by the thousands, starved down to living skeletons by Confederate cruelty. Don't preach to me about bravery, sir! I understand the meaning of the word."

As the gambler spoke Trey remembered bitter scenes from his first look at Andersonville. In the third year of the war he led a detachment of soldiers escorting three hundred Yankee prisoners across Georgia to the gates of Andersonville, and what he saw inside the barbed wire fences left a scar across Trey's soul. Thousands of starving men were crowded together in a city of mud and crude shelters. The site reeked of excrement. Half the prisoners were naked skeletons. They stared at the new arrivals with sunken eyes, dulled by despair.

"Union prison camps weren't any better," Trey replied. "There was a war going on, and none of it was easy."

"Agreed," the gambler said, his tone softer. "I merely wanted you to know that I saw my share of it. A lot of brave men died at Andersonville . . . they died as bravely as any soldier on the field of battle. I was there. I watched them die."

Trey stiffened, closing his mind to the unwanted memories. "Your point is made, Mr. Stiles. I will not, however, discuss the war with you, or anyone else. If you choose to discuss it, you'll have to find another listener. Now, ride clear of my fire and remember to keep your distance from here on. I don't want any company."

The gambler turned his horse and rode off into the dark. Trey listened to the sorrel's hoofbeats until they faded to silence, sipping the gambler's whiskey. He found himself thinking about the gambler with less rancor as he returned to his fire. His mood warmed by the whiskey, he decided against killing Stiles for no better reason than an intrusion into his solitude on the trail to Santa Fe. Perhaps the gambler wasn't such a bad sort after all, if he could learn to keep his distance.

Trey smothered his fire and rested against his saddle, enjoying the contents of his cup until the last swallow was gone. Later, he drew his pistol and covered his face with his hat. In minutes he was asleep.

Chapter Four

Just before noon he rode down to the shallow crossing, after a careful examination of the riverbank from a wooded crest above the Pecos. The map showed a military post a few miles west of the river, a place called Fort Sumner abandoned by the army where a handful of small ranchers and sheep herders now occupied the old army quarters. He'd been told there was a trading post when he asked about the road to Santa Fe back in Tascosa. At the trading post he would try to sell the outlaws' horses and gear, and buy fresh supplies before he entered the mountains.

The horses drank deeply from the river while Trey filled his canteen. Muddy wagon tracks and the fresher prints of shod horses covered the soft clay near the river crossing. A line of cottonwoods followed the river northward; Trey had scrutinized them for several minutes before he rode down to the water. Eastern New Mexico Territory was the emptiest land Trey had ever seen, a vast expanse of rolling prairie and empty canyons without a trace of habitation. "Lonesome place, hoss," he muttered, as the roan lifted its muzzle from the river. "I like it. It suits me."

He mounted and rode carefully through the shallows, watching for quicksand. After an uneventful crossing the horses shook themselves to rid the water from their coats. Trey hurried the roan up the opposite bank and then swung a look over his shoulder. In the distance he saw the gambler, and the gambler's haste puzzled Trey. A boiling cloud of caliche went skyward above the galloping sorrel. Why was Stiles in such a hurry?

The answer appeared in a larger cloud of dust. Half a mile behind the gambler, Trey saw horsemen moving rapidly toward the river. "Trouble," he said under his breath. "Nobody runs a horse in this heat without a reason."

He was sorely tempted to ride off and leave the gambler to fend for himself, yet Trey's dreams during the night had been filled with unwanted recollections of Andersonville Prison, and the war. Learning that Stiles was an Andersonville survivor softened Trey's hard line against the gambler. The card player had to be tough or he'd have died inside the prison's wire fences.

"Reckon I'll wait, to see what sort of predicament Stiles has gotten himself into," Trey said, wishing the dumb animal between his knees could speak its mind. "The fool has probably tried to cheat some cowboys with his dishonest deck, and now they're out to hang him from the nearest tree. I suppose I'll have to take a hand in it. Damn him anyway. If it wasn't for that jug of whiskey he's carrying. . . ."

The gambler spurred his sorrel toward the river in an all-out run, leaning over the gelding's neck, glancing over his shoulder. It required no special talent to see that Stiles had made himself half a dozen enemies. The cowboys were riding hard to catch up before Stiles could cross the Pecos.

The sorrel floundered into the water and stumbled, for the gambler still punished his mount foolishly with a spur. Stiles went flying over his horse's head as the gelding fell. Arms and legs outstretched, the

36

gambler splashed head-first into the river and promptly went below the muddy surface, only his hat remaining visible as the slow current swept it away from his fall.

Trey chuckled when the sorrel regained its footing. Suddenly the gambler's head exploded from the water; there was a gasping sound as Stiles struggled for a breath of air, hands clawing to be free of the water's pull. Trey laughed out loud at the gambler's plight, soaked like he was in his fancy frock coat and silky vest, standing in waist-deep mud and water. Stiles coughed as he fingered water from his eyes, whirling to look behind him when he heard the thunder of running hooves.

Seven men galloped over the rise in a cloud of yellow dust, spurring relentlessly down the embankment toward Stiles. Trey dropped the lead rope on the spare horses and touched the roan with a spur as he hurried down the opposite bank, filling his fist with his .44.

The cowboys slowed when they reached the water's edge. The man at the front of the bunch drew his pistol and spurred into the river after the gambler. Trey sent the roan into the shallows as the other cowboys splashed into the river. For a moment there was utter confusion . . . splashing hooves and angry shouts as the men rode down on Stiles.

The gambler's hand went quickly inside his coat, then out with his pistol before Trey could reach him. One of the cowboys aimed down at the gambler's chest with a long-barreled Colt, struggling for good aim aboard the back of his lunging mount.

Trey fired a warning shot over the riders' heads. "Hold off, boys!" he shouted, cocking the .44 quickly, reining the roan to a halt.

The gunshot drew the cowboys' attention. Horses were jerked to a stop in the churning water; then guns came to bear on Trey as the horses settled. For a

37

tense moment there was silence as the men eyed each other.

"Stay out of this, mister," a cowboy growled. "This ain't none of your affair."

Trey raised his Colt, aiming across the distance between them with his sights on the cowboy's chest. "I'm making it my affair," Trey snarled. "First shot gets fired, I'll kill you. Whatever happens, you can count on having a hole in your belly."

Another cowboy spoke. "This is between us an' him, that gent in the river. You're stickin' your nose where it don't belong, an' you damn sure can't count. There's seven of us an' just one of you."

Trey nodded once. "I appreciate the arithmetic lesson, but it doesn't change a thing. I'll kill the first man who uses a gun, so think about it . . . decide who wants to be first to go."

"I'll get one more, maybe two or three," a voice said, distracting the cowboys. Stiles stood with his gun aimed at the riders, a sorry sight in his water-soaked attire, but with a deadly serious purpose. "Colonel Marsh, you kill the men closest to you and I'll drop the pair in front of me. We'll have them in a cross fire."

Nervous looks were exchanged among the mounted men. A whiskered cowboy near Trey slowly holstered his gun. "Count me out," he said as he turned his horse. "I ain't lookin' to die for no ten-dollar-a-month job."

The cowboy trotted his horse out of the river. Then another swung his mount to ride behind him.

"The odds are changing, gentlemen," Trey announced. "Why don't you explain what all the trouble is about. Maybe there's another way to settle things."

The man who spoke first made a face. "This fancy-dressed gent was tryin' to steal one of the bossman's cows. We caught him red-handed."

38

Trey's glance fell on the gambler, questioning him with a look.

"There was a crippled calf down in this draw," Stiles protested. "I rode over to have a look . . . I didn't steal it."

The cowboy's face hardened. "You had a damn skinnin' knife in your hands, mister. Killin' a cow is the same as stealin' it. You was aimin' to make a meal at the bossman's expense."

The gambler looked sheepishly at Trey. "The calf had a broken leg. It would have died anyway, Colonel."

Trey clamped his jaw. "The beef wasn't yours, Mr. Stiles. It doesn't matter about the broken leg."

The cowboy now had a puzzled expression. "If you two fellers know each other, then how come you wasn't ridin' together just now?"

Trey let out an impatient sigh. "Mr. Stiles and I are only acquainted. His actions are his own. If he killed one of your calves, then I'm of the opinion he owes you for it. How about it, gambler? Can you pay the price for stolen beef?"

Stiles shook his head, wearing a look of disappointment. "I hoped you would take my side in this affair, Colonel. I did not kill the calf . . . there wasn't time, before these ruffians rode up on me and gave chase."

"You was plannin' on killin' it," the cowboy challenged. "We rode up just in time."

Stiles adopted his best indignant air. "You're only guessing at my intentions," he snapped.

"You had a damn knife in your hands," the cowboy replied. "Any fool could see what you aimed to do."

"Enough," Trey growled. "No harm's been done and no blood has been spilled. Ride back to your herd and we'll get on with our travels."

For a moment there was a silent standoff. The

cowboys looked at each other; then the leader shrugged and lifted his reins. "I reckon we'll let it alone this time," he said. "That skinny feller owes you. If you hadn't come along, me an' the boys was gonna string him up from one of them trees. In case you ain't heard, there's a range war in the making around here. John Chisum and his bunch are stealin' cattle from Dolan, and Jimmy Dolan's boys are taking cows from Chisum's herds. A man better have his brand on cattle if he's got 'em in his possession these days. I had this skinny feller figured for a cow thief, but now I can see he ain't nothin' but a damn fool in a fancy suit."

Trey lowered his .44. "Then, we're in agreement," Trey said as he looked over at the gambler. "Mr. Stiles is a fool for trying to take a beef that was not his."

"It had a broken leg," the gambler muttered, unable to meet Trey's level gaze.

"It doesn't matter," Trey snapped. "You made a fool's move, and it almost put your neck in a rope. You're a damn nuisance, Mr. Stiles. I should have let these men hang you. Now get on your horse and get the hell out of my sight. You're keeping me from the road to Santa Fe."

Trey noticed that the cowboy eyed him curiously. "You aim to go to work for Jimmy Dolan?" the cowboy asked.

"Hadn't planned on it," Trey replied, as the gambler staggered through the waist-deep water toward his horse. "Who is Dolan? And what kind of work has he got?"

The cowboy chuckled softly. "Figured you was one of them gunhands he's been hiring, judgin' by that low-slung holster. Dolan heads up the Catron interests up at Santa Fe. Figured that was why you was headed that way, carryin' a shootist's gun. The work is real easy to explain: you get paid to kill anybody who gets in Jimmy Dolan's way. Like I said, there's gonna be a war in these parts. Chisum don't back down from nobody, and neither does Jimmy Dolan. This country ain't big enough for both of them. It looks to be one hell of a fight."

Trey considered what the cowboy told him. "Who do you men work for?" he asked.

"We ride for John Cole, only some of us ain't gonna be inclined to stay on, once the shootin' starts. Me, I hired on with this outfit to be a cowboy. I ain't no gunslick, and I sure as hell ain't lookin' to die for this job. Ride careful, Colonel, or you'll wind up between a bunch of paid guns, you and that Stiles feller. Stiles looks like the type who'll get hisself killed right quick. You, you'll last longer, if you keep your eyes open."

The men swung their horses and rode out of the river. Trey holstered his Colt and reined the roan toward the far side. As he left the shallows he halted beside Stiles. Stiles was wiping mud from his coat sleeves.

"I shoulda let them hang you," Trey snapped. "From now on, I want you out of my sight. You've caused me enough trouble as it is, and I damn sure don't want any more. Stay behind me, Mr. Stiles. Understood?"

The gambler nodded. "Sorry, Colonel. The calf had a broken leg, and I thought we could use some fresh beef. It's a long road to Santa Fe, and the calf would have died anyway. Before you leave, let me offer you a drink of my whiskey, as a token of my gratitude for what you did back there in the river."

Before Trey could shake his head against the idea, he heard the gambler exclaim, "My whiskey!" The jug had broken when the sorrel fell, and now the burlap netting held only broken pieces of crockery.

"It appears you've lost your whiskey to the river," Trey remarked. "And your hat has drifted downstream. Have a pleasant trip, Mr. Stiles, and remember to stay out of my way on the road to Santa Fe."

Trey rode off leading the spare horses, leaving the gambler in utter despair beside the Pecos, mourning his broken jug. Once, on a hilltop, Trey looked over his shoulder. The gambler was walking down the riverbank, looking for his hat.

Fort Sumner was a collection of adobe buildings, a row of crumbling barracks, a few small huts, and an occasional house of clapboard. The road snaked its way through the tiny outpost. Here and there, rawboned milk cows were held in small corrals behind adobe huts. Burros grazed from stacks of hay while others stood in the shafts of sagging donkey carts overloaded with pottery and lambs' wool and goat skins. A pair of saddled horses waited in the shade of slender mesquites while Mexican children played ball beyond the trees. The village seemed asleep as Trey rode toward the empty parade ground where a false-fronted trading post sat beside the road. He was surprised to find a canopied black carriage beside the store; the conveyance was layered with caliche dust from its canopy to the running boards. A team of good-blooded bay horses stood in the harness, covered with dried sweat. Trey rode to a hitching post and swung down, eyeing the expensive carriage as he tied off the horses. The carriage seemed out of place in Fort Sumner, and he wondered about its occupants.

He entered the store and heard voices at the back. A woman spoke sharply in rapid Spanish to a man clad in vaquero's attire. When Trey saw the woman, his gaze lingered, for she was an uncommonly beautiful creature. He simply stared at her for a time, admiring the soft lines of her pretty oval face framed by flowing black hair that reached her shoulders. Suddenly the woman was aware of Trey's stare; her dark eyes flashed angrily when she looked away from her companion, and Trey was forced to look elsewhere.

A storekeeper wearing a white apron approached Trey. "How may I help you?" the man asked.

Trey glanced once more at the woman before he spoke, swallowing uncomfortably when he felt her eyes on him. "I've got a couple of extra horses to sell . . . some old saddles and a pair of pistols, if you're in the market to buy."

The storekeeper shook his head, taking quick note of Trey's gun. "I suppose you have a bill of sale?" he asked.

"I found the horses," Trey replied softly. "The men who owned them were dead from gunshot wounds. I claimed them, and the dead men's gear. I'll sell the outfits cheap, if you're interested."

The man gave Trey a cautious examination. "Look, stranger, I don't make it a practice to buy . . . questionable livestock."

Trey shrugged. "Suit yourself. I can sell them in Santa Fe. Somebody'll want to make the profits."

The storekeeper hesitated. "I'll take a look at the brands. Then maybe I'll give you my price."

"The little sorrel mare has a limp," Trey remarked. "A stone bruise, I reckon. The guns are hanging from the saddle horns. Make me an offer on everything."

The man left the store and walked to the end of the front porch. Trey turned to the shelves to pass some time, until he heard the woman approach. He turned when he heard her footsteps, admiring her unusual beauty again. He guessed her age at twenty-five when he saw her in better light. She wore a flowing green dress of expensive velvet. Trey smelled sweet perfume when the woman halted near his elbow.

"Pardon me, señor," she said softly, a throaty

43

sound hinted with accent. "I happened to overhear what you said to the storekeeper, and I'm curious as to the direction from which you came."

"Tascosa," Trey replied as he pulled off his hat in gentlemanly fashion to address the woman. "I just came up from Texas. I'm headed for Santa Fe."

There was disappointment on the woman's face. "I had hoped you could tell us about the road to Santa Fe. My driver and I are also headed north, and we worry about all the trouble. The outlaw gangs have grown worse in recent months, since we drove down to Chihuahua, and now we are told there are Apache troubles in the mountains again."

"I'm new to this country, ma'am," Trey said. "I wish I could help. A teamster told me that he saw a few Apaches on the way down from Santa Rosa, and some cattle drovers told me a little about the problems between Chisum and Dolan; but beyond that I know nothing more. Sorry."

At that, the woman smiled, revealing rows of perfect white teeth. "No need to apologize, señor. We face the same uncertainties along the way. Perhaps you are looking for work? I might be willing to pay you a reasonable amount to escort us to Santa Fe. I can tell by your proper manner and speech that you are not a common cowboy, and I see that you are carrying a gun. If Juan agrees that we can trust you, perhaps we can strike a bargain. Can you use the gun you are wearing, señor?"

Trey glanced to the back of the store. The old Mexican vaquero was watching Trey with hooded eyes. "I'm a decent shot, I suppose," he replied quietly. "I'm headed the same direction. Talk it over with your driver and let me know what you decide. By the way, my name is Trey Marsh, if it matters."

The woman bowed slightly. "I am Maria Valdez, and I will speak to Juan about . . . the arrangement. We have been waiting here all day, trying to find out about the dangers on the road before we risked the drive into the mountains. An armed escort will discourage bandits. Please give me a moment to speak to Juan."

She whirled toward the back of the store and hurried away. Trey watched her depart with a curious feeling of anticipation as his eyes fell to the sway of her hips. "I wonder what she's carrying in that buggy that requires an armed escort?" he asked himself in a whisper. "She's a pretty thing," he added, stirred by a moment of desire, a feeling he hadn't known for many lonely years.

Chapter Five

"I'd pay you twenty-five dollars in hard coin for all of it," the storekeeper said, hands shoved in his pants pockets as he gave the pair of horses a closer look. "The mare's a cripple, so she ain't worth much, and the guns are in pretty bad shape. Take it or leave it, stranger."

Trey's deliberations took longer than necessary. The outlaws' gear and saddle stock was worth twice the price the man offered, however Trey understood that he was in a poor bargaining position so many miles from the next trading post. The twenty-five dollars was "found" money, and it would see him through to Santa Fe. "I'll take it," Trey replied. "I'll need some food . . . some tins of tomatoes and peaches, if you've got them. Coffee and a little sugar. And a bottle of good whiskey."

The storekeeper eyed Trey suspiciously. "You killed the two gents who owned the horses, didn't you?" he asked.

Trey turned his attention from the horses. "That's none of your affair. If I told you the truth of the matter, it wouldn't make any difference. It would only be my word against theirs, and they won't be doing any more talking."

Again, the storekeeper's eyes fell to Trey's gun.

"There ain't much law in these parts, mister, so I reckon your word on things is enough. Come inside and get your money. I'll draw up a bill of sale while you pick out your supplies."

Trey turned for the store, to find the old vaquero watching him from the doorway. Hard black eyes appraised him, moving up and down his frame. Trey sauntered across the porch, halting in front of the Mexican blocking his path.

"Señorita Valdez wishes to speak to you," the old man said in a rasping voice, his face darkened with doubt. "I am called Juan, and we wish to offer you a proposition. But first, I have a few questions. The señorita is my responsibility, and I have given my word to her father that I will make sure of her safety. Porfirio Valdez is *mi patrón*, and he is also my friend. I must be certain that we can trust you, before the offer is made."

Trey nodded once. "Ask your questions. I mean no harm to you or the woman. I'm merely a traveler, on my way to Santa Fe."

Juan's brow knitted. "Then, explain how you came by the pair of horses and saddles. And the guns."

Trey glanced over his shoulder as the storekeeper went inside. He waited until the man was out of earshot. "Two men tried to steal my horse while I was camped along the road from Tascosa. I killed them. They came at me with guns and I had no choice. The mare one of them rode was lame, and I suppose they were looking for a replacement. They made a mistake, trying for my roan."

Juan's expression did not change. "The Territory is full of wanted men . . . dangerous men. Some will kill unsuspecting travelers for the weight of their purse. How can we be sure you are not a *bandido*, señor?"

Trey shrugged. "You can't. You'll have to take my

48

word that I'm an honest man. The choice is yours: you can take your chances alone on the road, or you can trust me. The men who jumped me got what was coming to them, and I owe no man an apology for putting an end to their lives. When someone tries to take something that does not belong to him, he puts his life on the line."

Juan shook his head, and now his look was softer, though still cautious. "Come inside with me, señor. I will tell the señorita what you told me, and then we can discuss our proposition."

Trey followed the old man into the store, deciding that the Mexican was merely doing his job as carefully as he could under the circumstances. A man Juan's age would be of little help if their party was attacked by Indians or a gang of bandits. The expensive carriage would be a lure to men with bad intentions, for it bespoke the wealth of its owner too plainly. Again, Trey wondered what the woman and the old man were carrying, a cargo valuable enough to warrant an armed escort through the mountains? Or was it simply concern for their own safety?

Maria was watching Trey as he approached the back of the store. Something stirred in Trey's memory, a recollection of long-forgotten desires when Marybeth was in his arms.

Juan spoke to Maria in Spanish. Trey listened to the words, understanding only a part of what was said.

"Juan tells me we must trust you," Maria explained, searching Trey's face as she spoke. "We really have no other choice, Mr. Marsh, for we were delayed too long in Mexico. I must return to my father's ranch as quickly as possible. If you agree to act as our escort, you will be paid twenty dollars in gold. I hope the arrangement will be . . . satisfactory. For both of us."

The offer was more than he expected. He meant to

make the ride northward anyway, thus the twenty dollars was an added windfall. "I accept," he replied, "but let's understand each other. I will accompany you to Santa Fe, and to the best of my ability I will make sure that no harm comes to you. However, in the event we are attacked by Indians or a band of outlaws, you both must agree to do exactly as I say. I can't defend you if you act on your own."

Maria gave him a strange smile. "You sound like a soldier, Mr. Marsh. Are you telling us we must follow orders?"

Distracted by the woman's beautiful smile, Trey was slow to give an answer. "All I'm saying, ma'am, is that you'll have to listen to me when the trouble starts. You can't outrun men on horseback in that carriage. In order to set up a proper defense I'll need your cooperation."

"You will have it," Maria said quickly, glancing at Juan. "How soon can we be on our way?"

Trey looked over his shoulder. The storekeeper was preparing the bill of sale on his countertop. "I'll settle up with the store and buy a few supplies. Half an hour, and I'll be ready. The day's half gone, but I figure we can make the foothills before dark."

"Done, then," Maria said, extending a slender hand.

Trey took her palm and held it briefly, unable to take his gaze from the woman's deep chocolate eyes. When the following silence lasted too long, Juan scuffed a boot toe on the floor.

"I will see that the horses are watered, señorita," he said.

Maria nodded, still staring into Trey's face. "Let us know as soon as you are ready, Mr. Marsh," she said softly.

Trey released her hand, oddly uncomfortable under the woman's stare. "Half an hour," he muttered; then he turned and walked to the counter where the storekeeper was counting out his money.

"I'll need your name for this bill of sale," the man said, stacking silver dollars in front of Trey. "And some sort of place for an address, wherever you call home."

Trey pursed his lips, still conscious of the woman's gaze. "The name is Trey Marsh, and I used to call Galveston my home."

Trey fastened the burlap bags behind his saddle, being careful to put the whiskey in his saddlebags, within easy reach. A small bag of grain would see the roan across meager grazing, and the tins of peaches would make a nice addition to his meals. He spent seven dollars in the store, adding a box of cartridges for the rifle, and the whiskey, totaling five dollars more. When his gear was in place he led the roan to a water trough. The gelding drank deeply while Trey refilled his canteen. He was thinking about the woman, remembering her beautiful smile, when a sound distracted him. A boy of nine or ten climbed down from the back seat of the carriage wearing white homespun. The boy looked at Trey, then averted his eyes.

"Nobody told me there was a kid," Trey muttered unhappily. The child would present an added risk if there was trouble along the road to Santa Fe, another member of the party in need of protection.

Maria and Juan appeared from the doorway into the store.

"We are ready, Carlos," Maria said.

The boy nodded once, glancing toward Trey again.

"*Quien es?*" he asked, indicating Trey.

"A man who will keep us safe," she replied.

Carlos stared at Trey a moment longer; then he turned for the carriage.

"You didn't tell me about the boy," Trey said, fastening his canteen to the pommel of his saddle.

Maria came over to the trough. She glanced over her shoulder and lowered her voice. "Carlos is my nephew, Mr. Marsh. My brother and his wife were killed by the Yaquis in Mexico. We are taking him back to the ranch to live with us. My father and I are the only family he has now."

Trey looked into Maria's eyes. "I understand. Must have been hard on the kid to lose his folks . . ."

Tears crept into the corners of Maria's eyes suddenly. "It was a Yaqui massacre. He watched the *Indios* butcher his mother and father. Only a *niño*, and yet he saw such terrible things. He does not talk about it now. Sometimes, he wakes up crying in the night, remembering."

The objections Trey meant to raise about having the boy along were forgotten quickly. "He won't be a problem," Trey replied. "If we aim to make those foothills, we'd better get started. I intend to ride out front a ways to scout the road. Tell Juan to keep the team back. If we run into any trouble, I'll ride back in a hurry. I figure we've got five or six hours of daylight left. Let's get moving."

He swung aboard the roan and waited for Maria and Juan to climb in the carriage. Juan flicked the reins over the team and wheeled around the back of the store. Trey roweled the roan to a soft trot, reining north out of Fort Sumner. Soon the barracks and adobes were behind them.

On a rise above town he turned back, wondering about the gambler. The road southeast was empty. "Maybe those cowpokes changed their minds and strung him up," Trey mumbled, urging the roan forward again.

Miles of dusty road crossed the dry prairie. In the distance he saw the shapes of rocky peaks surrounded by foothills. A hot wind blew in his face, adding to his discomfort as he sent the gelding across empty land.

He thought about the woman as the miles passed beneath the roan's easy gait, judging his chances. He found himself oddly fascinated by her dark beauty, renewing forgotten sensations deep inside. Thus he indulged in flights of fancy, wondering how her lips would feel if the Fates gave him a chance to kiss her. Since the war, he had all but given up on the notion that he might ever feel atraction to a woman. Losing his beloved Marybeth had left him without the capacity to love another woman, of that he'd been sure. Yet there was something about Maria Valdez that awakened a sleeping part of his nature. He tried to imagine what it would be like to hold Maria in his arms.

Now and then he glanced back to check on the carriage, always finding it in his wake below a cloud of caliche dust. Knowing the woman was behind him, he found himself in a brighter mood, even looking forward to their night camp, where he might get to know her better. "Maybe I'm gettin' foolish in my old age, hoss," he said, "but damned if that ain't the prettiest woman a man could want."

The roan snorted, rattling its curb chain, flicking its ears back when Trey spoke.

"About time you started listening to me." He chuckled, stroking the animal's neck.

The road began to twist and turn through gentle hills. Higher up, the hills loomed larger, dotted with scattered stands of scrub pines and mesquites. Trey put aside his thoughts of the woman to scout the road, a task for which he had agreed to accept payment. "Time I started earning my money," he whispered, scanning the distant trees for shapes that did not belong.

The sun became an orange ball on the western horizon. Here and there the road bent sharply to climb steepening ridges. Trey studied the flight paths of birds, hopeful that a night camp could be found with water. More dry hills stretched northward, offering little hope of creeks or springs. Doves and sparrows winged high above his head, showing no signs of coming down to roost in the land through which Trey and his party would travel.

Dusk purpled the hills, lengthening shadows beneath the trees around him. He knew he would be forced to select a dry campsite very soon, before darkness fell.

On a little knoll he found a thicket of slender pines that would hide the carriage and their horses. Reining off the road, he rode through the trees cautiously, finding nothing amiss. A tiny clearing in the thicket was perfect for shielding their campfire from anyone who rode the hills in the dark. Satisfied, he trotted the roan back to the road to wait for the carriage.

Juan hauled back on the team, sleeving dust from his face, questioning Trey with a look.

"We'll pitch camp up there in those trees," Trey remarked, noticing that Maria had covered her face with a veil. "No water for our horses, but we'll be out of sight. There's a clearing in those pines. Follow me."

He led the way up the knoll, then into the trees. The sky had begun to fill with the first bright stars of evening as Juan brought the carriage to a halt in the clearing. Trey swung down to help with the harness team, when the boy suddenly jumped down from the seat to lend Juan a hand with the trace chains.

Maria stepped daintily to the ground, took off her veil, then gave Trey a smile. Juan was watching from the corner of his eye.

"I'll picket the horses close to camp," Trey said, stripping his saddle from the roan.

"I can help," the woman said, lifting her skirt

before she walked away from the buggy.

"No need," Trey replied as she drew near. "I can manage it."

Maria tilted her face, and now there was an edge to her voice. "I am not a helpless woman, Mr. Marsh," she snapped.

A slow grin lifted the corners of his mouth. "Never said you were, ma'am. Just said I could manage it alone. No need to get your tail feathers up about it. Carrying that skirt appeared to be a full-time job."

She let the dress fall from her fingers. Anger still smoldered behind her eyes. "For your information, I work with the rest of the vaqueros at my father's ranch. I ride a horse as well as most men, and I know how to use a rope."

Her sudden outburst caught him off guard. "Didn't mean any offense," he muttered, trying to hide his grin.

Juan led the team away from the wagon tongue. Carlos followed closely behind the old man.

"The boy can help picket the horses tonight," Trey suggested, watching the youngster hang back when Trey looked at him. "Give one of the horses to Carlos and we'll find these animals some grass."

The boy kept his face to the ground, but he took the reins on one of the bays and followed Trey away from the clearing. Trey could feel Maria's eyes on his back until they were out of sight beyond the trees.

"Down here," Trey suggested, walking down a slope to a grassy swale below the knob. "They'll be close enough so I can keep an eye on them tonight. Wouldn't want to lose 'em to Apache horse thieves."

Working in pale starlight, he fitted hobbles on his roan and the harness team. All the while Carlos stared at him, paying particular attention to Trey's gun.

"That oughta do it," Trey said, glancing around the hills where the horses grazed. Then he turned to find the boy.

"Are you a *pistolero?*" Carlos asked softly, watching Trey's face.

"Not exactly, son," he replied, wondering if the label might fit. "I was a soldier once. A long time ago."

The boy swallowed, preparing another question. "Then, why do you carry a *pistola,* señor?"

Trey let out a whispering sigh as he thought about his answer. "For protection, mostly. Some men need to be persuaded to mind their own business."

Carlos stared at the gun a moment. "Would you teach me how to fire a *pistola?*" he asked, speaking so softly Trey had to listen closely.

"Maybe. If your Aunt Maria gave her permission."

Now Carlos smiled. "I would be very grateful, señor," he said quickly. "*Tia* Maria will give her permission, of that I am certain."

Trey tousled the boy's black hair and started back toward camp with Carlos at his side. Only fleetingly, Trey was reminded that Billy Marsh would have been about the same age as the boy. He quickly pushed the memory away, fearing the pain of any further recollections from his past.

Chapter Six

He had difficulty keeping his eyes off the woman, stealing glances when her attention was elsewhere. In the soft firelight her face seemed even lovelier, and her eyes sparkled with reflected flames. While she busied herself with a supper of bacon and fry bread, he admired her unusual beauty, her flawless skin and high cheekbones, her dainty, slightly aquiline nose. Now and then she seemed to feel his stare, looking up from her cooking to warm him with one of her smiles.

"You are a very quiet man," she said once, noticing the look he gave her.

"I never was much at idle conversation," he replied.

"Would it be idle conversation if you told us about yourself, Mr. Marsh?"

He shrugged, palming a tin coffee cup for its warmth. "Not much to tell, I'm afraid. You wouldn't find it very interesting."

She mocked him with a surprised look. "You said you were a soldier . . ."

Trey's gaze fell. "I never talk about the war, señorita," he said in a quiet voice. "I've tried my best to forget about it."

"I'm sorry," she replied softly. "A war must be a

terrible thing."

"It was," he said, after a thoughtful pause. "I lost a lot of good friends . . . I watched a lot of brave young men die. I try not to think about it. My wife and son were killed when the Yanks burned Galveston."

"Please forgive me, Mr. Marsh," she whispered, furrowing her brow. "I should have known not to ask a soldier about a war . . ."

Juan was seated across the fire. He shook his head knowingly, staring absently at the flames. "All wars are bad," he said with feeling. "I fought in the revolution when I was a boy. I saw many terrible things."

Carlos had been listening closely. "I have always dreamed of becoming a soldier," he said, "like the men at the *presidio* who have the beautiful uniforms and ride prancing horses through our village. *Madre!* If you could only see them!"

Trey shook his head, listening to the distant bark of a coyote in the hills. "It takes more than a uniform to be a soldier," he told the boy. "When you're older, you'll understand."

Carlos watched him across the fire, wearing a puzzled look. "Some day, I will become a soldier," he said with resolve. "I will carry a rifle and a pistol, and a long saber, like the brave soldiers of our *presidio* in Chihuahua. Then I will lead my men against the Yaquis. . . ."

At first light the horses were harnessed to the carriage. Carlos helped Maria pack their gear while Juan assisted Trey with the horses. An uneventful night had passed, giving Trey a chance to doze against a tree trunk, standing guard over the horses. When the camp was cleared Trey mounted the roan to lead back to the wagon road. Juan said the Pecos River was only a few miles west in a steep-walled canyon. The road would soon take them to the river, then north to Santa Rosa. Juan also warned that the climbs would steepen as they entered Apache country.

Thus forewarned about what lay in store, Trey headed north in front of the carriage. All around them, empty hills arose from the foot of a mountain range. Summer-dry grass covered the hills, yellowed by infrequent rains and the ever-present dry wind. In spite of the danger of roving Apache bands, Trey found himself at peace. Unsettled country suited him, allowing him to forget about his beginnings.

By mid-morning they were climbing high, wind-swept ridges, only to face steep declines into rocky canyons before the road climbed again. In a box canyon antelope grazed beside a canyon wall, lifting their heads to watch the horses pass, unafraid. "We can have a little fresh meat," Trey told the roan, deciding against a hunting foray for the present. There would be more wild game at the river by sundown when they made their night camp.

Passing time, he thought about the woman again, wondering if he should shave his chin stubble to make himself more presentable. Maria's dark beauty kept working into his brain whenever his mind was idle. He worried that he might make a fool of himself if he showed any sign of his interest in her, thus he put aside the notions of shaving and taking a bath at the river. She would guess his motives.

Following a series of switchbacks, the road turned sharply westward. Cresting a rise, he could see the river below. A line of cottonwoods stood along the riverbank, providing inviting patches of shade. Wagon ruts coursed down into the canyon to where the river flowed, then north again beside the Pecos. Trey scanned the bluffs on all sides before urging the gelding down the slope.

He found cattle tracks along the river's edge, but

no prints made by horses. Thus he signaled Juan to bring the carriage down to the river, satisfied that they were alone.

The horses drank from the shallows as soon as the carriage rolled to a halt. Carlos jumped from the seat and was soon splashing his face with cool water. Juan helped Maria down from the buggy seat, then to a shady spot beneath some cottonwoods. As soon as the roan had its fill in the river, Trey reined over to the trees and swung down. Juan backed the team away from the river and drove into the shade.

"We'll rest here a few minutes," Trey said, examining the opposite riverbank. "It looks safe enough. For now."

Maria opened the top buttons on her dress to cool her skin, a distraction Trey couldn't help but notice. The boy was still playing beside the river, skipping stones across the surface. But Juan was watching Trey closely. As Maria's guardian he was never far away.

In spite of his earlier decision to avoid shaving and bathing for Maria's benefit, he took his razor and shaving cup from his saddlebags, then a clean shirt, to go downstream. He selected a flat rock near the water's edge where he knelt to scrape off his beard stubble. When he saw his reflection on the water he grimaced and hurried to soap his chin.

Later, he pulled off his soiled shirt and washed himself. He knew Carlos was watching him, and wondered if the woman was doing likewise.

When he was properly dressed, with a clean-shaven chin, he sauntered back to the trees to put his belongings away.

"That is a terrible scar on your back," Maria said.

Trey remembered the musket ball that had very nearly cost him his life. "A Yankee sharpshooter," he replied offhandedly, stuffing his shirt into his saddlebags, then the razor and cup. "I didn't know you were looking."

When he turned around, she was smiling faintly. Juan had walked down to the river to fill their water keg.

"A woman's curiosity," she said.

Their eyes met briefly. Trey sensed that her interest might be more than simple curiosity.

"How is it that a beautiful woman like you is without a husband?" he asked boldly, while Juan was out of earshot.

Maria's cheeks colored before she answered. "The right man never asked, I suppose."

Juan came struggling up the riverbank carrying the water keg, forcing Trey away from the conversation with Maria to lend a hand with the barrel.

They lashed the keg to the back of the carriage, then took tortillas and strips of jerky for the noon meal. Trey kept watch on the bluffs above the river while they ate.

"Carlos asked me if he could learn to shoot a pistol," Maria said. "He told me you would teach him."

Carlos was beaming as soon as he heard the remark, looking from Trey to his aunt.

"I offered to show him," Trey replied. "If you've got no objections . . ."

She glanced over to the boy. "A young man must know these things," she said, "although Carlos is still very young."

"I'm old enough!" he protested.

Maria smiled. "If Mr. Marsh is willing, then I have no objections to the lessons."

Carlos jumped to his feet. "Can I take the first lesson now?" he asked.

Trey's attention was drawn suddenly to a movement on the far side of the river. On a limestone bluff to the northwest he saw a fleeting shadow; it could have been a horse and a rider.

Trey's muscles tensed. He came to his feet, squinting to see the spot clearly. "We've got company," he said, resting a palm on his gun butt. "Maybe I ought to ride over and have a look around."

Juan was shading his eyes with his hand, looking the same direction. "I don't see anything," the old man said.

"He's gone now," Trey replied carefully. "Whoever it was, he saw us down here." Then Trey's features pinched in a frown. "What worries me most is that he didn't want us to get a look at him."

"You saw only one?" Juan asked, still watching the bluff.

"Couldn't be sure," Trey replied. "I reckon we better get on the move. This ain't the best place to be if we have to defend ourselves."

Carlos gave his aunt a worried look.

"Get back in the carriage," she said quickly.

Juan helped the woman to the buggy seat and then shook the reins over the bays. Trey waited a few moments longer, examining the spot where he'd seen the horseman; then he stepped aboard the roan and roweled away from the river.

The road followed the riverbank northward. Trey moved out in front, studying likely places for an ambush in their path. To the east the canyon wall offered few hiding places. Across the river to the west lay more dangerous ground. Boulders fallen from the canyon rim could provide countless hiding places for a gunman. In spots the road would take them perilously close to sheltering rocks where a bushwhacker might lie in wait for unsuspecting travelers.

He knew nothing about Apaches and their fighting tactics. If the rider he'd seen across the river canyon was an Indian, it was a safe bet that more were close by. Texans claimed that Comanches were the most formidable Indian adversaries, the best horsemen and the fiercest fighters among the plains tribes.

But the closer Trey came to Apache country, the more stories he heard about the clever Apaches and their bloody raids across New Mexico Territory. The war had taught him never to underestimate an enemy. John Bell Hood's Texas Brigades had won numerous battles until they met General George Thomas at Franklin, Tennessee. The Union Army had soundly defeated Hood's Confederates at Franklin, and then again at the fall of Nashville. General Hood had seriously underestimated the Yankees' will to fight. Thus Trey would make no judgments about Apaches until he knew them on a battlefield.

The road twisted beside the Pecos. Trey watched the bluffs above the river, and the rock piles below, as he guided the carriage north. He stayed close to his party, wary of a surprise attack from either flank, as the miles passed beneath the roan's hooves. Once, he glimpsed a tiny swirl of dust on a bluff to the west of the river. It could have been only a dust devil swept skyward by the wind. Or it might have been an Apache pony.

Soon the sun fell below the canyon wall. Shadows darkened the westward side of the bluff. Sometimes his eyes played tricks on him: a shadow seemed to move across the river, though it was only an illusion. As the hours passed, Trey began to worry about selecting a defensible spot for a night camp. He knew he would have to pay particular attention to guarding their horses tonight, lest they wind up in Apache hands in the dark. He wondered if he was being overly cautious. He was certain that he'd seen a rider on the rim of the river canyon. Had it been an Apache scout, hurrying off to alert a raiding party? He wasn't sure enough of what he'd seen to do much more than guesswork.

Rounding a bend in the river, he found a widening in the canyon that offered his best chances of setting up a defense. A stand of cottonwoods grew in the middle of a sand bar. Dry washes floored with gravel beds surrounded the trees. A horse, or a man on foot, would have to cross thirty or forty yards of open ground to reach those cottonwoods. The Remington would make short work of anyone who tried to slip up on their camp across the gravel beds.

He signaled Juan and rode for the trees, discovering ample grass for their horses beneath the limbs. With the carriage parked inside the cottonwood grove, Trey's party would have as much protection as possible from an all-out attack or a raid by horse thieves.

Juan drove the carriage into the cottonwoods and hauled back on the reins. "It is early, señor, to stop for the night," he said.

"Maybe," Trey replied, scanning the bluffs, "but this is damn sure where we're gonna camp. If that was an Apache I saw this afternoon, you can bet they'll make a try for our horses when it gets dark. I agreed to take this job under my conditions, and this is one of them. We stay here tonight, so I'll have a chance to see who's out there if somebody comes slippin' up on us in the dark."

Juan was looking at Maria unhappily, but the woman nodded and started down from the carriage.

"We have entrusted Mr. Marsh with our safety, Juan," she said, stepping lightly to the ground. "We will do as he asks."

Juan's face registered impatience, though he said nothing. He climbed down from the carriage seat and started unfastening the harness. Carlos hurried to the front of the team to help the old man while Trey tied the roan to a tree limb and then loosened the cinch on his saddle.

He walked to the edge of the cottonwood grove, balancing his rifle in his left hand, studying the rocks on the far side of the Pecos, examining every shadow and niche. It was only a guess that someone would try

64

an approach from the far side of the river. He meant to give the bluffs on both sides careful scrutiny before darkness came.

He heard the woman behind him. "You are a very cautious man, Mr. Marsh," she said.

He didn't bother turning around to answer her. "It keeps me alive. Careless folks usually wind up in trouble. I'm only trying to earn the money you're paying me."

"You must have been a very good soldier," she said.

Trey shrugged off her remark. "I lived through four years of war, if that means anything. It pays to know who's gettin' too close to your backside."

Maria stepped closer to his shoulder. "Carlos has been begging me all afternoon about the lessons with a gun. I promised that I would ask you about it when we stopped for the night."

Trey shook his head quickly, never taking his eyes off the cliffs. "Wouldn't be a good idea tonight, ma'am," he said. "A gunshot is liable to draw unwanted company. Hadn't figured on a fire tonight either. Too risky."

"I see," she said. Her voice had turned cold. She whirled away from the edge of the trees and went back to the carriage.

Trey wondered what had unsettled her. He was only thinking of their safety when he made his decision about the fire and the shooting lessons.

Chapter Seven

The cloudless sky purpled with dusk. A handful of stars shone down upon the river canyon before Trey finished his examination of the cliffs east of their camp. Walking cautiously among the huge rocks at the base of the cliff, he looked for hiding places that would shield an Apache warrior's approach. Upon his return to the cottonwoods, he was met by resentful stares from Maria and Juan.

"There will be a chill tonight in these mountains, señor," the old man said. "Without a fire, the woman and the boy will be cold."

The remark angered Trey. "Better cold than dead," he replied. "A fire silhouettes whoever is sitting around it. Best way I know of to get your head shot off is to sit real close to a fire when you're in enemy territory."

Juan's expression grew even darker. "You only thought you saw an Apache this afternoon," he said. "How can you be sure?"

Trey turned to face Juan, fighting to control his temper. "I'm not sure, old man. Don't know who it was I saw up there. But I make it a practice never to take anything for granted. I was told this is Apache country. I don't aim to lose my scalp because I wasn't sure the man I saw was an Indian."

"Enough!" Maria snapped, addressing Juan. "Mr. Marsh is right about the fire. We must think of Carlos' safety. My father wishes to see his grandson. Say no more about the cold. We have blankets in the trunk behind the carriage."

"Sí, señorita," Juan replied softly, bowing his head. He went to the rear of the buggy and opened the large wooden trunk.

Trey shouldered his rifle and walked toward the horses. The harness team was secured to tree limbs by lengths of rope that allowed both horses to graze. Trey inspected the knots in the ropes, then went to the roan and fitted a pair of rawhide hobbles around its front feet.

He saw the boy standing in the shadows beneath a tree. Carlos was watching him. When he was finished with the roan, he came over to the boy. Butt-first, Trey drew his Colt .44 and placed it in Carlos' hands.

"Get the feel of it," he said.

"It is very heavy," the boy whispered.

"Packs a hell of a kick when you shoot it. That's a .44, and it'll knock you over on your back unless you know how to fire it."

"Will you show me, Señor Marsh?"

Trey shook his head. "Soon as it's safe. Tonight, we're liable to have company . . . maybe Apache horse thieves. Don't want any gunshots to tell 'em just where we are."

"I understand," Carlos whispered, shaking his head as he stared down at the big Colt pistol. "But I must learn how to use a gun. One day, I will become a soldier, like you, señor. Then I will go back to Mexico and look for the Yaquis who killed my father and mother. Before I go, I must learn the ways of a *pistolero*." Then the boy looked up at Trey's face. "Juan says you are a *pistolero*, Señor Marsh. He can tell by the holster you wear, the way the leather is cut at the front, so the gun will come quickly when you ask for it."

Trey lifted the pistol from the boy's hands. "I was a soldier, son. Don't reckon you could call me a gunfighter." He dropped the .44 into its leather berth and then rested his palm on the butt of the gun. "I'll teach you how to fire a gun . . . when the time is right. I understand how you feel about those Indians that killed your folks, but I'll tell you straight that being good with a gun ain't enough, sometimes. A man has to outsmart his enemies to stay alive when the odds are against him. If you aim to learn how to shoot, you'd better learn a few other things. Otherwise, all a gun is good for is an invitation to get you shot. There's always somebody who's a fraction faster."

A twig snapped behind Trey; he was wheeling toward the sound reflexively, with his hand clawing for his Colt, before he saw the woman coming toward him. He froze, and let the .44 fall back in its holster. "Sorry," he mumbled. "Heard a noise."

Maria stopped quickly. She smiled. "I was listening to what you were saying to Carlos. I wanted to thank you."

Trey shook his head, thankful for the dark so that the woman would not see his sudden embarrassment. "Time I found a spot to watch that river," he said. "Never can tell . . ."

He walked softly to the edge of the cottonwood grove and made a careful inspection of the canyon floor. Beyond the river, in the pale light of a sliver of moon, he watched the rocks at the foot of the cliff. Settling against a tree trunk, he sat down to wait for daylight, allowing his thoughts to drift back to his first meeting with Maria Valdez.

A shadow moved; he was sure of it. An inky form crept from a boulder across the shallow river to another hiding place. Trey had been dozing, and he

69

cursed his carelessness silently when he saw the dark figure moving toward the riverbank.

Knowing he was hidden by the deeper shadows below the tree limbs, he raised his rifle slowly and rested the stock against his shoulder. "Keep coming, fool," he whispered to himself. "I'll make you pay in blood . . ."

The shadow slipped away from the rocks and entered the moonlit current of the Pecos on soundless feet. A crouching man with a rifle crept slowly into waist-deep water. Silhouetted by the pale limestone cliff, Trey saw the outline of an Indian. A shaggy mane of shoulder-length hair touched the warrior's bare shoulders. Trey sighted in on the Indian's chest, holding his breath to steady his aim, then gently squeezed the trigger.

The sharp clap of the rifle echoed from the canyon walls as his bullet struck the warrior's breastbone. A muffled cry followed the gunshot. Trey worked the firing mechanism and sent another cartridge into the chamber, watching the Indian fall back upon the river's surface, making a soft splash. Trey's ears were ringing from the explosion so near his face, and he almost missed the guttural shout from the rocks below the canyon rim.

A bright muzzle flash appeared across the river. Molten lead whispered into the cottonwood leaves above Trey's head. In the same instant, a rifle barked, and the sound traveled up and down the canyon. A horse snorted in the trees behind Trey, spooked by the gunshot.

Then he heard heavy boots thumping toward him; he knew it would be Juan. Seconds later the old Mexican stopped running and whispered, "Where are they, señor?"

He could see the old man's face beaded with sweat. "Across the river," he answered softly. "Go to the other side and keep your eyes open. This may only be a diversion. They may be coming from the east."

Juan cradled his rifle and moved away. Trey watched the far side of the river intently, awaiting the Indians' next move. At least one more warrior was hidden in the rocks, but the river, and the open ground around the cottonwood thicket, would force anyone who wanted their horses to cross dangerous yards to reach the prize.

The silence in the canyon grew heavy, the only sound a soft gurgling of the river where water passed over submerged rock. Trey saw the dead Indian float to the surface; then his body was caught in a swirling eddy, spinning him slowly toward a rocky shoal jutting from the opposite bank.

Minutes passed slowly, without a sign of the second warrior among the rocks below the bluff. Trey guessed the Indian was creeping away before daylight trapped him without a way to escape. Juan was silent on the far side of the grove, apparently without a target for his rifle. Trey found himself hoping that the old Mexican's eyesight was good.

An hour dragged by with painful slowness. The dead warrior had washed up against the shoal, and now his body bobbed up and down with the river's flow. Trey sat motionless against the tree trunk, unwilling to be the first to move, thus making a target of himself. Frozen to the spot, he judged time by the stars and waited for the first gray skies of dawn.

Carlos stared down at the body. Juan stood beside the boy to view Trey's victim.

"He is Apache," Juan remarked. "See the headband they wear. This one is very young. They are taught to fight at a very early age, señor."

A jagged hole was torn in the flesh of the Apache's back where the big .50/.70 slug had exited. Chips of flinty bone at the edges of the wound gave evidence of

71

the Remington's power. Trey bent down and rolled the warrior over on his back. Carlos gasped when he saw the dead Apache's face, the obsidian eyes staring blankly at the morning sky, and the warrior's mouth frozen in a perpetual snarl. A dark, round hole in the Apache's chest seeped blood into the river shallows. Trey's bullet had been a perfect shot through the Indian's heart at close range, hardly more than target practice with an accurate rifle like the carbine.

"Little more than a boy." Trey sighed, straightening up from the corpse with bitter memories of the Confederate boys, some not yet sixteen, who had died in the battle to hold Franklin in '64.

The woman was standing across the river while the men examined the Apache. Her face turned anxiously up and down the canyon until Trey started back toward camp.

"Looks like the other one pulled out, ma'am," Trey said, when he joined Maria at the carriage. "Could have been more of them, I reckon. We'll count ourselves lucky that they didn't rush us last night if there was a war party close by. If I had to guess, I'd say they sent the boy across the river to see if he could steal a horse without getting caught."

"A test of courage," Juan agreed. Then he turned to Trey. "You were right to be prepared for them, Señor Marsh," he said in a voice that told of his embarrassment. "I am sorry I argued against you yesterday. From now on, I will do exactly as you say without questioning your reasons."

Trey shook his head. "Let's get the horses harnessed and clear out of this canyon. That other Apache may have gone to round up some of his friends."

They needed only a quarter hour to break camp and get under way. Trey led from the trees with his rifle resting across the pommel of his saddle, scanning the bluffs above them as he rode north at a steady pace. His stomach grumbled for food and coffee as they made their way up the canyon, knowing a fire would be like a beacon to a band of roving Apaches. Half an hour along the road he opened his saddlebags and took out a strip of jerky, tasting its salty nourishment with little satisfaction. A mile farther on he removed the whiskey and savored its delicious burn. He could not shake the gnawing sensation that someone was watching them from the canyon rim. "Maybe those Apaches will find that gambler and take his scalp instead of ours," he said aloud. Woodrow Stiles would certainly be no match for Apache warriors, and his carelessness would make him inviting prey for a war party. Trey wondered what an Apache would look like, dressed in the gambler's expensive eastern coat. Surviving the hardships of Andersonville Prison would be nothing compared to a fight with naked savages in the wilderness of New Mexico Territory. Curiously, Trey felt a touch of pity for Stiles, should he happen upon an Apache band. Stiles had shown traces of human decency when he'd risked his life to ride foolishly toward the gunshots that night, as the two drifters tried to steal the roan. Stiles was still a crooked gambler, to be sure, but he had courage.

Morning sun quickly filled the river canyon, driving away the mountain chill. Barren peaks rose higher to the north and west, promising steeper climbs when the road left the Pecos at its headwaters. Scrub pines clung to the rocky slopes in front of them, and now a gentle wind carried the pines' scent to the canyon floor. No travelers had come this road in recent weeks, Trey judged, for he found no sign in the caliche.

The sun was almost directly overhead when Trey found a turn in the wagon ruts climbing away from the Pecos toward higher ground. He kicked the roan to a trot and rode to the east rim of the river canyon.

The road still followed the river northward, twisting into jagged peaks. Far to the north, a mountain range loomed against a clear blue sky.

"Here's where the traveling gets chancy," Trey said aloud. He listened to the carriage rattle up the steep incline behind him. If the Apache who had fired on their camp last night meant to try his luck again, Trey judged it would happen as they crossed the slopes in their path. The uneasy sensation that they were being watched was still with him; he looked around and found nothing to support the feeling, though it lingered just the same.

He waited for Juan to drive alongside. When the carriage came to a halt, Trey pointed to the rocky passage they would follow into the peaks. "Stay close, and keep that rifle ready," Trey said. He tried to sound casual, so as not to worry the woman and the boy.

Juan nodded. His Sharps lay across his lap.

Trey roweled the gelding to a trot, sweeping the landscape as he urged the roan north. A sixth sense warned that they were headed into trouble, and he couldn't shake the feeling, no matter how empty the rocks seemed on either side of the road. The horse sensed something, too, for its ears were pricked forward. Now and then, the gelding snorted softly and bowed its neck.

The attack came suddenly in a narrow pass between sheer rock cliffs. A gunshot popped from a ridge above the road. The roan shied from the sound, just as a lead slug cut a furrow of caliche near its front feet. Trey shouldered his rifle quickly, trying to settle the roan for a shot at the wisp of gunsmoke lifting above the ridge, when a movement on the far side of the pass caught his attention. A swirl of dust followed the charge of five wiry ponies from a niche in the rock. Gunshots banged in rapid succession from bare-chested warriors aboard the galloping ponies. Speeding lead whistled past Trey, cutting through the air with a deadly whine, then the dull crack of bullets against rock and a singing ricochet somewhere behind him.

He wheeled the roan and spurred toward a pile of boulders at the edge of the road, shouting to Juan, "Follow me!" Another staccato of gunfire blasted from the passage. A bullet tore through the canvas carriage top, harmlessly high, as the other shots went wide. Trey swung a look over his shoulder as the roan raced toward the boulders. The Apaches were reloading their single-shot rifles as they closed the distance. Trey knew the Remington would be too slow; he wouldn't have time to reload himself, facing five fast-moving targets bearing down on him.

He swung the roan around the boulders and leapt from his saddle in a flying jump as he clawed the Colt from its holster. Trey stumbled when his boots landed, and he came dangerously close to falling; but then he righted himself and took aim with the .44, running toward a rock that would shield him from the Apaches' guns. Tossing the Remington to the ground, he steadied his aim on a warrior's chest and pulled the Colt's trigger. The explosion of the big-bore pistol shook his fist. An Apache, bent low over his mount's neck, cried out and flipped off the pony's withers as Trey swung his gunsights to the chest of another copper-skinned warrior. Trey's second shot lifted an Indian off the rump of his pony into the cloud of dust behind the charge. To Trey's left, Juan was wheeling the carriage into the rocks. The Apaches shouted yipping cries to each other, bearing down on the boulders at a flat-out gallop. Two more shots rang out. A bullet whined overhead and cracked into the cliff behind the carriage.

Trey sought a target amongst the churning dust and flying manes of the speeding ponies. Now the warriors lay flat on the animals' backs, hidden from view. Trey was suddenly faced with hard choices, to drop a pony and slow the charge, or wait for a warrior to appear in his sights.

Juan's Sharps bellowed from the rock pile. His bullet kicked up a tiny puff of dust in front of the ponies. Trey glanced over his shoulder; Maria was standing in front of the harness team to quiet them and hold them behind the boulders, making a target of herself.

"Get down!" Trey cried. A rifle banged, and Trey was forced to face the charge again, for now the Apaches were very close to the rocks.

A warrior brought his rifle to his shoulder at the front of the attack. Trey aimed and fired too quickly. His shot caught the shoulder of the sorrel pony beneath the Apache and knocked the animal off stride. The pony tumbled, hooves flailing, as the two remaining warriors galloped their ponies past the pile of boulders. A rifle spat flame in one warrior's hands; then the ponies raced out of pistol range to the south, yelling their odd coyote cries above the patter of unshod hooves.

Trey wheeled back to the fallen pony, knowing its rider was still in the fight. A cloud of dust was settling over the spot where the sorrel had fallen, but there was no sign of the Apache.

Chapter Eight

"Get the woman out of the line of fire!" Trey cried. "Put her and the boy behind those rocks!"

Juan's aim was so poor he could offer little in their defense, Trey knew. The shot Juan had fired at the Indians had been a waste of gunpowder and lead. The pair of Apaches circled their ponies to prepare for another charge, and there was still the downed warrior to worry about, and at least one more high on the ledge, the first to fire when Trey started into the passage. Juan would be needed to protect the woman and the child, should the fighting come down to close quarters. The woman was foolishly standing in plain sight to hold the harness horses. A stray bullet might cut her down in the next volley from the Indians.

Trey scanned the rocks and brush where the sorrel had gone down, feeling a momentary pang of guilt for the hasty shot that had struck the pony. Had Trey's aim been a little better, he wouldn't be worried now about the missing Apache, doubtlessly creeping up on the boulders at this very moment. Trey knew he faced at least four more Indians. Two were hidden, thus his best choice lay in firing at the pair aboard the ponies, the two he could see. He picked up the heavy

Remington and shouldered it. The mounted Indians were about to resume their charge toward Trey's position, and he meant to make them pay for their bravery.

He had his sights on an approaching warrior when he noticed that Maria was still standing at the front of the harness team. Had Juan chosen to ignore the warning?

"Get the woman down!" he shouted.

Juan was hurrying toward the carriage, speaking to the woman in Spanish. But Maria shook her head and stood firm with her hands on the reins. There was no time to argue with her; the thunder of running hooves was coming closer to the rocks.

Trey braced himself for the rifle's kick and squeezed off a careful shot. The roar of the Remington drowned out every other sound as the stock slammed into Trey's shoulder. He watched as a body twisted off the withers of a racing pinto pony, the Apache's arms outstretched like bird's wings, a rifle falling from his hands. The blast of the gunshot died while Trey worked the rolling block to fit a shell into the firing chamber. One last mounted Indian charged toward him aboard a little dun pony. Sunlight glinted off the Indian's rifle. Trey took aim and waited until he was sure of the bullet's placement. Suddenly, there was a blur to Trey's right, a dark shape lunging from the rocks. Trey knew it was the Apache who had fallen from the sorrel. And he knew there was no time to swing the rifle around.

With his life hanging on his reflexes, he sent his right hand toward his holstered Colt as the Apache jumped from his hiding place a few yards away. It was the woman who had distracted him, just long enough for the Indian to make his move toward the boulders. Now precious fractions of a second would

78

determine who would live, and who would die.

Trey's thumb found the hammer of his Colt as he jerked the gun from his waist. Cocking and firing the gun was a reflex; he'd had years of practice, to make it a mechanical action. The Apache flew at Trey's face with a dreamlike slowness as Trey swung the .44 and pulled the trigger. The Indian shouted his animal scream and dove at Trey with a Bowie knife in the same instant that Trey's Colt exploded. The gun barrel was inches from the Apache's stomach when it fired.

Just briefly, as time was measured in spilled blood, the Apache and Trey glared into each other's eyes. Trey saw pure hate on the Indian's face, then sudden surprise when the molten ball of lead pierced his skin and shattered his spine. In mid-flight, the bullet jerked the Apache backward. His knife clattered to the rocks before he sprawled on the side of a boulder, grunting when the air left his lungs. Trey watched the warrior slide down the face of the rock, leaving a smear of blood where the .44 exited his back. The Apache slumped to the ground with a soft plop and went still.

A gun banged, awakening Trey from his trance as he watched the Indian fall. Hot lead whispered past Trey's face and then whacked into the top of the carriage, startling the harness team. Maria and Juan tried to hold the horses in place. Trey puzzled over the whereabouts of the boy.

The dun pony galloped past the rocks. Trey lifted his pistol and snapped off a shot at the Apache clinging to the pony's mane. He heard his bullet whine across the road. The Indian was headed back to the niche. It would give Trey time to reload his Colt.

He worked the ejection rod as quickly as he could. Empty shell casings tinkled musically around his

79

boots. Fingering fresh loads from the loops in his cartridge belt, he glanced over his shoulder. Juan and Maria were trying to settle the pair of bays in the aftermath of the gunshots. Carlos was peering from the floor of the carriage. All three had been easy targets for the Apaches' rifles in the heat of the attack. Why was the carriage so important? Was it worth placing their lives in jeopardy?

When the gun was loaded, he picked up his rifle and scanned the rocks along both sides of the passageway. The Apache on the dun pony was nowhere in sight. Trey examined the ridge where the first shot had come from. Now a heavy silence lingered. Four dead warriors lay in the sun's glare where Trey's bullets had felled them. Had the short fight been enough for the rest of the Apaches? Trey wondered how many more were hidden near the pass.

He waited a few moments more, then holstered the Colt and turned for the carriage, balancing the Remington in his fist. As he approached the buggy, he heard Juan and Maria talking to each other in Spanish.

"Why did you disobey my orders?" he asked, pausing a few yards from the pair. "I warned you to take cover. I can't protect you when you stand out in the open. I thought we had an understanding . . ."

Maria glanced at Juan. "We must tell him the truth," she said.

The old man nodded.

"We are carrying a valuable cargo, señor," she began.

He guessed she was talking about the boy. "The kid should have been taken to the rocks," he snapped.

Maria swallowed uncomfortably. "I am not only talking of my nephew. There is a small chest hidden under the seat of the buggy. We must trust you with this information, and pray you will not rob us. The

80

chest contains gold, Señor Marsh. The money belongs to Carlos. It was his father's wealth, and now it belongs to him."

At last, Trey understood. "You should have told me about the chest," he said. "It was foolish, what you did. Those Apaches could have killed you. That boy needs you more than he needs a chest full of gold."

"We were afraid," Juan said softly. "Afraid of you, señor. But when we saw how you risked your life to save us, we decided that you should be told everything. The chest is filled with gold pesos. We are placing ourselves at your mercy. The boy, and his inheritance, must make it safely to Santa Fe. And now you know the truth."

Trey had wondered about it before, what it was that Maria and Juan seemed so anxious to protect. At first, he'd thought it was merely concern for Carlos. "I'm glad you told me," he sighed, turning to glance up the pass. "From now on, we'll take special precautions with the money." Then he looked at Maria. "You have no choice, as I see it. You'll have to trust me. I can't protect the three of you, or that gold, the way things are. You'll only get yourself killed, standing out in the open like that. When I tell you to take cover, I want you to do exactly as I say. The chest will have to come out of that carriage when trouble starts. That'll be your job from here on, Juan. You keep that chest with you while Maria looks after the boy. If there's any fighting to be done, I'll do it. But that carriage can't be protected if we get in a tight spot, so the chest has to come out. Understood?"

Maria and Juan nodded their heads.

"Agreed," Maria said quietly. Then she stared at the pass. "How will we get through, Señor Marsh?"

Trey examined the ridge again, and then the niche. "Maybe we won't," he said. "Maybe we'll have to

81

find a way around. Right now, we wait for their next move. Depends on how many of them there are, whether they'll rush us again."

"We can't stay here forever," Maria protested. "My father expects us in Santa Fe very soon."

Trey's impatience was growing. "I suspect your father would rather have you alive. We wait here until I think it's safe to move. If you're in a big hurry, you can pay me my twenty dollars and drive straight through that pass anytime you get ready."

When he turned back to Maria, she was fuming. Her eyes were flashing when she spoke. "You can be very impudent, Señor Marsh!"

Her remark angered Trey even more. "Let's get one thing understood," he said coldly. "I'm not your personal servant, or anything of the kind. I agreed to protect you. If I sound impudent, it's because I've been trying to reason with you and you won't listen. I told you from the beginning . . . we do this my way, or not at all. I'll be the one to decide when we move, and when we wait."

Maria whirled, turning her back on him. She said something to Juan in Spanish, then marched to the other side of the carriage and spoke to Carlos.

Trey was surprised to find Juan grinning. "You have much to learn about Mexican women, señor," he said. "They are hot-blooded creatures. They should be handled gently."

"I'm only trying to save your lives," he argued. "If we try to make it through that pass before those Apaches ride off, we won't be much more than target practice for a sharpshooter up in those rocks."

"I understand," Juan replied softly. "And so does Maria. It has been hard for her, to bury her brother in Mexico and take the responsibility for the boy, and the gold. Give her time."

Trey glanced over to the carriage. He could see the

woman's outline in the shadow of the canopy. "I'm only trying to do the job she hired me to do. Those Apaches mean business."

He went back to his firing position in the boulders. Juan removed the chest from underneath the carriage seat and carried it to a shady spot beside a boulder. Maria and the boy came to sit beside the chest while Juan tethered the harness team. All was quiet for a time as Trey studied the rocks and the ledge above the passageway through the mountains.

A loose pony wandered across the road, a scrubby pinto with its hipbones jutting through a thin hide. Trey could make out a splatter of blood on the pony's withers. Green-backed blowflies had begun to swarm over the dead warriors, lifting in unison to hover above the corpses, then settling back to feed. Trey listened to the buzzing of the insects, remembering battlefields where the flies grew so thick above the rotting dead that soldiers couldn't see enemy lines.

Juan caught Trey's roan and led it to the carriage. In Trey's saddlebags was the box of shells for the rifle. He got up and went to the roan, glancing over his shoulder, to pocket a handful of cartridges for the Remington.

"Will they come back, señor?" It was Carlos who asked. He was crouched behind a rock at Maria's side.

"Hard to say, son. If there's just two of them . . ."

He walked back to the boulder and squatted behind it, worrying that the Apaches would play a waiting game until dark. The position he had to defend offered no protection for the horses. If shooting started after nightfall, a stray bullet could easily drop one of the harness team, or his roan. Slowed down by the carriage, it would be risky to fall back down the road seeking a safer place to fight. Moving out in the open, without knowing the strength of the enemy, would be a mistake.

He heard the old man creeping toward him.

"What will we do?" Juan asked, "if they wait for the sun to go down?"

"Pick 'em off one at a time, I reckon," he replied. "It's the horses I'm worried about. They could send a rifleman up to the top of the pass and shoot our horses. That way they know we'll be here until they decide what to do about us. If they aim to rob us, they'll shoot our horses. But there's a chance they were after our horses in the first place, and maybe our guns. Hard to say what an Indian will do . . . I haven't had much experience with 'em."

"All Apaches are thieves," Juan said. "You are right to think they want our horses and weapons. They would not know about the gold we carry."

Trey grunted, having no more opinions on the subject, never taking his eyes from the pass. The carriage made it impossible to choose a route around the mountains. The road was the only choice they had, and if the Apaches were lurking behind the ridge, the road would have to be cleared before it would be safe. Trey wondered about his chances, of slipping around the back side of the ridge after it got dark. But that would leave only Juan to defend the woman and the boy, and Juan had already shown he couldn't hit a moving target with his rifle.

An hour dragged by. Trey listened to the buzzing flies and studied the ledges above the pass. The pinto pony grazed quietly across the road, lifting its head now and then to sniff the air and nicker to the horses tied to the carriage. Had the Apaches pulled out? He wondered about the risks of finding out, circling their position in broad daylight. How long could they wait? As long as he?

He reasoned that an attack was most likely to come at night. The young Apache he'd killed the night before had chosen the cover of darkness. Trey knew he needed sleep, to remain alert after sundown, but could he risk dozing now?

He found a spot of shade below a boulder and rested his head against the cool rock. Last night's long ordeal had begun to take its toll on his eyelids.

"Keep your eyes open," he mumbled sleepily. "I'll try to get a little shut-eye before it gets dark."

Juan shifted his rifle and peered across the rocks.

Chapter Nine

A moving body causes a stirring that can't be explained by the senses. It isn't a sound, or an easily recognizable movement, no matter how slight. Some men believe it is a gentle current of air against their cheeks, though it seems a farfetched explanation if the movement is thirty yards away. But Trey felt that stirring in the dark and keened his senses. At Second Bull Run he had known a Union advance was coming in the dark long before the first shot bellowed near Confederate trenches. He could never have explained how he knew. He'd felt, rather than seen, a stirring along the Union lines.

He felt a stirring now, somewhere in the night, the whisper of moving bodies near the entrance into the pass. There was no movement he could see, but he knew the Apaches were coming for them.

"Get ready," he whispered, crouching behind the rocks. "I figure we're about to have company."

Juan shouldered his rifle, aiming toward the pass. "There is nothing," he answered softly.

Trey focused on a shadow below the pass. Was there movement in the shadow? He couldn't be sure.

Then the roan rattled a soft warning from its muzzle, and Trey knew he'd been right. The gelding pricked its ears forward, listening to the passageway.

Carlos gave a soft whimper, startling Trey, distracting him briefly. The woman had Carlos in an embrace, trying to comfort him. Trey guessed the boy was remembering the Yaqui attack that took the lives of his parents.

Trey scanned the moonlit ridge above the pass, searching for a shape that didn't belong. He had figured all along that the Indians would send a sharpshooter to the highest ground, to pin them down with rifle fire when an attack was launched.

He glanced behind them, to the carriage and the open expanse the Apaches must cross to reach the horses from the east. Without any cover, it would be a foolish choice for the Indians. If Trey was any judge of tactics, they would come from the pass and make use of the shadows and rocks. Trey's nerves grew raw-edged when the silence continued.

A shadow moved on the ledge, a mere shift to one side which only a trained eye would see. "There you are, you tricky bastard," he whispered, never once taking his eyes from the shape as he brought the Remington to his shoulder.

He sighted down the barrel, making tiny adjustments for the range, then held his breath and feathered the trigger. Like a clap of thunder, the rifle boomed, shattering the night quiet.

A shrill cry quickly followed the shot. There was a clatter atop the ridge before the cry ended, a rifle falling off the rim while Trey ejected the spent shell and thumbed another into the chamber. The rifle bounced somewhere on the floor of the pass, and the silence returned.

"*Madre,*" Juan whispered, tensing his arms with the rifle to his shoulder.

Carlos uttered a muffled sob, his face pressed into Maria's blouse.

"Be silent," the woman scolded. "We are safe."

Once, Trey thought he heard the whisper of

running feet at the mouth of the passage, but he found no target among the deep shadows. Motionless, Trey waited, listening to the quiet.

A quarter hour passed without incident. A horse stamped a hoof behind Trey, rattling a harness chain. Sweeping a look all around, he saw nothing and heard no sound. He tried to relax his aching muscles, frozen in one position too long with the rifle.

An owl hooted somewhere, a distant sound.

"Is it over?" Maria asked softly, the faintest of whispers.

"I'd only be guessing," Trey replied. "It's quiet. For now, but I wouldn't want to count on things staying that way. I gave them a little something to think about."

Trey heard his roan nibbling grass, bumping the shank of its bit against the ground. Something had relaxed the horse, and a horse's senses were much keener than a man's if the animal was range-bred.

He lowered the rifle and rested against the boulder, still watching the pass, wondering if the enemy had withdrawn. Only a fool gambled with his life, thus Trey did not allow himself any conclusions. Several hours of darkness remained, enough time for the Apaches to find different approaches. The waiting game would go on until dawn.

The Apache's skull was split open, resting in a pool of blood a few feet back from the ledge. Trey examined the ground briefly, looking for more footprints. He found only the tracks of the lone warrior coming from a footpath up the side of the ridge.

By all appearances, the Apaches had pulled out sometime during the night. But Trey meant to be sure the pass was clear before he allowed the carriage to move through it. He went cautiously down the steep footpath to the floor of the pass, covering his progress with the rifle against his left hip and the Colt in his right fist. He approached the niche carefully, slowly, noticing the hoofprints of unshod ponies leaving the crevice. On the balls of his feet, he entered the niche, to a hollow basin in the side of the mountain. Fresh horse droppings littered the bottom of the tiny canyon. The Apaches were gone.

He went back to the carriage, still wary, examining their surroundings. "All clear," he said, to the question on Maria's face. "Get the chest back under the seat and we'll ride through quick as we can. Juan, stay close behind me 'til we're out of that pass."

When everyone was loaded in the carriage, Trey swung aboard the roan and rode away from the boulders at a walk. He watched the rim on both sides with the rifle resting against his leg, not yet quite convinced that their troubles were over. As the buggy rolled out of the pass, he let out a ragged breath and booted the Remington. The road twisted and climbed ahead of them. There would be more narrow passes and tight places in the mountains looming in their path, spots where another ambush might be waiting for them. At least one more Apache was out there someplace, the warrior who'd escaped on the little buckskin pony. It seemed doubtful that one Indian would try to attack Trey's party, yet there was always the likelihood that the Indian would come back with more of his friends.

"It's that damn fancy carriage," Trey grumbled, riding fifty yards in front to scout the way. "That contraption is an invitation to every bushwhacker we run across, white men or red. A blind man can tell these folks have got more money than they've got good sense."

Just once, Trey wondered about Woodrow Stiles. Was the gambler's scalp dangling from an Apache's belt somewhere behind them? The crafty easterner would meet his match if he ran across a band of Indians on the way to Santa Fe. It would be one scrape he couldn't talk his way out of. The Apaches wouldn't understand a word he said to them, and they damn sure wouldn't be interested in a cut from the gambler's deck of cards.

The road wound its way higher into the peaks, where the air was cooler, more heavily scented with pine. On some of the slopes where grass grew thicker, deer grazed, lifting their heads to see the noisy intruders into their quiet domain. There were no tracks along the wagon ruts, proof that the road was seldom used. Was it because of the Apache troubles? Trey wondered about it as they climbed higher. According to Juan, the little village called Santa Rosa was two days farther north. Would Apaches jump them again before they reached the town? From Santa Rosa, they would swing northwest, facing more of the same empty country. And more Indian troubles, if the storekeeper at Fort Sumner was right about what lay in store for them farther on.

When the sun was directly overhead, Trey called a halt for the noon meal. "No fire," he said, studying the trees on the slopes around them. "Too risky to let the Apaches know where we are."

Maria came down from the carriage, her expression softer now as she came over to Trey with a cold flour tortilla and a strip of dried meat. She gave him his lunch and smiled. "I am sorry for the way I behaved," she said. "My father tells me that I am spoiled. Perhaps he is right?"

Her smile beguiled him. "It's forgotten, ma'am. I'm only tryin' to do my job."

"I know," she replied, very softly, eyes downcast. "I acted like a child. Please forgive me."

"You're forgiven," he chuckled, admiring the soft

lines of her face, her smooth skin the color of cream, without a flaw. Maria was an unusually beautiful woman by any man's standards, and once again he found himself strangely attracted to her in much the same way he had been to his beloved Marybeth so long ago.

He took a bite of his tortilla, noticing that the woman did not return to the buggy, as if she had more she wanted to say.

"You are a very brave man," she said finally, after a moment of silence. She was looking at his face now.

He shrugged. "Just tryin' to keep us alive," he answered, as his cheeks began to feel hot. When Maria was staring at him he felt unaccountably ill at ease.

"It was our good fortune . . . that you came to Fort Sumner when you did," she went on. "Had it not been for you, the Apaches would certainly have killed us and stolen everything."

"These are dangerous times for a woman to be traveling without protection." He lowered his voice. "The old man isn't much of a shot with that rifle."

Maria nodded. "But he is a good man. A trusted friend of my father. Juan has worked for us for many years. His loyalty is beyond question. My father knew that Juan would give his life to save us from bandits and thieves."

Trey hooked a thumb in his gunbelt. "Trouble is, he can't protect you if he can't shoot, ma'am. On a journey like this, you need someone who can hit what he aims at." He took another bite of his food, hoping the woman wouldn't see the color in his face.

She took a step closer to him, adding to his sudden discomfort. "Please call me Maria," she said, touching his arm with a dainty hand. "And if you have no objections, I would like to call you Trey."

"No objections," he replied, feeling his arm tingle where her hand rested on his sleeve.

"It would make me happy," she said. Her smile widened, and her eyes sparkled when she looked up at him.

He felt a mixture of pleasure and discomfort, standing so near the beautiful woman. "Time we got back on the road," he said.

She drew her hand away, tilting her face as though she meant to read his thoughts. Then she turned for the carriage.

Trey tightened the saddle cinch and stepped aboard the roan, giving their surroundings a careful examination. Juan helped the woman into the carriage. Carlos hopped onto the back seat just as the buggy rolled away from the trees.

Trey led them northwest at a walk, scanning the road for spots where an ambush might be waiting. He passed the time thinking about Maria's pretty face, and the beginnings of an attraction he felt toward her. Not since Marybeth had he felt such a pull in a woman's presence. He wondered what was so special about her, as the roan plodded in front of the carriage.

The afternoon passed. As sundown drew near, he began to look for a campsite with adequate defenses. The road twisted and turned through bleak mountains. Above them grew thick pines where they saw deer and antelope grazing steep slopes. Slowly, Trey began to trust the feeling that they were alone. There had been no sign of Apaches, no unshod hoofprints and no telltale swirls of dust in the distance. As the sun fell below the peaks, he allowed himself to relax. Perhaps the lone Apache had moved on to easier pickings.

He found what he wanted at a bend in the road. A stand of pines offered protection from all sides. He rode into the trees and felt some satisfaction. He could defend the position, and there was cover for the horses and the members of his party.

The carriage halted inside the pines. Juan aided Maria down from the seat and then took the chest while Carlos helped with the harness team. Trey skirted the little pine grove before he swung off the roan, making sure of things, sweeping the mountains before the last rays of sunlight faded.

"We'll risk a fire tonight," he said, slipping hobbles on the roan's forefeet. "Make it small, and circle it with rocks. Soon as the cooking's done, I want it smothered."

Carlos nodded. "I can gather wood for the fire," he said, starting away from the trees.

"Don't go alone," Trey warned, halting the boy with his uplifted palm. "Wait for Juan. I'm still not satisfied that we're all alone up here."

Dark came quickly. Trey circled the pines with his rifle while Juan boiled coffee and fried strips of salt pork. The air turned colder, and he shivered once, walking the perimeter of the camp in a chill night breeze washing down from the slopes.

He heard footsteps behind him some time later, and he knew by the sound that it was Maria coming toward him. He smelled coffee before he turned around.

"I brought you something warm," she said, handing him a tin cup that gave off steam when he held it to his lips.

"Thanks, Maria," he said gently. He liked the sound of the name when he said it aloud.

"You are welcome, Trey," she answered, beaming one of her wonderful smiles.

She stood very close to him while he sipped his coffee.

"I've got some whiskey in my saddlebags that'll sweeten this stuff," he said. More than anything else he was searching for things to talk about, though the

94

whiskey would take the edge off his nerves when Maria's eyes were on him. He found it increasingly strange that she had such a profound effect on him. What was there about her that stirred him so deeply?

"I don't approve of whiskey," she said darkly. Her expression had changed quickly. She turned away and walked back to the fire with her shoulders rounded against the chill.

Once again, Maria's mood had changed suddenly, leaving Trey puzzled by it. Maria was full of contradictions. One minute she was smiling; then some off-handed remark would erase her smile without apparent cause. Was it her unpredictable nature that he found so fascinating? She was very different from any woman he had ever known.

He drank coffee and gazed up at the stars. He couldn't allow himself to develop feelings for Maria. His plans did not include settling down with a woman. He wasn't the type. Not now.

Chapter Ten

Santa Rosa sat on the banks of the Pecos River, a dusty little village surrounded by foothills and thick forest. Adobe huts and a few clapboard stores lined a single road through town. To the northwest, purple mountains jutted into a cloudless sky. As Trey led his party to the outskirts of the village, he noticed herds of sheep grazing the wooded hillsides, attended by cotton-clad boys of Mexican descent. Donkeys brayed from makeshift corrals behind some of the adobes, greeting their arrival. A few townspeople stopped to stare at the carriage when Juan drove the horses to the heart of Santa Rosa.

Trey halted the roan in front of a mercantile. The carriage rattled to a stop behind him. An adobe cantina beside the store was Trey's destination. A handful of dust-laden horses stood hipshot at the cantina hitch rails. Travelers passing through from Santa Fe would seek the cantina, to cut the dust from dry throats.

He turned to Juan. "I'll ask around about the road north," he said. "Shouldn't take but a minute."

Maria was watching him. "We will buy supplies at the store," she said, smiling at Carlos. "My nephew has been begging for a piece of peppermint candy."

Trey tied off the roan and walked across the road. A guitar strummed softly from the cantina's open doorway. Out of old habit he lifted his .44 in its holster, to make for an easier pull if he needed the gun; then he stepped into the cool interior of the adobe and sighted along the bar.

A pair of whiskered cowboys stared at him. Shotglasses of whiskey stood before them on the bar. The two men showed him no friendliness when he approached a smiling bartender. His spurs made a soft rattle on the hard-packed dirt floor.

"I'll have a whiskey," he said to the barman, tossing a coin on the heavy wooden plank atop two barrels. "And some information about the road to Santa Fe."

The barkeeper bowed politely and reached for a bottle on the shelf behind him. The little cantina was quiet.

"The road is very dangerous now," he said, pouring a shot of amber liquid into Trey's glass. "Apache raids have grown worse in recent months. The territorial governor has called for more militia to patrol the road. Patrols come from Fort Stanton to chase the Apaches, but the Indians are too clever." He corked the bottle and glanced out a window. "Are you escorting the big black carriage to Santa Fe?" he asked.

Trey nodded. "We had a run-in with some Apaches above Fort Sumner. Only a handful of 'em, trying to steal our horses, I reckon."

Trey could feel the two cowboys watching him while he spoke. He took a sip of his whiskey and looked over his shoulder. The men wore gunbelts. They had a look about them that warned Trey of trouble. He met their stares with his own level gaze, then turned his attention back to his drink.

"That's damn sure a pretty woman in that buggy,"

one of the men said. He was leering when Trey glanced back.

"You've got good eyes," Trey said softly. He could feel the tension mounting in the cantina.

"Appears she ain't yours, or you'd be ridin' on that buggy seat with her," the cowboy continued.

Muscles tightened in Trey's cheeks. "I work for the lady," he replied evenly.

The second cowboy had his hand near the butt of his gun. He appraised Trey with a guarded look. "Don't reckon you'd mind if me an' Carl went out and had a word with her, seein' as you just work for that woman."

Trey turned slowly from the bar. When he was facing the pair, he spoke. "That would be up to the lady," he said. "If she had any objections, I'd have to send you packing." He took a deep breath. "I'll give the two of you some free advice . . . stay away from that lady. She's in a hurry to get to Santa Fe."

The cowboy named Carl stiffened. He glanced at his friend and then back to Trey. "Didn't ask fer no goddamn advice from you, stranger. If we take the notion to talk to that woman, we'll do it without gettin' permission from you."

Trey lowered his voice to a whisper. "That wouldn't be healthy, boys. I might have to kill you."

Carl's partner curled the fingers on his gun hand. "That's mighty big talk, stranger, comin' from just one man. In case you can't count, there's two of us."

Trey's temper was on the rise. "Wouldn't matter if there was half a dozen," he said, fighting to control his anger. "It's my guess you need some help when it comes to counting. A Colt .44 carries six slugs."

The two cowboys shared a moment of indecision. It was all the time Trey needed. With one sudden movement he drew his pistol and cocked the hammer in the cowboys' faces. Neither man had time to reach for his gun.

"You'd both be dead right now," Trey hissed, clenching his teeth, "if I wasn't in such a forgiving mood. Think about it, boys, before you say anything to that lady across the street. A word from either one of you, and I swear I'll kill you. You've tangled with the wrong man this time. Now turn around and finish your drinks, and be thankful there ain't a hole in your belly so the whiskey don't run out."

Carl lifted his palms, with a changed expression on his face. "No offense, stranger. Just havin' a little fun, was all. I never saw a man draw a gun so quick. I'd be obliged if you'd put that gun away."

Trey lowered the hammer on the Colt. He gave both men a lingering stare, then holstered his pistol and turned back to his whiskey. The bartender was staring at Trey with rounded eyes.

"You had me worried," the barman said with a half smile.

"How's that?" Trey asked, without really caring.

"I figured there was gonna be blood on my floor," he answered quietly, glancing down the bar. "Glad I didn't have to go fetch the mop." He swallowed. "About that road to Santa Fe, stranger," he continued, "you ain't gonna have no problems. A gent like you, so quick with a sidearm, won't have much to worry about. Now, it ain't none of my business, but I was wondering . . . you said you was headed to Santa Fe. You aimin' to hire out your gun to Jimmy Dolan?"

It was the second time he'd been asked the question. "I work for the lady. Never met this Dolan, but I hadn't planned to take a side in a range war." He downed the rest of his drink. "I appreciate the information about the road," he said, turning away from the bar. He glanced at the two cowboys. Their heads were bent down to their drinks. Trey knew they wouldn't give him any more trouble.

He walked outside as Juan was loading bags of supplies into the back of the carriage. Carlos had an armload of packages, and a lump of candy in his cheek that made him all smiles when Trey crossed the road.

Maria came out of the store, and the change in her appearance caught Trey's attention. She had changed out of her green dress, and now she wore tight denims and a soft white blouse. Men's work boots reached to her knees, with her pant legs stuffed into the tops. He knew he was staring at her, the swell of her hips and her tiny waist. She carried a valise under her arm.

He grinned when their eyes met. "Not many women can look good in a man's outfit," he said. "You look pretty just now."

She gave him a smile in return. "I know you are only being kind. I was tired of wearing a dress. Now tell me, what did you find out about the road?"

He let out a sigh and glanced north. "More Indian troubles, according to the bartender. He said the army sent patrols out, but they weren't having much luck finding Apaches."

Maria's face darkened. "I worry about the boy. He has seen so much in his short lifetime. He remembers what the Yaquis did to his parents, and sometimes, he wakes up in the night from terrible dreams. My brother and his wife were very foolish to settle so far up in the mountains. They paid for it . . . with their lives."

Trey looked over to the boy, who was helping Juan put packages in the trunk tied behind the carriage. "Life can be hard, Maria," he said softly. "Death is a tough thing to understand. Given time, he'll stop remembering."

She touched his arm. "He likes you, Trey. He talks about you while we follow you in the carriage. He

101

wants to be like you when he is older." Then she tilted her head and gave Trey an amused look. "He asks me why I do not marry you, so you will stay at my father's ranch after we arrive."

Trey wondered if his embarrassment showed. "I reckon he's too young to understand how those things work," he replied.

Maria's smile widened. "How do they work?" she asked.

The question caught him off guard. He toed the ground with his boot and tried to think of an answer that would satisfy her. "I suppose a man and a woman have to fall in love first," he said weakly.

She dropped her hand from his sleeve, though her eyes still twinkled with humor. "I've never been in love," she said in a quiet voice. "These are things I know nothing about. How do you know when you've fallen in love?"

His mouth had gone suddenly dry. She kept probing him for answers, and he wondered why. "You get this funny feeling in your chest when you're around the person you love, I reckon. You think about them all the time. I'm no expert on the subject."

Maria's face changed. "You were in love with your wife," she said. It was a statement.

He nodded. "That was a long time ago."

"Could you fall in love with another woman now?" she asked. "If the right woman came along?"

He knew his ears were turning red. Maria's boldness put him on the defensive suddenly. "I'm not the same man I was back then. The war came along . . ."

She nodded. "I understand, Trey. I shouldn't be prying, but there are times when I wonder about you." Then she smiled again and said playfully, "Besides, I promised Carlos that I would say yes if

102

you asked me to marry you. I will try to explain what you told me about falling in love, about the funny feeling in your chest. I'll tell Carlos that you are waiting for a funny feeling to happen inside. Carlos must learn to be patient.''

She whirled toward the carriage and walked around to the back to inspect the packing, leaving Trey to puzzle over what Maria said. Was she only having fun with him? Or was there a hint of seriousness behind her questions? Did she suspect that he found her attractive? Did his feelings show?

He went to the roan and stepped in a stirrup, thinking about the woman as he swung a leg over his saddle.

Northwest of Santa Rosa, on a stretch of open prairie, Trey made a chilling discovery. The tracks of better than twenty barefoot ponies crossed the wagon road. He halted the roan and got down to examine the prints. The impressions were sharp-edged, no more than a couple of hours old.

"Bad news," he whispered, glancing around him. The hoofprints angled northeast. Were the Indians flanking the road, scouting for easy prey?

They were ten or twelve miles away from Santa Rosa, and the sun was lowering, making the return to the village impossible before dark. Twenty armed warriors would be tough odds to handle under the best of circumstances. The Indians would be drawn to the expensive carriage, certain it would contain booty. The old man's aim was so poor he would be of little help in an all-out attack. Trey found himself wondering if the woman could shoot a gun.

He swung back on the roan and began a serious search for the best possible defensive position along the darkening road. Were the Apaches watching him

103

even now from the wooded hills to the east? Or were the tracks merely evidence of the Indians' movements to another destination?

Facing the prospects of another sleepless night, he roweled the roan into the deepening twilight along the wagon ruts. He decided to spare his party the grim news about the pony tracks, thinking about the boy.

He found what he was looking for an hour past sundown. A dry wash crossed the road. The carriage would be hidden by steep cutbanks on both sides, offering a breastwork for good firing positions to the north and south. It was the best he could do, under the circumstances. If the Indians came at them down the wash from either side, they would face the attack unprotected. As Trey guided the carriage into the dry streambed, he found himself hoping that he was making a good guess for a night camp.

Juan was down from the carriage seat before Trey was finished with his inspection of the spot.

"Should I build a fire, señor?" he asked.

Trey meant to sound casual. "No sense inviting trouble," he answered. "Come sunrise, if we haven't had any visitors, we can make a breakfast fire and boil some coffee."

The old man seemed puzzled, but he went about unharnessing the team without comment. Carlos helped with the team as Trey fitted hobbles on the roan's forefeet and then loosened his saddle cinch.

Maria came over to him before he finished his tasks. She stood very close to his elbow and asked, "Why did you leave the back of your horse this afternoon? I saw you looking closely at something on the ground."

He looked past her, to be sure the boy was out of earshot.

"I found Indian tracks," he said softly. "Maybe

104

twenty of them. Didn't want to say anything that might worry Carlos, but I figure we may be in for a spot of trouble pretty soon. Never thought to ask you this before, Maria . . . can you shoot a gun?"

She shook her head. "My father gave me target practice with a rifle. It was a long time ago."

He tried not to show disappointment. A fast-moving Apache was nothing like target practice.

Chapter Eleven

A cold night passed without incident. When dawn came, Trey allowed Juan to build a small fire. Later, they drank coffee and ate pan-fried bread with tins of peaches.

Trey's uneasiness over the unshod hoofprints still lingered as they broke camp and left the ravine. He scanned the hills around them with his usual caution and found nothing amiss. A herd of deer grazed on a distant hillside, proof that the way was clear to the northwest. A half mile west of the road, the Pecos River caught early morning sunlight. They would follow the river for days, according to Juan, until they reached a mountain range east of Santa Fe.

All morning, Trey kept a nervous eye on his surroundings. The road showed signs of recent travel, deeper wagon tracks in the powdery caliche, and the hoofprints of shod horses. Trey searched the dust for Indian sign and found nothing. Thus, as the day wore on, he began to relax and think of other things.

When the sun was directly overhead, they encountered a sharp bend in the road where the trail turned almost due west. Now the road was much closer to the river, in places only a stone's throw from the rocky banks. Off in the distance, they could see towering mountains, the highest range Trey had seen on his travels westward. Ever so slightly, the road began to climb again, and the air turned cooler. Steep foothills appeared in their path. The Pecos cut deep gorges where it passed through the rocky hills. A few puffy white clouds drifted across the sky. At these higher elevations, the pines grew taller. Trees with curious white bark grew in thick stands across the hillsides.

They made camp at a clear running stream where it flowed to join the Pecos. Trey's concerns over the Apaches were less, and he allowed a fire below the edge of the creek bank. Soon Juan was frying pork and opening tins of tomatoes. The crisp mountain air was scented with boiling coffee as darkness came.

Trey slumped against the creek bank to eat his supper, worn down by sleepless nights and miles of travel. The horses grazed on a stretch of level ground thick with grass. For a time, there was only the sound of the horses, and the pop of a wood knot in the firepit followed by the hiss of hot sap.

"This is mighty lonesome country," Trey said, sipping coffee laced with whiskey when his meal was finished. "Let's hope it stays that way."

Maria understood. She shook her head and made no comment, listening to the distant call of a coyote.

Trey rested his head on the grass. Moments later he was asleep.

The roan snorted and lifted its head to the east. Dawn grayed the sky above the eastern hills. Deep shadows still hid the forest floor where stands of pine dotted the hilltops and dark valleys. Trey knew the roan sensed something moving in the trees, perhaps hearing a sound too faint to be detected by a man.

Trey tightened the cinch on his saddle and drew the Remington from its boot, sweeping the dark hills with slow, lingering looks. What was it the horse heard? The gelding flared its nostrils and held its gaze on a particular spot between two hills. The horse was trying to find a scent it could identify. The animal snorted again and pawed the ground with a forefoot.

"Trouble," Trey said under his breath. The horse might be scenting a mountain cougar. Or an Indian.

Trey looked over his shoulder quickly. "Smother that fire," he snapped. "Looks like we've got company. Get the team close to the carriage and tie them to a wheel. Can't tell what's out there just yet, but this roan don't like the smell."

Juan hurried up the creek bank to get the horses. Carlos trotted along beside him. Maria threw cooking utensils and foodstuffs into the back of the buggy, aiming worried looks at the hills.

Trey balanced the rifle in his fist and watched the spot that held the roan's attention. In the half dark, he couldn't see any movement in the shadows beneath the trees. The distance to the tree line was roughly a quarter mile.

"Wish the hell the light was better," he grumbled, straining to see. What had alerted the horse?

When the horses were tied behind the carriage, Juan came to the creek bank with his Sharps and a cartridge pouch. He peered over the top of the embankment. "Do you see anything, señor?"

Trey kept watching the shallow valley between the hills, forming a plan for their defense. With the river behind them, an attack would come from three sides. The embankment offered some protection. "Nothing yet," he said softly.

A minute passed, then two. The roan gelding flared its nostrils once more and then emitted a warning rattle through its muzzle. A shadow moved at the edge of the tree line. In the space of a heartbeat, it seemed the trees were alive with moving bodies.

"There they are," Trey whispered.

Juan lifted his head. *"Madre!"* he said quickly. "Apaches!"

Trey went to his stomach and fitted the rifle to his shoulder, then spread a handful of cartridges on the grass within easy reach. "Tell Maria and the boy to stay down!" he shouted, levering a shell into the firing chamber. "Leave the money chest where it is. We're in for one hell of a fight just now. I count twenty-one Indians riding down that slope. Make every shot count, and keep an eye on our left flank in case they try to circle us. I got a feelin' they'll test us first."

The sudden sighting of so many Indians had taken Trey's mind from the horse, but when the roan snorted again, he pushed up to a crouch and led the gelding to the rear of the carriage. As an afterthought he opened his saddlebags and removed the rest of the shells for his Remington. By the time he reached the embankment he could see the Apaches clearly, spread out in an uneven line across the slope leading down to the river. The warriors made an unforgettable sight. Wiry ponies carried dark-skinned men with shaggy manes of coal black hair toward Trey's position. Rifles bristled in the warriors' hands. The Indians were advancing slowly, holding their ponies to a walk as though they felt no need to hurry making an attack.

"They're confident bastards," he told himself. "Comin' down that hill as casual as you please, like they had all the time in the world to get the job done."

The sky above the river brightened. Rays of golden sunlight appeared above the trees behind the warriors. Trey sighted down his rifle barrel and waited for the right range, feeling his hands moisten around the rifle stock. He knew the battle would be furious, with so many targets to turn away from the creek bank where he and Juan were hidden. He would need to reload quickly, and make sure of the placement of every bullet before he sent it on its way.

Juan cocked his Sharps carbine and opened his bullet pouch, scattering shells near his elbows. *"Dios!"* he said hoarsely. "There are so many!"

Trey hoped the old man could keep his wits about him in the heat of the fight. "Take your time. Shoot the closest Indian and reload as quick as you can, but make sure of your target before you fire. Only thing that matters is how many of 'em you can kill."

"Sí, señor," the old man replied in a tight voice.

A cry echoed from the slope. One warrior raised his rifle and kicked his pinto pony to a lope. More cries sounded back and forth along the line of Indians as they heeled their mounts to a run.

"Wait 'til they're in range," Trey shouted, trying to be heard above the eerie barks and cries coming from the line of charging Apaches. "Put your sights on one and make damn sure he's close enough to kill before you pull that trigger."

The multicolored ponies were racing down on them at full speed when Trey selected a warrior for his first shot. When the Apache's chest was in his gun sights, Trey feathered the trigger.

The .50/.70 slammed into his shoulder with an ear-splitting roar. The Indian was torn from his pony as though his body had met a solid wall, tumbling behind the pinto's heels. An empty casing tinkled to the ground near Trey's right shoulder. He thumbed a fresh cartridge into the firing chamber and swung his sights to another warrior.

Juan fired, and cursed softly when his bullet missed. Guns popped along the line of charging Indians, causing a sizzle of flying lead above the embankment.

Trey fired quickly. An Indian slumped over his pony's back and dropped his rifle to clutch his

111

wound. Trey merely glimpsed the effect of his shot, intent upon reloading and seeking yet another target.

Juan's Sharps thundered, and a warrior screamed at the front of the charge. A coppery body slipped sideways and disappeared.

A whistling lead ball plowed a furrow of dirt near Trey's face, and he flinched reflexively. Rifles banged and bullets hissed in the air above him. Trey trained his gun muzzle on a rider aboard a speeding black pony and pulled the trigger. The Apache jolted when Trey's bullet struck his ribs. There was a splash of crimson as the Indian fell out of sight.

The charging Apaches were fifty yards from the creek in an uneven line when Trey fired again. A pony stumbled and tossed its rider skyward. The Indian fell in front of another racing pony, and Trey heard the sharp crack of splintering bone when the little sorrel tumbled on its chest, spilling its rider to the ground.

A warrior atop a black-and-white pinto sped toward Trey with his rifle aimed for the embankment. The Apache was almost hidden by the pony's flying mane. Trey tightened the stock against his shoulder and held his breath, gently squeezing the trigger when his sights were on the Indian. In the same instant, the Apache fired. Trey saw gunsmoke billow from the muzzle of the warrior's rifle; then the Apache disappeared off the side of his mount.

Trey's ears were ringing. The firing chamber of his Remington was red-hot when he thumbed a shell into place. Juan's rifle spat flame to Trey's left. Now the Indians were upon them, and reloading the rifles was much too slow.

He pulled his Colt and pressed flat against the dry grass to present as small a target as possible. Resting the pistol on his forearm, he took a shot at a warrior near the front of the charge. The Apache swerved his pony, untouched by the bullet.

Facing the brunt of the attack at close range now, Trey fired into the pack of screaming warriors as rapidly as he could, fixing his sights on first one Indian, then another. Five more times he threw lead into the charge, until his gun clicked empty. Racing ponies were all around them. Juan's rifle cracked, and a warrior yelled.

Trey dropped below the cutbank, working the ejection rod to empty the spent casings from his Colt. The whine of bullets and the bang of rifle fire was everywhere. A speeding slug sizzled past his ear. He fingered fresh cartridges from his belt loops and rammed them into the cylinder, hunkered down to escape flying lead.

An Apache aimed his galloping pony for the cutbank. Trey swung his .44 and triggered off a hasty shot. The Colt bucked and spat fire, lifting the Indian from the pony's back less than ten yards from Trey. The warrior tumbled lifelessly to a halt at the edge of the rim where Trey was hiding. A trickle of blood came from the Apache's mouth and nose as dust settled over the body.

Warriors at the forefront of the charge suddenly veered to the right, heeling their ponies away from Trey's deadly fire. Pressed flat against the necks of their mounts, the Indians made poor targets. Trey's gun blasted just once more, when he drew his sights on a fast-moving rider. The Indian cried out when Trey's slug found its mark, dropping his carbine to cling to his pony's mane while the animal raced out of range.

Juan fired at a retreating Indian, wide and too high. The Apaches galloped away, yipping their war cries. Trey quickly counted a dozen mounted men fleeing into the trees along the south bank of the stream.

A wounded Indian stirred on a grassy flat beyond the cutbank. Trey waited for the warrior to rise on his hands and knees; then he triggered a shot that sent the Apache sprawling on his face with a muffled groan.

Then he turned to Maria and the boy. They were huddled near the carriage, trying to settle the harness horses. Neither was hurt, and the old man had escaped injury. For the time being, Trey was satisfied.

"They'll be back," he said, peering above the rim. Dead warriors were spread over a vast expanse. A crippled pony limped off trailing its jaw rein, with a bloody smear down its withers. The smell of burnt gunpowder hung above the stream, bringing water to Trey's eyes.

On a rise south of the Pecos, Trey saw a lone horseman, and he heard a gunshot. A cowboy came spurring along the stream, firing a pistol over his shoulder toward the trees where the Apaches had ridden. "Who the hell is that?" Trey asked. The distance was too great to see the man clearly.

A sorrel horse galloped hard in the direction of the cutbank, and Trey suddenly recognized the man aboard its back. Woodrow Stiles, dressed in his fancy frock coat, came racing toward Trey firing his pistol at the Indians.

"It's that damn gambler," Trey muttered. "The fool is trying to get himself killed, and those Apaches will damn sure oblige him if he don't hurry."

Stiles fired once more, though it was a wasted shot since the Indians were not giving chase. The gambler drummed his heels into the sorrel's ribs, glancing backward, until he reached the cutbank and then slowed his horse.

Trey frowned when Stiles reined his horse to a halt. "You must be tryin' to lose your scalp, gambler," he said. "That was a fool's move just then."

Some of the color returned to Stiles' face. "I heard all the shooting and came as quickly as I could to

114

lend a hand. Didn't know it was you 'til now. Good to see you again, Mr. Marsh." Then he gazed across the battlefield. "Looks like you gave a good account of yourself, Colonel. If you happen to have another rifle, I'll throw in with you before they come back."

Trey let out a sigh. It seemed he was destined to have this gambler on his coattails all the way to Santa Fe. "Climb down, Stiles," he said in a tired voice. "I suppose we could use one more gun if those Apaches try us again."

Chapter Twelve

Trey studied the battleground before them, the still bodies of downed Apaches scattered across the flats leading to the stream, as Stiles tied his winded sorrel behind the carriage, out of harm's way. Trey heard Juan reloading his Sharps, and when he turned to look at the old man, he could read the fear on Juan's face.

"That was very close, señor," Juan said. There was a slight tremor in his voice. Juan looked over his shoulder. "You know this man? You called him . . . gambler?"

Trey shook his head. "We had the misfortune to meet back in Tascosa. It wasn't my idea."

Juan shrugged. "We do not have another rifle, as he asked."

Trey sighed and turned back to the battlefield. "He probably can't shoot straight anyway. Maybe the distance across a crowded saloon."

Juan lowered his voice. "But he has offered to help us fight the Apaches, señor . . . and that is a very brave thing."

"Maybe," Trey replied softly, wondering about the gambler's motives.

Stiles approached the creek bank with a question on his face. "Do you have a spare rifle?"

Trey wagged his head side to side. "Just these two. If you take the notion to lend us a hand, you'll have to do it with that peashooter of yours. A .41 caliber isn't liable to help much, but if you've got the inclination . . ."

Stiles stood beside Trey, searching his face now. "You don't seem too happy to see me again Colonel. And I wonder why, when you're surrounded by hostiles."

Trey's impatience was growing. "I told you before, I didn't want any company, Stiles."

"I heard the shooting," Stiles answered. "And I could see you were badly outnumbered. I wasn't expecting gratitude, but you could at least drop the unfriendly tone."

Trey clamped his jaw to silence his tongue, wondering why the gambler irritated him so. "We're obliged," he said finally. "I reckon my nerves are on edge."

Stiles rodded spent shells from his pistol and went about the task of reloading. "I can watch our flanks," he said, with a look back toward the creek where the woman and the boy took shelter behind the carriage. "If they come around either side, I'll be in a position to halt them."

"Suit yourself," Trey said, still struggling with a keen dislike for Stiles and men of his ilk. "Wish you hadn't busted that jug of whiskey right about now. Mine's about dry."

At the edge of the trees where the Apaches had ridden, Trey saw a shadow move. "Looks like they're gettin' ready for another try," he said. "Find some cover, and make sure the woman and the boy keep their heads down back there."

"Done, Colonel," Stiles replied, wheeling for the carriage.

"And cut out that colonel business, Stiles," Trey added. "The war is over, in case you've forgotten."

"Then, what shall I call you?" Stiles asked.

Trey had begun to chew his lip, anticipating the next charge by the Indians. "Don't make a hell of a lot of difference to me." He sighed heavily. "My given name is Trey."

Stiles grinned, though it was done weakly. "I'm called Woody by my friends," he said.

Trey's temper was on the rise. "We ain't friends, gambler. Make no mistake. I don't make friends with card cheats."

Now it was Stiles' turn to grow angry. "I do not cheat at cards," he said hotly. "Thus I shouldn't have to take your insults over my chosen profession."

Apaches had begun to materialize in the shadows beneath the trees, and Trey wanted no more conversation. He ignored Stiles and watched the Indians, until the gambler walked off.

"I count eleven," Trey said. Juan rested his rifle on his forearm, squinting at the trees.

Behind Trey, he heard Stiles introduce himself to Maria and Carlos. "The damn fool probably figures he's a ladies' man," Trey muttered under his breath.

Eleven slender ponies started down a slope leading away from the pine forest. In the early morning sunlight, they made a fearsome sight, copper skin turned red by the sun, rifle barrels glistening.

"They'll be smarter this time," Trey said, glancing over to Juan. "They'll come at us from all sides, now that they know we can shoot. We made 'em pay dearly for that charge. They won't be dumb enough to try that again."

"An Apache is not dumb, señor," Juan said. "The warriors are very brave. Their honor is at stake in battle. Some will ride foolishly right at us again, as proof of their courage to the other Apaches."

Trey grunted. "Then, let 'em come," he said, squaring his jaw. "Bravery and stupidity are two different things in a war."

Now the multicolored ponies were in a trot, fanning out across the slope. The Indians were silent, making Trey wonder when they would begin their animal cries again. The sound added to their fearsome appearance during an all-out charge. Trey knew it would send fear into the hearts of most enemies, in much the same way that a Rebel yell drove Union infantrymen back at Gettysburg, even when the Confederate forces were badly outnumbered.

The first yipping coyote call sounded from the slope, and in spite of Trey's experience in the heat of battle, the cry made the hairs prickle down the back of his neck.

"Dios!" Juan whispered, sighting down the barrel of his Sharps with the color draining from his cheeks.

Trey put his rifle sights on a distant warrior and waited for the right range. He knew the Apaches would try something, a trick to draw enemy fire.

Suddenly, five warriors broke off to the north, shouting their war cries, shaking rifles above their heads while heeling their ponies to a lope.

"Wonder what they're up to now?" Trey muttered, glancing north to watch the progress of the five Indians.

The riders disappeared over the bank of the creek, and Trey knew what the Apaches meant to do. "They're coming down the stream," he said, wishing for just one more accurate marksman to slow down the attack from the creek bed.

"Coming up the flank!" It was Stiles' voice.

"I see 'em," Trey answered. He looked over at Juan. "Get to that pile of rocks. I'll hold them off here. Pour as much lead up that stream as you can!"

Juan crawled away from the cutbank and crept to a pile of rocks where the stream made a turn. When he was crouched down, he sighted over the boulders and aimed up the creek.

A cry distracted Trey momentarily. The Apaches came at a full charge, shouting, drumming their heels into their ponies' sides. He fixed his sights on the closest warrior and nudged the trigger on the Remington.

The blast of the shot rocked him back. His ears were ringing as he watched a rider fall to the grass. Working another shell into the breech, he heard Juan's rifle explode with a sharp crack that echoed off the walls of the cutbank where Juan was hiding.

The Apaches' rifles pounded an answer. Gunshots crackled up and down the line of warriors racing toward Trey. Then, to the left, he heard the pop of rifles coming from the streambed. Slugs were singing overhead. A bullet ricochetted off the rocks where Juan was crouching. Trey swung his rifle to the form of a warrior atop a galloping gray pony bearing down on the cutbank, squeezing off a careful shot when his sights were steady.

The boom of the Remington filled Trey's ears. Across the battlefield, there was a scream. There was no time to feel satisfaction for having taken two Indians out of the fight, for the Apaches had closed the distance to less than a hundred yards.

Juan's rifle sounded; then a horse whickered behind the carriage, and there was a rattling of harness chain. From the corner of his eye, Trey saw the gambler run toward the pile of rocks where Juan was shooting, clutching his plated revolver.

Trey fired at a swiftly moving rider aboard a pinto pony and cursed his carelessness when he knew the shot was a miss. Thumbing a cartridge into the chamber as quickly as he could, he aimed and fired again when a buckskin pony flashed before his sights.

A warrior was torn from the back of the buckskin. The Apache's thick black hair lifted from his shoulders when the force of the slug jerked him from his pony's withers. Reloading mechanically, Trey was only dimly aware of gunshots near the jumble of boulders where Juan and the gambler put up their fight.

In a brief moment of silence when only the thunder of galloping hooves could be heard, the gambler's pistol snapped once, then again, and a third time. A muffled cry came after the shots; then a riderless pony raced past the rocks in an all-out run.

There was no pause in the next roar of gunfire. Rifles cracked and thudded in front of Trey and from the streambed to his left. Answering shots crackled from Juan's Sharps and the gambler's .41-caliber handgun in a staccato. Trey triggered off a slug that drove the rifle stock into his shoulder. An Apache screamed and dropped his rifle to reach for a wound in his thigh. Three speeding ponies veered away from Trey's firing position as he was fumbling a fresh shell into the breech. A rifle thundered from the back of one pony that sent a bullet whistling above Trey's hat. Before Trey's big Remington was ready to fire, the three Indians galloped out of sight beyond a swell.

Trey whirled toward the fight at the rock pile, just in time to see Stiles rise above a boulder to fire point-blank into the face of a shouting warrior. The Apache's shout ended with a strangled groan as he went toppling off the rump of his mount, arms and legs landing limply on the rocky creek bank where he tumbled and came to a sliding halt near the rocks where Stiles was standing.

"Get down, fool!" Trey cried, as two galloping ponies bearing warriors thundered past the boulders.

Stiles seemed briefly immobilized; then he crouched down and took a passing shot at the backs of the Indians. Neither Apache was touched by the hasty shot. They bent low over their ponies' necks and raced down to the river, then out of sight around a bend.

The sounds of running hoofbeats faded; then an eerie quiet came over the battle scene. Somewhere in the tall grass beyond the cutbank, a wounded Apache groaned. Trey sleeved acrid gunsmoke from his eyes and looked around him. By his quick count, five Indians had survived the attack. Were they foolhardy enough to return?

He heard the woman sobbing softly behind the carriage. He got up in a crouch and peered across the battlefield, toward the moans from the wounded man. Before he dared risk letting down his guard, he had to make sure the warrior was no threat.

Inching up the cutbank with his rifle cradled, he walked toward the sound of the voice on the balls of his feet until a sudden loud explosion sent him whirling around, clawing for his Colt.

The gambler stood over the body of a bare-chested Apache, smoke still rolling from the barrel of his pistol.

"What the hell was that all about?" Trey asked, tensed for more trouble.

Stiles pointed down to the Indian. "This one tried to get up," the gambler said. He looked at Trey. "He had a knife . . . he was crawling toward the woman and the child. I had no choice but to finish him."

Trey gave a nod. "There's one more out here someplace who ain't done yet." He turned and started toward the moans again, approaching cautiously, aiming his .44 in front of him.

When he found the source of the cries, he lowered his pistol to his side and shook his head. A thick-muscled Apache was sprawled on his back in a patch of bloodstained grass with a gaping hole in the flesh below his ribs. The .50/.70 had torn through the warrior's stomach, and it was just a matter of time before he bled to death. It would have been more merciful to end the Apache's suffering, but with the woman and the boy present, Trey decided against the idea.

The coppery scent of blood filled Trey's nostrils as he started back to the carriage. The close-quarters fight left him drained. Keeping an eye out for the five remaining Indians, he crept back to the cutbank, then down to the carraige.

Maria was weeping openly. Carlos cried and shivered against her shoulder, wrapped in his aunt's arms.

"I think it's over," Trey said softly, trying to comfort them the best he could.

Stiles came toward the carriage. He seemed a little unsteady on his feet, and his face looked drawn.

"They came straight at us," the gambler said in a faraway voice. "They weren't afraid of our guns at all."

Trey glanced at Juan. The old man was hunkered down behind the rock pile, looking upstream. "Looks like we made it through without a scratch," he said. "We were lucky." Then he looked at Stiles. "You showed guts just now, gambler. More guts than I figured you had. Maybe I got you all wrong. These folks owe you a debt of gratitude for throwing in with us."

Trey holstered his Colt and swung a cautious look over the battlefield, then at the trees, and the river where the pair of warriors had ridden. Morning sun warmed the cool mountain air, and when Trey took a deep breath, the air felt good in his lungs.

"What about the ones that got away?" Stiles asked, reloading his pistol while Trey's back was turned.

"I don't figure they'll be back," Trey replied. "We gave 'em a pretty good dose of lead poisoning." He thought about the trail ahead. "They might try to jump us farther north, but for the time being, I'd say we're okay."

Maria's crying had stopped. She was fingering

tears from her cheeks when Trey looked at her.

"They came so close," she whispered hoarsely. She looked at Stiles. "Thank you, for helping us, sir."

The gambler gave her a lopsided grin, tucking his revolver in his waistband beneath his coat. "It was nothing, really," he replied. But when his eyes met Trey's, Trey saw the traces of fear buried behind them.

Stiles approached Trey a moment later, as Trey scanned the trees around their camp.

"If it's all the same to you," the gambler said quietly, "I'd like to ride along to Santa Fe with you and your party. There's safety in numbers . . ."

Following Stiles' display of raw courage, Trey found himself without choices. "I reckon it's okay by me, but you'll have to ask Señorita Valdez about it."

Stiles shook his head. "She's a beautiful woman. She shouldn't have tried to travel this road without protection."

Trey's spine stiffened slightly. "She has some now. I'm escorting her to her father's ranch. You can ride along, so long as you conduct yourself like a gentleman."

Stiles looked Trey in the eye. "I understand. You've got my word that I'll behave myself."

Trey grunted unhappily. "If I take your word, it'll be the first time I've ever taken the word of a gambler on anything."

Chapter Thirteen

They proceeded warily over a twisting mountain road, slowing at every spot where an ambush might occur. Trey was still uneasy. His first experience fighting Apaches in open warfare had proven several things about their nature. They were fearless and downright reckless in the face of an enemy. Atop a racing pony, their aim was as bad as might be expected. They seemed to rely on sheer force of numbers to overwhelm an enemy, rather than a battle plan. Still, Trey found himself dreading another engagement with Apache warriors. Experience had taught him that luck often played a role in fighting success. The next time they met, if there was to be a next time, the Apaches might have luck on their side.

Stiles rode beside Trey, silent the first few miles away from the stream. Trey was forced to admit that he now held the gambler in higher regard, after the courage he had demonstrated against the Indians.

"I've been thinking," Stiles said later, as they crossed a wooded ridge. "It might be safer if I rode behind the carriage, sort of a rear guard, in case those redskins try to surprise us."

Trey looked over his shoulder. He'd been keeping an eye on their backtrail, but the gambler's idea made sense.

"It would be smarter," Trey agreed. "This is the emptiest country I ever saw, so we can't count on anybody else scaring off Apaches until we get where we're going."

Stiles slowed his horse. "I'll ride back. If you run into any trouble, I'll stay close to the buggy."

Trey wondered if the gambler had designs on befriending Maria. He also worried that the gambler might learn about the chest full of gold. Then Stiles would bear watching closely. Most any man would be tempted by a fortune in Mexican money.

Stiles swung back to ride past the carriage. Trey saw him tip his hat to the woman, then move farther back down the trail.

"That gambler'll make trouble before we get there," Trey told himself. "He'll make advances to Maria. He's that kind."

To keep his mind occupied, Trey studied the deepening pine forests on either side of the road. In spite of a close call with the Indians, he found that he liked New Mexico Territory, its vast open spaces where a man could be alone with his thoughts.

"Might be we'll stay here for a spell," Trey said, watching the roan's ears to see if the animal was listening. "There's good grass for horses, and it's cool in these mountains."

The roan gave no sign that it heard him, plodding up a turn in the trail, swishing flies with its tail.

"Wish you wouldn't ignore me," he said with a grin, patting the gelding's neck gently. "You'd make better company if you acted like you were listening now and then."

The horse flicked its ears, a gesture Trey appreciated, rewarding the roan with another pat on its withers.

Darkness moved steadily over the mountains,

purpling the slopes, blackening forest shadows. An hour earlier, they'd seen a herd of longhorn cattle grazing in a grassy meadow, proof that someone did a little ranching close by. Yet the road held no sign of travel along its ruts, not since the last rain. Trey wondered if anyone ever journeyed to Santa Fe by this route. Or was it the outbreak of Apache trouble that kept everyone out of the mountains?

Searching for a campsite, he slowed the roan at every bend to scout for a defensible position. This kind of thinking took him back to those years fighting for the Confederacy, when every move depended on being able to outguess an adversary. Though he had seen no sign of the Indians since morning, he was still troubled. Following the hoofprints of the unshod ponies, he knew the five survivors of the fight had ridden northwest along the river, which headed them in more or less the same direction.

A rocky outcrop on the side of a mountain offered the best campsite he could find before full dark. Halting at the edge of the road, he waited for the carriage, to direct Juan to the spot he had chosen for a night camp.

Maria gave him a warm smile when the buggy halted.

"We'll camp up there," Trey said, pointing to the rocks.

Juan shook the reins over the team and swung the carriage off the ruts. Trey glimpsed the boy's face in the shadow beneath the canopy when the buggy rolled past.

Stiles came riding up. "All's quiet back here," he said, after a look behind them.

"This is the quietest place I ever saw," Trey answered. "Except when we run across Indians."

The gambler nodded. "Why would a woman and a child attempt a journey like this?" he asked. "Surely

129

they have a good reason."

Trey thought about the chest of gold. "The boy is the woman's nephew. His parents were killed in an Indian raid down in Mexico. She's bringing him back to live with her, and her father. They didn't know about the Apache troubles, I don't suppose."

But Stiles' face was still pinched. "They should have waited at a safe place. If you hadn't come along, by now they'd have been Apache prisoners. Or dead."

Trey decided against a further discussion with Stiles. The less the gambler knew about what was in the black carriage, the safer everyone would be. It wasn't that he didn't trust the gambler around the woman; he could be made to mind his manners in the presence of a lady. But the gold might make Stiles take big chances, and right now, things were chancy enough with the mountains being full of warring Apaches.

Juan stopped the carriage inside a pocket of the outcrop and climbed down stiffly to begin unharnessing the team. Carlos did not offer to help the old man this time, hanging back, staying close to Maria while the work was being done with the horses.

While Trey hobbled the roan, he thought about the boy, what the experience of the Apache attack must have brought to mind. Carlos would never completely escape the recollection of his parents' death, any more than Trey had escaped the loss of Marybeth and his son. He supposed the death of loved ones remained in everyone's thoughts, but reminders like the savage battle this morning would make a painful memory harder to put aside.

In the half dark, he saw Maria coming toward him. Carlos was with Juan near the carriage.

"Juan wonders if we may have a fire tonight," Maria said, as she slipped a buckskin jacket around her shoulders.

"Might be risky," Trey replied, scanning the

slopes around them.

"Carlos is cold," she whispered. "Perhaps a part of it is fear of the dark."

"Maybe a small one," Trey said. "If we shield it in those rocks and surround it with stones."

A smile brightened Maria's face. She stood very close to Trey. "This morning . . . it was so terrible, when the Apaches came close. Woodrow Stiles is a very brave man, like you."

Trey nodded once. "I'll admit he surprised me. Never had much use for card players." Then he lowered his voice. "Don't mention the chest when you're around him. I still don't trust him, and neither should you."

Maria's expression darkened. "Shall I tell Juan to leave the chest under the seat of the carriage?"

"For now," Trey replied, after a moment of thought. "It wouldn't be a good idea to let Stiles see it."

The woman bowed her head. "I understand. I will speak to Juan, when we are alone. And to Carlos."

"The boy took it kinda hard this morning," Trey said. "I reckon it reminded him of the day he lost his folks."

Maria shuddered, and Trey couldn't be sure if it was from recollection or the chill air. "We were both very frightened," she said softly, shivering again.

Glancing toward the rocks, Trey stepped forward and put his arms around Maria's shoulders. It was a bold move, yet he risked it anyway, in part due to opportunity. "You're cold," he said, looking down at her lovely face. "Tell Juan to build a fire, so you and the boy won't freeze."

She tilted her face then. Her eyes sparkled in the light from dim stars in a blackening sky. "It feels good," she said in the quietest of voices, "when you put your arms around me."

He stared into her eyes. "You are a beautiful

131

woman, Maria. I haven't wanted to put my arms around a woman since . . ."

"Since you lost your wife in the fire?"

He shook his head. A strange tingling filled his chest, and there was a curious weakness in his knees. "Not since then," he whispered hoarsely, thickly, as though his tongue was coated with cotton.

"I hope you will do it again," she replied softly. "When no one else is around."

"Maybe I will," he answered. "Now that I know you approve."

"I . . . approve," she said, smiling now.

A sound near the carriage made Trey drop his hands to his sides. The gambler was walking toward them.

"We've got company," Trey said.

Maria looked over her shoulder. "Too bad," she said playfully. "Just when I was getting warm." She turned for the rocks. "I'll tell Juan what you said about keeping the fire hidden. We can fry some salt pork and warm a few tortillas for supper."

"I'm starved," the gambler said, overhearing her remark. "A cup of coffee would help with the chill." He stopped in front of Trey. "I'm almost out of provisions. As you already know, I've fallen on some hard times lately."

"You can share what we have, Mr. Stiles," Maria said.

Stiles took off his hat and bowed politely. "Please call me Woodrow. No reason to be so formal now, is there?"

"All right, Woodrow," she replied. "Trey has given his permission for a small fire tonight. I'll put coffee on to boil."

She walked past the gambler, rounding her shoulders against the growing cold. Stiles gave Trey a knowing look, and spoke when the woman was out of earshot.

"I interrupted something," he said, a question.

"Just a friendly talk," Trey answered, perhaps a bit too quickly while he watched Maria's back. "Those Apaches frightened her, and her nephew. Understandable, under the circumstances."

Stiles shook his head. "To tell the truth, I was scared."

Since the war, Trey had no fear of death, but he understood. "It's natural. They came at us hard and fast. I never trusted a soldier who wasn't afraid of dying. There's courage, and a thing called stupidity."

He heard Maria instructing Juan about the fire. Off in the mountains, a coyote called to its mate.

"Can we be friends now, Trey?" the gambler asked, sticking out his hand for a shake. "After this morning?"

Trey let out a sigh. "I reckon so," he said, taking Stiles' hand, examining his face in the starlight. "You showed some backbone. I'll shake your hand and call you a friend. But don't ever doublecross me, Stiles, or you'll regret this handshake, and the day our trails crossed. Consider it a friendly warning."

When Trey released the gambler's hand, Stiles said, "I understand. You'll soon discover that I'm neither a card cheat nor a doublecrosser. You've been wrong about me from the start."

A flame came to life inside the pocket of rocks, illuminating the carriage, Juan and the boy, silhouetting the horses tied to the buggy wheels.

"That's too much light," Trey warned, glancing around him. "Be like hanging up a sign to every Indian within fifty miles."

He started toward the fire, with Stiles at his heels. By the time they arrived at the flames, Juan had smothered some of the fire with handfuls of dirt.

Maria knelt beside the circle of stone, nestling the tiny coffeepot near the heat. Trey became aware that

133

Carlos was staring at him. Tears stained the boy's brown cheeks, glistening in the firelight. Trey walked around the fire and tousled the boy's hair.

"Rough day," he said. "We were all scared out of our wits this morning."

The boy nodded weakly, sniffling. "You were very brave, señor," he said softly. "But I was not brave at all. I cried, and hid my face in *Tia* Maria's blouse."

"Bein' brave comes with age, Carlos," he answered. "When a man becomes a soldier, it takes a while to learn courage. Right at first, everybody's scared. So was I, in the beginning."

"Is it true?" Carlos asked, watching Trey's face in the firelight. "At first, you were afraid?"

Trey grinned. "Scared to death the first time I heard a gun go off. My knees were shaking so hard I couldn't run and hide."

The boy then wiped tears from his face with the palm of his hand. "I will learn how to be brave," he said. "And I will also learn how to shoot a gun, if you will teach me."

"That's a promise," Trey said. "When we get someplace where a gunshot won't draw unwanted company, I'll show you how to shoot a Colt .44, and a rifle. We'll borrow Juan's Sharps, on account of that Remington of mine has got too much kick. My shoulder's still sore from firing it this morning."

From the corner of his eye, Trey noticed that Maria was watching him. Unaccountably, the tingling returned to his chest when he felt her stare.

The boy's mood had brightened considerably. "I can hardly wait for the lessons," he said, smiling now. "I will study what you show me very carefully, señor. I will be a good shot. You have my promise."

A pine knot popped in the flames, hissing hot sap, spewing sparks. The scent of boiling coffee arose from the pot, accompanied by a soft bubbling sound.

Trey looked up at the peaks around them. "I'd

134

better stand watch," he said. "I'd be obliged if you'd bring me some of that coffee later on," he added, speaking to Maria as he turned to go.

She flashed him a warm smile. "I'll bring some tortillas and bacon as soon as it's ready," she said.

The tingling filled him as he walked away into the dark to get his rifle.

In the shadows of pine thicket, he sipped scalding coffee and gazed into her eyes, without appetite for the food she brought him in a folded linen napkin. They stood very close, hidden by darkness.

"Once before," Maria began in a soft whisper, "you told me that I should expect a funny feeling when I meet the right person and begin to fall in love."

"That's what I said," he replied carefully, wondering where the conversation was headed.

"I never had the feeling before, so I don't know what it is like," she continued.

He gave her a slight shrug. "You'll know . . . when it happens to you," he said.

She looked up at him and said nothing more, but he was sure there was a message behind her shining eyes.

Chapter Fourteen

Trey's muscles tightened. On the far side of a tree-studded valley, a column of horsemen came toward him along the road. At first he couldn't make out the riders' identities, until a closer look told him the men wore matching blue tunics. They were soldiers.

He turned back in the saddle and signaled Juan. The harness team labored up a slope behind him. Farther back, the gambler rode his sorrel as a rear guard.

"Territorial militia," Trey muttered, relieved to find friendly faces in this empty wilderness. He roweled the roan down a steep grade and struck a trot toward the slow-moving column making its way to the valley floor.

A bearded officer rode at the front, his face hidden in the shadow of a slouch hat. A captain's bars adorned the man's blue tunic. The uniforms the soldiers wore were not regular army issue.

The captain drew rein and signaled a halt when Trey came abreast of the column.

"Mornin', Captain," Trey said, counting the troopers behind the scowling officer before he looked back to the captain's face.

The captain did not answer at first, looking past Trey to the black carriage rattling down the wagon

137

ruts. "Who's that?" the captain asked after a moment of silence.

"Maria Valdez, her nephew, and one of her father's ranch hands," Trey replied uneasily. For militiamen, the soldiers had a slovenly appearance.

"Whose side are they on?" the officer asked sharply.

"Whose side of what?" Trey countered. Was he talking about the range war.

"The cattle war," the captain spat, glaring at Trey.

Trey took a deep breath. "I don't think they take sides," he answered. "You can ask her when the carriage arrives."

"Seen any 'Paches?" the captain asked.

Trey nodded. "Tangled with a bunch of them farther south down the Pecos."

"How many?" the soldier inquired, peering under Trey's hat brim.

"Counted about two dozen the second time. Eight or nine the first time they hit us."

The captain arched an eyebrow. "You fought 'em off?"

"Killed a few," Trey replied, wary of the officer's tone.

The captain gave Trey a look of appraisal. "You must be a hell of a fighter, mister," he said. "Goddamn 'Paches don't scare off none too easy."

"I've done my share of fighting . . . during the war," Trey said.

The soldier's eyes bored through Trey. "You sound like a southerner. Texan, if I had to guess."

Trey nodded. "I was with Hood."

The captain seemed satisfied for the moment. His gaze drifted to the approaching carriage. "Don't seem like you know about the cattle war. Lincoln and San Miguel counties are 'bout to bust wide open. Big John Chisum has gone up against Jimmy Dolan's bunch over the cattle contracts. There's big trouble over it, so I figured any folks way off in these mountains had a side in it."

"We're on our way to Santa Fe," Trey said, as the sounds of the carriage drew closer. "Maria's father has a ranch north of Santa Fe, and she's on her way back home."

"You work for 'em?" the captain asked.

"Just temporary . . . seein' the woman safe 'til she gets home."

The captain's eyes fell to Trey's holster. "Judgin' by the look of that pistol rig, I'd say you was a hired gun. Fast draw artist, by the look of that cutaway holster."

Trey was growing weary of the soldier's accusations. "I know my way around a gun, if that's what you mean."

"Then, you'll be hirin' out to Jimmy Dolan when you get to Santa Fe," he said flatly. "That Catron outfit pays good, an' Dolan hires the best money can buy."

Trey wagged his head side to side. "Never said I'd hire out to anybody, except to Maria Valdez. Like I told you, it's just a temporary thing."

The captain made a face. "Which way'd them 'Paches ride?"

"Same as us," Trey answered. "Tracks followed the Pecos, far as they went."

The soldier looked west, in the direction of the river. "We'll see if we can find 'em. Ain't likely, though. Goddamn murderin' bastards can just disappear into thin air when they take the notion. But we'll look."

The carriage came to a halt behind Trey.

"How's the road north to Santa Fe?" Trey asked.

The captain was looking at Maria and didn't answer the question right at first. "Clear, mostly," he replied, after a silence. "If you ain't had no trouble with J.J. Dolan, then you'll make it okay."

"Never met this Dolan," Trey replied. "We hadn't

planned to give anyone any trouble, so long as they let us pass."

The captain seemed amused. "Maybe they will, an' maybe they won't," he said. "Depends."

Just then, Trey did not care what the trouble depended on, growing tired of the soldier's attitude. "We don't ask for any trouble, just clear passage to Santa Fe," Trey remarked, an edge creeping into his voice. "But if they want trouble with me, I'll damn sure oblige them. Can't say as I ever met the man I'd run from."

The officer looked back at Trey. "That's mighty tough talk, stranger."

Trey gave a slight shrug. "I'll back it up, if they force my hand. Be seein' you, Captain. Watch out for those Indians when you get close to the river. It figures they're still mad about the whippin' we gave 'em." He reined his horse away from the column and laid a spur gently into the roan's ribs.

Several of the militiamen gave him hard looks when he rode past. They were a ragtag outfit, unshaven and unwashed, a sight that would rankle a military man. Trey supposed theirs was a job few men wanted, chasing Apaches and cattle thieves across unsettled land, most likely for low pay.

Behind him, he heard the carriage rattle forward. Turning back once, he glimpsed Stiles in conversation with one of the soldiers. Thinking back to what the captain said, he wondered why the officer warned him about running across men who worked for the man named Dolan. Were the two factions in the cattle war riding roughshod over everyone in the Territory? The soldier made it sound like they could expect trouble from Dolan's men. "Just what we didn't need," Trey groused, "with a chest full of money to worry about."

*　　*　　*

Just before noon, the road turned sharply west-ward, climbing into wooded peaks. Here and there, tiny offshoot trails reached the main road, and now there were recent signs of travel, the hoofprints of horses and an occasional wagon track. Cattle tracks skirted the road in places, then veered off mysteri-ously.

"Plenty of activity in these parts," Trey said aloud, reading fresh sign where a small herd of cattle had crossed the road in a tightly packed bunch. The hoofprints of two horses followed the cattle tracks.

Later, high on a grassy mountain slope, they encountered a herd of longhorns. The half-wild cows lifted their heads and moved away from Trey and the noisy carriage.

Still, they saw no one on the road as the sun moved across the sky. Birds fluttered from tall grasses beside the ruts, disturbed by the horses. Now and then, a deer would trot across a clearing into the pines. At a clear running stream, Trey's horse startled five antelope away from the water. Trey watched them run downstream with a peaceful feeling. "Pretty country," he said to himself. "A man could live up here and never be bothered by humanity."

More cattle tracks crossed the overgrown ruts farther to the west, a large herd, better than fifty animals by Trey's rough guess. He found the hoofprint of a horse flanking the cow tracks. "Somebody's sure movin' a lot of cattle around," he whispered.

He let his mind drift, to the moment last evening when he put his arms around Maria. "She said she approved of it. Hoped I'd do it again, she said, when nobody else was around." He remembered the strange feeling in his chest when he held her. He could almost summon up the feeling again when he thought about her. "It'll be a damn complication,"

141

he told himself. "Gettin' all moon-eyed over a female."

He heard the gambler's horse coming at a lope and whirled the roan around in the trail, expecting trouble. But Stiles gave a friendly wave, and Trey calmed himself until the gambler arrived.

"Hadn't seen a soul all day," Stiles said. "Except for those soldiers. They were a seedy-looking lot." Stiles looked over his shoulder. "Just thought I'd ride up. I was getting restless back there with nobody to talk to. I decided not to talk to the lady without your permission." The gambler grinned. "I don't know you well enough to know if you're the jealous type."

The remark angered Trey a little. "I'd have nothing to be jealous about," he said, with heat in his voice. "I'm not courting the woman. She's free to talk to whoever she likes."

It was plain the gambler noticed the edge to Trey's denial, and he shook his head. "I should have put it another way," he replied with a shrug. "Sorry."

"Let it drop," Trey snapped.

"I seem to make a habit of getting on your nerves," Stiles said apologetically.

The carriage was coming closer, within earshot.

"I'll admit to being a little edgy in these mountains," Trey said, heeling the roan forward.

Stiles swung his sorrel beside Trey's mount. "A shot of good whiskey would help," he offered. "If I hadn't broken that jug in the river . . ."

Trey turned back and reached in a saddlebag. The bottle he'd purchased in Fort Sumner had a mere two fingers of liquid in it now. Trey pulled the cork with his teeth and held the bottle out to Stiles. "I remember I owe you a drink," he said. "That cup of whiskey you gave me tasted mighty good that night. Take a swig of this and we'll finish it off."

Stiles seemed genuinely grateful for Trey's generosity. He took the pint and sent a swallow down his throat, then gave it back to Trey and took a deep breath. "Thanks," he said, his voice tight from the burn. "I'll return the favor at the next town we come to . . . Las Vegas, I think it's called.

"You said you were broke," Trey said.

The gambler shrugged. "I am, but I've saved a coin or two for hard times. After that Indian fight, I'd say we've been through a hard time."

Trey lifted the bottle to his lips. The whiskey was like sweet nectar on his tongue. The rattle of harness chain reminded him of something the woman had said. "Maria doesn't approve of whiskey," he said. He corked the bottle and tucked it away among his belongings.

"One of those soldiers asked me if you were a shootist," the gambler said, as though the question had amused him.

"And what was your answer?" Trey asked, when Stiles did not offer any more on the subject.

Stiles was grinning broadly. "I told them you were the fastest draw I'd ever seen, and that you had more notches on your gun than Tom Spoon or Wilson Young. The soldier wanted to know your name right off. I told them you went by several aliases . . . that your real name was a dark secret known only to a few. The officer looked worried after I told them. He kept turning around to watch your back."

Trey wagged his head. "You're a liar as well as a card sharp, Woodrow Stiles. You shouldn't have said such a thing about me."

The gambler's expression grew serious. "I figure I told the truth," he said quietly. "I've seen a few shootists in my time working the gambling establishments. That holster you wear isn't just for decoration. I'll admit I was having a little fun with those soldiers, but my guess is that I have you pegged correctly. You are a gunfighter by trade. Am I wrong?"

"Dead wrong," Trey snapped, glaring at Stiles. "Loose talk like that tries my patience. I'm not a hired gun."

Stiles shrugged. "Then, you have my sincere apology. Like I said, I was only guessing."

Trey's face had turned hard. "Don't do any more guesswork around me," he said. "Now get back behind that carriage and keep your eyes open. I've listened to about all of your loose jabbering I intend to hear." He touched the roan with a spur and trotted away from the gambler.

Later, reflecting on what Stiles had said, his temper cooled.

Chapter Fifteen

He heard the lumbering freight wagons long before they rolled over the crest of a hill. A pair of heavy mule-drawn wagons came toward him under the crack of the drivers' whips. Trey roweled his horse to a short lope and met the first wagon before it began the descent from the hilltop. The driver of the wagon, a bearded mule skinner, hauled back on his spans of mules, giving Trey a wary look.

"How's the road north?" Trey asked.

The driver eyed him silently for a time. "Clear of Injuns, if that's what yer askin', stranger."

Trey glanced over his shoulder. "I'm escorting a woman and a child to Santa Fe. We had a scrape with Apaches at the river. Just being cautious."

The driver seemed to relax. The second wagon rolled to a halt. "This can be dangerous country," he said, appraising Trey guardedly, but without his previous concern. "Some of Dolan's boys are prowling the mountains, but if you're neutral in the contract business, you won't have no trouble."

"We're neutral," Trey said. "Just trying to make it to Santa Fe without losing our scalps."

The driver nodded, then frowned. "How far south did you meet up with them 'Paches?"

Trey considered his answer. "Back where the road

runs along the Pecos. They jumped us where a creek enters the river. The first time, we had trouble with them at a rocky pass. Narrow spot, if I remember right."

"I know the place," the mule skinner said. "We make this road every month or so. Liable to be makin' it more often now, with John Tunstall openin' his store. The regular run is whiskey to Beaver Smith's saloon down at Lincoln Township. We carry the red-eye most of the time. But now, with that Englishman openin' up a store in Lincoln, we'll be runnin' this road pretty regular."

"Are you carrying whiskey?" Trey asked, remembering the pint almost empty in his saddlebags.

The driver shook his head and aimed a thumb over his shoulder. "In the other wagon. Gallon jugs, mostly."

"I'd like to buy a bottle or two, if you can spare 'em," Trey remarked, hopeful that the purchase could be made.

The mule skinner's beard parted in a grin. "We carry a few spares, just in case me an' Roy get thirsty. Sell you a bottle fer five dollars, hard money. It's right decent whiskey. Comes from over in Kentucky, where they make good corn squeeze."

Trey went into his pocket for the money. "I'll take one if it's Kentucky," he replied.

The driver reached under his wagon seat and withdrew a labeled bottle. He wiped the dust off with his shirt sleeve and extended his palm for Trey's money.

When the coins rattled in the mule skinner's hand, he handed Trey the jug. "Won't be no headaches tomorrow mornin' if you're careful," he said, chuckling, putting the money away.

"I'm obliged," Trey answered, holding the whiskey up to the light to examine its color.

Then the freighter scowled. "Watch out for Dolan's bunch," he said, eyeing the carriage. "They're mostly a gang of owlhoots who ain't got no respect fer a woman. Gunslicks hired by the cattle ring up in Sante Fe to throw a scare into Chisum's men. If you give 'em the chance, they'll work you over real good. They wear badges and call themselves lawmen. Only law they know anything about are the laws they break."

Trey digested the news. "I won't take a side, but if they try to harm the woman . . ."

"Ride careful," the mule skinner said, lifting his reins and the blacksnake whip beside his leg. "Don't bite off more'n you can chew."

Trey waved to the driver as he cracked his whip above the backs of the mules. Amid the creak of axles and the rattle of doubletrees and harness chain, the wagon lurched forward. Trey watched the wagon pass, fisting the jug of whiskey.

"Everybody's warning us about Dolan's men," he said, thinking out loud. "Just my luck to land square in the middle of a war."

The driver of the second wagon touched his hat brim in a lazy salute when he came abreast of Trey, then pulled back on the brake lever as the mules started down the grade. Crockery jugs of whiskey packed in straw filled the wagon bed. Trey watched the wagon start down the hill, packing the bottle away among his extra shirt and denims. At the bottom of the slope, both freighters swung off the road to let Juan pass in the carriage.

As the gambler rode past the last wagon, he stared wistfully at the whiskey jugs, and Trey could almost imagine seeing Stiles lick his lips.

Westward, the mountains were a lush green. Trey sent his horse down the road at an easy walk, thinking peaceful thoughts. And thoughts about Maria, her smooth skin and flashing smile.

"Damn," he grumbled moments later, when

Maria's image floated before his eyes. "You're actin' a fool, Trey. Get that woman out of your head."

The admonition didn't work.

At dusk, in a hollow beside a sparkling stream surrounded by tall pines, he swung out of the saddle and stretched his legs. In the distance he could hear the carriage. He led the roan down to the stream for a drink, cupping cool water in his hands to quench his own thirst. Then he remembered the whiskey and opened his saddlebags to drink the last swallow from the pint. Savoring the delicious burn down his throat, he opened the quart bottle with his teeth and drank again. Back in Tascosa, he would have enjoyed the same mouthful of distilled spirits greatly. But hard times and circumstance had prevented him from good whiskey that day, and right then, prospects had seemed gloomy. But now, his pockets jingled with money, and there was a twenty-dollar payday when he reached Santa Fe with the woman and her precious cargo. On the whole, things were on the mend.

Since the war, there had been more bad times than good in the life of Trey Marsh. He wondered if things were about to change. Was it the woman brightening his mood? Or simply the money in his pockets?

The carriage rolled down to the stream and came to a stop.

"We'll camp here," Trey said, when Juan gave him a questioning look.

"A fire?" Juan asked.

Trey nodded. "That mule skinner said things were quiet along the road. No Apaches, but we might have a run-in with some of Dolan's men."

Maria's face darkened. "Dolan's men are ruffians," she said, climbing down from the buggy seat aided by Juan's arm. "My father ordered them away from our

148

ranch in the spring. They wanted us to sell our fall calves to Catron, for the contracts. My father said he wouldn't sell to special interests, that we had nothing against John Chisum."

"It's best to stay out of politics," Trey agreed.

The gambler rode up and stepped down tiredly. "I'm stiff all over," he complained. He saw the quart of whiskey in Trey's fist, and his face softened. "I see you purchased a remedy for stiffness from those wagons," he added. "That was a most beautiful sight, all that whiskey in the back of that wagon."

Trey offered Stiles the jug, knowing Maria would not approve. Maria's dark eyes followed the bottle from Trey's hand to the gambler's mouth.

Stiles took a big swallow and let out a sigh. "That is truly wonderful stuff," he said, smacking his lips together. Then he noticed Maria's stare. "Hope this doesn't offend you," he said. "Every now and then a man needs refreshment, and it's good for the digestion, so I'm told."

Maria turned her back without a reply and helped Carlos down from the carriage.

Trey took the jug back from Stiles and took a swallow for himself, corking the neck when he was done. "This sure is a peaceful spot," he said, looking at the forest around them, inhaling the clean aroma of pine. "Hope it stays that way."

Juan started to unfasten the team. Carlos was right beside him, helping with the chains. Stiles led his horse down to the stream and allowed it to drink. Above the clearing, a few early stars sprinkled the heavens. Off to the north, an owl hooted in the trees.

"I could enjoy life out here," the gambler said, hooking his thumbs in his pockets. "The air is clean. It would be a good place to settle down."

Trey stripped his saddle from the roan's back. The horse grazed hungrily on lush grass along the creek bank. Stiles began unsaddling his sorrel and fitting hobbles to its forelegs. Soon Juan had the team tied to low pine limbs by lengths of rope that would permit them to graze.

Near the carriage, Maria touched a sulfur match to a pile of pine cones inside a circle of small stones. Carlos carried the coffeepot to the stream and filled it. In short order, their camp was ready for the night. Juan settled an iron skillet over the flames and cut strips of salt pork. Coffee beans gave off a wonderful smell when water began to bubble in the pot.

Darkness settled swiftly over the mountains. Trey unbooted his rifle and made a circle above the stream while Maria and Juan prepared food. When Trey crossed the shallow creek to walk south, he found Carlos waiting for him.

"Señor," the boy began, hands folded behind his back, "may I come with you?"

Their campsite seemed safe enough, so Trey gave in to the boy's request. "C'mon along," he said gently. "I'm just taking a look around, to be sure we're alone."

"Do you think there will be more Indians tonight?" Carlos asked.

"Not likely, but it pays to be careful. That mule skinner said they hadn't seen any sign, and neither had the soldiers."

Carlos fell in beside Trey as he walked away from the stream. "One day, I will wear a uniform," he said, trying to keep pace with Trey's longer strides.

"You've got a lot of years left before you have to decide," Trey answered. "Being a soldier can be hard sometimes."

Trey saw the boy's shoulders stiffen. "I will be a soldier," he said with resolve. "Of that, señor, I am sure."

They walked to the edge of a stand of pines overlooking the road to the south. By the light from the stars, Trey could see empty mountainsides and quiet valleys.

"Looks mighty peaceful," he said, after a look around them. "I'm hungry. Let's go back and see what there is to eat."

Carlos stopped and looked up at Trey. "May I hold the pistol again, señor?" he asked.

Trey grinned and pulled his .44. Carlos held out both hands to accept the gun. When the weight of the Colt rested in the boy's palms, he smiled.

"It is indeed very heavy," he said softly, staring down at the revolver. He closed his right hand around the gun butt and tested the feel. "With this," he whispered, "I could become a brave soldier."

"Being brave has nothing to do with guns, son," Trey said quietly. "It has to do with what's inside a man's heart, not the weapons he carries."

Carlos looked up quickly. "I do not understand, señor," he replied.

Trey chuckled and put his hand on the boy's shoulder. "You will. Give yourself time. There is much to learn about bravery. It takes a while."

"Will you teach me about being brave?" Carlos asked.

"I doubt if I'll be around that long, son. After I see you and your aunt safely to Santa Fe, I plan to move on."

The boy swallowed, and by the look on his face, Trey judged he was summoning his nerve.

"Perhaps you will stay at my grandfather's *rancho* for a while," he said. "If you . . . if you plan to marry *Tia* Maria."

Trey laughed softly again. "I don't think your aunt wants to get married, Carlos. She wouldn't want to marry someone like me."

"But why not, señor?"

Trey took a deep breath, deliberating his answer before he gave it. "I'm a drifter. I move around a lot. I'm not the kind of man who stays in one place very long."

151

"I don't . . . understand. Why would you go to another place?"

Trey let his shoulders sag. "It's just my nature, I reckon. I get the urge to move along now and then . . . see different country, like this. A woman wants a man who stays close to home."

Carlos blinked. "But if you truly loved *Tia* Maria, then you would want to stay."

Trey knew the boy was narrowing in on the truth. If he fell in love with Maria Valdez, he wouldn't drift from place to place the way he had since the war. Since Marybeth passed away. Since Billy died in her arms. "I suppose you're right," Trey sighed, gazing up at the stars. "If I loved her, I'd stay."

Carlos was grinning now. "Then, I hope you fall in love with *Tia* Maria very soon," he said.

Trey was amused by the boy's innocence. "Works both ways," he said, turning for the fire. "Your aunt would have to feel the same way about me."

Carlos walked next to Trey, speaking in a conspiratorial tone. "I think she already does, señor," he whispered.

The gambler was seated across the flames, sipping coffee when they got back to camp. He searched Trey's face. "See anything out there?"

"It's quiet," Trey replied, taking a tin cup offered by Juan. Pouring coffee, he glanced toward Maria as she folded tortillas around strips of bacon. Juan opened a tin of peaches with his knife and passed the tin to Trey.

"It will be cold tonight," the old man said, looking up at the stars. "We have been climbing higher all day."

Trey squatted above the flames and put a slice of peach in his mouth. It did not escape his notice that Carlos was close beside him, their elbows almost touching.

Maria came over with tortillas and pork. She

152

smiled when she handed Trey his food, after giving a tortilla to Carlos. "I see my nephew has decided to help you keep an eye on things," she said.

"I'm learning how to become a *soldado*," Carlos said, before Trey could answer. "And we were talking, about guns, and things such as that . . . things soldiers talk about."

"I see," Maria answered, gazing down at Carlos. Trey could see the love and admiration in her eyes.

"Maybe tomorrow," Trey began, "we'll have the first shooting lesson, if we can find the right place."

The boy's face beamed while he chewed his supper.

Chapter Sixteen

A sixth sense told him the men spelled trouble. Five riders pushing a small herd of longhorn steers came across a narrow valley coursing between a pair of tall mountains. Trey saw them long before they saw him, and he didn't like the cut of them right off. All five wore low-slung gunbelts, and when Trey rode up on them where the road crossed the valley, he took note of the expressions on their faces when they saw him. To a man, they were sure of themselves, giving him haughty looks. They meant to push him. If they could.

"What's your business up here, cowboy?" The man who asked the surly question had a tin star pinned to his chest. All of them wore badges, and Trey knew at once these would be Dolan's men.

Trey examined their faces silently for a time. The man who spoke was a barrel-chested sort, with angry green eyes that seemed to be mocking Trey. Flanked by a pair of riders on each side, the man's impatience grew when Trey did not answer.

"I asked you a question, cowpoke!" the man snapped, jutting his chin. "What's your business?"

"Traveling," Trey replied evenly, his right hand resting near the butt of his .44. "Any law against that?"

"Maybe," the man answered. "Might depend on where you're goin' and what you aim to do when you get there."

Trey heard the carriage rattling closer behind him. The herd of steers the men were driving drifted across the road, untended for now.

"I don't see that's any of your affair," Trey said coldly, with an eye on the five men and the placement of their gun hands.

The barrel-chested gent tilted his head, then aimed a thumb at the badge he wore. "This star makes it my affair. We're duly sworn peace officers. Answer my question, or you're liable to wind up in the Las Vegas jail for suspicion of cattle rustling."

Trey chuckled, but there was no humor behind it. "You've got no evidence," he said, fighting to control his temper. "Looks like you're the one drivin' cattle. As you can see, we don't have any, so the charge won't stick. Now let us pass."

The leader of the five gave his companions a wicked grin and then nudged his horse closer to Trey's, blocking the middle of the road. "You're a smart-mouthed son of a bitch," he growled, with a dare behind his eyes.

Trey hesitated a moment longer, though deep inside, he knew what the outcome would be. He'd always had a problem with the temper he'd inherited from his father. Keeping it bridled was a lifelong chore that had only worsened with age. He took a deep breath, listening to the sounds of the carriage; then his palm closed around the butt of his Colt with a suddenness that came with years of practice. He drew the .44 and cocked it in the leader's face; then his lips pulled back in an angry snarl. "I'll blow your goddamn head off if anybody reaches for a gun!"

The draw came too quickly for any of the five to react. With Trey's gun leveled between the leader's green eyes, all five men froze in their saddles, glancing nervously to each other.

"Nobody calls me a son of a bitch!" Trey hissed, clenching his teeth, finger poised against the trigger. "I'll kill the first man that moves, right after I blow your goddamn head off your neck for calling me a name. I hope you understand just how close you are to dyin', 'cause I'm gonna kill you first if anybody twitches a finger."

Behind Trey, a horse galloped closer. In the following stand-off, five men staring at Trey's gun, the gambler rode up beside Trey with his revolver aimed at the riders blocking the road.

"Trouble here?" Stiles asked, when his sorrel slid to a halt.

"Not anymore," Trey growled, "not unless these gents are as dumb as they look."

White-hot anger burned behind the leader's eyes. "You can't threaten an officer of the law like this. Put down that gun or you'll go to jail."

Trey's cheek muscles worked furiously. "Shut your goddamn mouth or you'll go to an early grave, fool. I'm threatening you, and I don't give a damn who pinned that tin star on you. You called me a son of a bitch, which offends me. You'll apologize, or your friends will be down off their horses picking up what's left of your head. Understood?"

The green-eyed leader swallowed. "You're makin' a big mistake, pardner, a mistake you'll regret."

Trey's anger seethed inside him. To Trey's right, the gambler kept his gun aimed at the group.

"You boys are the ones who've made a mistake," Stiles said earnestly. "You insulted the wrong man. It would appear that you don't recognize the man you just aggrieved. Perhaps he isn't quite as well known here in the Territory. But I can assure you of one thing, gentlemen . . . you can consider yourselves lucky to be alive right now. The man who's holding a gun on you isn't usually this generous. I'd say you

157

caught him in a good mood today. Otherwise, all five of you would be dead."

The gambler's speech took its effect on some of the faces staring at Trey. And while it was an amusing story, like the one Stiles had told the soldiers, Trey wasn't pleased with the result. He still battled blind rage swelling inside him, of a kind that had always gotten him in trouble.

"Who are you, mister?" the leader asked, and now his voice held a softer tone.

"My name doesn't matter," Trey snapped, waving his gun barrel menacingly. "I want that apology, and I damn sure won't wait much longer."

"What is the problem, Mr. Marsh?" Maria asked from the seat of the carriage.

Trey heard footsteps; then Juan came to stand beside Trey and the gambler with his Sharps cradled in the crook of his arm.

"It's nothing, ma'am," Trey replied over his shoulder, without taking his eyes off the five riders. "Just some fools who ask too many questions. Damn near got themselves killed over it, too."

The leader shrugged. "I reckon I owe you," he said softly. "Sorry 'bout callin' you a son of a bitch, mister. You must be new in these parts, or you'd know you can't pull a gun on us like you done. When Jimmy hears about it, there'll be trouble."

Trey shrugged. His expression softened some. "I can handle trouble," Trey replied evenly. "I'm used to it. Now ride off this road and let us pass, or your troubles have just begun."

The men lifted their reins and swung their horses to ride off, but not before the leader spoke again. "You'll be hearin' from Jimmy Dolan about this matter," he said. "It ain't over."

The five spurred their horses off the ruts and rode to the rear of their herd of steers. Trey and the gambler kept them covered with their guns until they rode out of range down the grassy valley.

"What was that all about?" Stiles asked, tucking his pistol inside his coat.

Trey tented his shoulders and tried to relax, letting out a breath before he answered. "They demanded to know our business. I told them it was none of their affair. That's when the big gent made a wrong guess about my ancestry. There's some things I'll tolerate. Bein' called a son of a bitch ain't one of them."

Stiles was studying Trey's face. "It took a lot of nerve to pull a gun on five armed men, Trey," he said.

Trey looked over to the gambler. "One thing I've got plenty of is nerve," he replied, as Maria hurried from the carriage to find out about the difficulty.

"What was that about?" she asked when she reached them.

"Some of Dolan's men," Trey sighed. "They wanted to know what we were doing on this road. I told them it was our business. One of them took exception to my remark. I was forced to persuade him to keep moving along with his cows."

Maria was watching the five riders in the distance. "The situation has grown worse," she said darkly. "I hope my father has stayed out of it. I hope he is safe and well." She turned to Juan. "We must hurry, Juan. *Andele!* I fear for my father's safety. Get back to the team."

Trey waited until the woman and the old man were back in the carriage; then he nudged his horse forward. "Keep your eyes open back there," he said, leaving Stiles at the edge of the road.

Slowly, the anger of moments before flowed out of Trey, leaving him drained. It was always like that, he remembered, when sudden rage got the best of him and pushed him into a fight. He had never been able to get a grip on his temper, not since childhood. There was too much of his father's blood in his veins.

159

Crossing the valley floor, they started up a steep slope. Midway up the incline, Trey turned around in the saddle, finding no sign of the five men who had confronted him earlier. Down in his gut, Trey knew the men wouldn't let things lie. Somewhere farther up the road, there would be more trouble from the Dolan men.

To put his mind on other things, he studied the landscape, the tall pine forests, and meadows thick with grass. On a tree limb near the road, a blue jay uttered a harsh cry and then fluttered to a higher limb. The jay seemed to be scolding the humans for entering its quiet domain. The scent of pine needles made the crisp air even more enjoyable. Trey wondered why he'd waited so long to ride west into this pristine country. Here, he felt at peace . . . when he was left alone to enjoy it.

One of the roan's thin horseshoes had begun to rattle, a reminder of the blacksmith's warning back in Tascosa. At Las Vegas, he would buy new iron for the gelding and have it properly set.

Nightfall found them in a steep-walled valley surrounded by pines and slender oaks. Trey allowed a campfire, where Juan boiled beans and warmed tortillas. While the camp preparations were being made, he felt Maria's eyes on him as he went about his chores. It made him wonder if Carlos could be right about the way she had begun to feel about him. Her lingering stares, however, no longer made Trey feel uneasy.

Las Vegas sat on a broad, flat plain at the foot of a towering mountain range. Adobe huts and clapboard shacks were scattered about along dusty streets. Several freight wagons sat beside adobe stores in the heart of the city. Children played on quiet side roads, close to houses where colorful laundry dried on lengths of rope in a gentle breeze. Here and there, dogs barked. Pens full of goats bleating added to the odd mix of sounds. Near the center of town, Trey spotted a weathered, two-story building advertised as the Las Vegas Hotel.

"A bed and a warm bath," he told himself, his mood brightened by the prospects.

He worried about secreting the chest. A town of this size would have hard characters, men who would take risks to get their hands on a chest full of Mexican gold. Moving the chest would alert Stiles to its existence. Could he trust Woodrow Stiles? It wasn't Trey's nature to trust men, for he understood them. Understood men's greed.

"I can toss a bedroll down close to the carriage." He sighed, putting aside the notion of arranging for a bed at the hotel. The risks were too great, moving the chest up to one of the rooms. It was better to leave the money hidden below the carriage seat and keep an eye on it there.

He led the way into town at a walk, judging the time at two hours before sundown. Dark-eyed Mexican goat herders watched the carriage roll into Las Vegas, and Trey knew word would quickly spread that a rich woman had arrived in town.

"That fancy buggy only makes matters worse," he said under his breath. "Everybody knows it don't belong to some sheep herder or a traveling drummer."

Maria's unusual beauty made the carriage an added attraction, drawing the stares of every cowboy in the place, the way it had back in Santa Rosa, where he'd been forced to draw a gun to cool the two cowboys' interest in the pretty occupant of the carriage.

He rode toward the hotel, with a watchful eye on hitch rails in front of the cantinas and saloons they went past. At a little place called El Torito, he

161

glimpsed the first signs of potential trouble. Seven branded horses stood hipshot at the rail in front of the little cantina. By the saddles and coiled ropes the horses carried, Trey knew their owners were cowboys. And with a cattle war in the making, the cowboys would represent one side or the other.

"Hope they ain't Dolan men," he said quietly. "I've had about all the interference I'll tolerate from their kind."

As he led the carriage past the front doors of El Torito, a cowboy in heavy leather chaps came to the opening to watch Trey and his party proceed down the street. Trey met the cowboy's gaze and held it, glancing down briefly to examine the man's gun. A gunbelt was tied low on the cowboy's right leg. The man's eyes followed Trey, then the carriage, to the front of the Las Vegas Hotel.

"Won't be much sleep tonight, I don't reckon," he said, swinging a leg over the roan's rump to step to the ground. "Some of that bunch inside El Torito will come nosin' around later on, to find out who the woman is . . . why she's here in this fancy buggy."

He waited for Juan to help Maria down from the seat, keeping one eye on the front of the cantina. As he had predicted, more cowboys came out on the boardwalk in front of the place to stare at Maria and the carriage.

The gambler rode up beside Trey and lowered his voice. "Couldn't help but notice we've got an audience," he said, swinging down. "It's this expensive conveyance she drives," he added, tying off his sorrel with a loose rein.

Trey grunted and shook his head. "It stands out," he agreed. "I figure I'll sleep close to it tonight, to keep folks honest. I judge there'll be some around here who'd steal this buggy if it wasn't watched close."

Stiles loosened the cinch on his saddle. "I'll join

162

you," he said cheerfully. "I don't have the price of a room anyway. What money I have will be invested in a bottle of cheap whiskey." He looked up at the hotel with a wistful expression. "A soft bed would be nice, but whiskey sounds even better."

Trey aimed a thumb toward his saddlebags. "We can share the jug I bought from the mule skinner tonight. There's enough to keep us both warm, I reckon."

Chapter Seventeen

When arrangements for shoeing the roan had been made at a blacksmith's shop down the street, Trey sauntered down the boardwalks of Las Vegas, passing store windows, idling away time before dark. At all times, he kept an eye on the carriage, where Juan had parked it beside the hotel in a vacant lot after leading the harness team to a nearby livery. Trey had warned Maria that the chest would not be safe if anyone saw it being carried up to one of the rooms.

"I'll sleep near the carriage tonight," he had promised her, and the promise evoked a sudden smile.

"Should I trust you with my nephew's gold?" she asked then.

Her remark would have angered him otherwise, but when he saw her playful smile, he could only shrug and answer, "What do you think, pretty lady? Can I be trusted with your money?"

Her expression turned serious. "We have already entrusted you with our lives, Trey," she whispered. "If you wanted the money, you could have taken it easily many times before this. So my answer is yes . . . I trust you with my nephew's inheritance. And with my life. All our lives."

He wondered if his cheeks were coloring.

"Thanks," he muttered.

He knew that she meant what she said, about trusting him. More and more, he had begun to sense a difference in the way Maria looked at him. There was a subtle difference in the sound of her voice when she spoke to him, too. Was she falling in love with him? And was he falling in love with her?

As dusk fell, handfuls of local citizens came by the hotel to stare at the carriage, some strolling casually by, others stopping a few yards away to whisper amongst themselves. Trey stayed near while Juan and Carlos carried luggage to an upstairs room. For now, the cowboys inside El Torito stayed out of sight, though Trey worried that the condition was only temporary.

When the last items of clothing had been removed from the buggy, Trey pulled Maria and Juan aside.

"Get a bite to eat and then go up to your rooms," he said. "I don't like the looks of that bunch over at the cantina. Could be Dolan men, or Chisum cowboys. Either way, we won't invite any trouble. Me and the gambler will pitch our bedrolls near the carriage tonight and keep an eye on . . . things."

"I understand, señor," Juan answered, "but do you trust the gambler?"

"Not very far," Trey sighed. "But he'll be an extra pair of eyes, and he doesn't know about the money."

Maria rested a palm against Trey's chest. "Be careful, Trey. I'll bring you something to eat when we find a cafe."

Trey glanced across the road, down the street, to the cantina. "Stay wide of that place. It'll be dark soon."

Carlos was watching Trey's face. "Are those bad men in the cantina, señor?" he asked softly.

"We're not taking any chances," Trey said, noting that the gambler was approaching from a side street. Stiles seemed to be in a hurry.

166

Stiles walked up to the group and tipped his hat to Maria, but there was a look on his face before he spoke, a look of concern.

"I had a word with the gentleman who owns the newspaper here," Stiles began. "More difficulties are brewing down around Lincoln, and it extends to Santa Fe. We may run across open warfare on the Santa Fe road. That cowman John Chisum is hiring gunslicks to see that his cow herds are left alone. According to the proprietor of the paper, there has been a lot of rustling across the Territory. Powerful men at the territorial capital have sided against this fellow Chisum, and they have their own hired guns. Those men you had difficulty with earlier today are special posse men working for a gentleman by the name of Thomas Catron."

"Tom Catron is no gentleman," Maria said quickly. "He sent men to my father's *rancho*, telling us that we had to sell our calves to Dolan." Then she glanced west, toward the darkening horizon. "I worry more than ever about my father. We must hurry back to the ranch." She looked at Trey. "We will be ready to leave just before dawn. We must not waste any more time."

Trey nodded. "We'll be ready. Now get something to eat, and get to your rooms. Those men down the street will get rowdy with bellies full of whiskey. I don't suppose it matters which side they work for. There'll be trouble as soon as they drink up a bellyful of courage."

Juan took Maria's arm. "I will go for the food," he said in a gentle voice. "Come, we will go upstairs, and when you are safe, I will find something to eat."

Maria started to object, then agreed silently and allowed Juan to escort her to the front door of the hotel. As soon as the three were inside, Stiles turned to Trey.

"The old man at the newspaper warned that we

shouldn't travel the road to Santa Fe until a military patrol accompanies us," he said darkly. "There have been killings. Half a dozen or so in the past few weeks. The governor is trying to keep a lid on things; but there aren't many federal troops at Fort Stanton, and the militia is suspected of favoring the powerful men in Santa Fe."

"Looks like we've ridden into a powder keg." Trey sighed. "If we stay neutral, maybe they'll let us past unmolested."

Stiles gave him a half grin. "You were hardly neutral back when you held a gun on those five deputies."

Trey's face tightened. "Nobody calls me a son of a bitch, Mr. Stiles. Nobody."

The gambler shrugged. "It was just my observation that those men aren't likely to let it rest. If we see them again, we can expect more difficulties."

Trey hooked his thumbs in his gunbelt. "I'm accustomed to having difficulties, gambler. Seems Lady Luck has decided to hand me a good-sized share of them. I've learned one thing from the experience . . . a man who has nothing to lose can handle difficulty better than anybody else."

Stiles looked at him strangely. "But you could lose your life if the odds get too long against you."

Trey's hard gray eyes came to rest on the gambler's face. "Like I said, a man with nothing to lose isn't afraid of the odds, or much of anything else."

By Stiles' expression, Trey knew the gambler did not understand.

"You're not afraid of dying?" Stiles asked.

Trey had grown weary of the discussion. He turned his back on the gambler and started toward the blacksmith's shop, where he could see his roan tied out front, finished with its shoeing.

The smithy eyed him carefully, first his face, then his gun. "You're new 'round here, ain't ya?" he asked.

Trey nodded, digging in a pocket for the two dollars he owed the blacksmith. He handed the smithy two silver dollars and turned for the roan.

"Who's the lady in that fancy buggy?" the smithy asked.

Trey ignored the question and started back up the street with his gelding in tow. Across the road, loud voices echoed from the doors and windows of El Torito.

Approaching the carriage, he noticed that the gambler had tied his sorrel to a rear wheel. Stiles was leaning against one side of the buggy, watching the street.

"I wonder what he'd do if he knew there was a chest full of gold under the seat behind him," Trey muttered, leading the roan to a stretch of soft grass not far from the carriage at the rear of the vacant lot. Deep shadows fell across the spot from the hotel and a mercantile on the other side of the lot. Trey knelt and fitted rawhide hobbles on the roan's forefeet, briefly admiring the new iron shoes nailed to the horse's hooves.

When Trey returned to the carriage, he removed the Kentucky whiskey from a saddlebag and pulled the cork, offering the bottle to Stiles.

The gambler grinned. "That's good whiskey. You'll spoil me. I'd been forced to develop a taste for bad red-eye." He took the bottle and held it to his lips. A generous swallow bubbled into his mouth. "Damn that's good," he said, returning the jug, his voice tight from the burn.

Trey took a swallow, savoring it, rolling the whiskey across his tongue to fully enjoy it. Like liquid fire, the whiskey scalded his throat on its way to his belly. "That is some of the finest," he said, when he could talk. He took another drink and passed the bottle back to Stiles.

Down the street, raucous laughter came from the

cantina, then the sound of breaking glass. Stiles jumped when the glass broke, and he turned a worried look at Trey.

"Some of them were staring at us when we rode in," he said, as though Trey hadn't heard him the first time. "I fully expect them to come out later on, perhaps to challenge us, to see which side of this cattle business we're on."

Trey knew the gambler spoke truth. He, too, expected trouble from the cowboys down at the cantina. Facing the prospects of yet another sleepless night, he leaned back against a carriage wheel, resting the whiskey bottle on his bent knee. "I 'spect you're right," he said. "Don't look like we'll get much shut-eye tonight, having to guard this fancy wagon."

Stiles peered down the street, to the saddled horses in front of the El Torito. "By my count, there's seven of them, and just two of us, not counting the old man," he said thoughtfully. "Lately, it seems the odds are always stacked the wrong way. Those rascals who chased me to the river had us outnumbered. Then there was that Indian attack, and the five deputies. And now this."

"You worry too much about the odds, gambler," Trey replied, when Stiles fell silent.

Stiles looked over at Trey. "You've forgotten that it's the way I make my living. I never bet into long odds."

Trey chuckled softly. "Appears you have this time, Mr. Stiles."

His muscles stiffened when he heard the clump of heavy boots and the rattle of spurs. He'd been dozing against a carriage wheel, and the sound startled him awake. Gazing down the street, he saw dark shadows moving along the boardwalk in front of the cantina.

170

"Here they come," he said softly.

The gambler had been sitting on the ground. Trey's warning brought him quickly to his feet. He reached inside his coat and drew his nickle-plated pistol, then let it dangle beside his pant leg.

"I see four of them," Stiles whispered, craning his neck for a better view of the street.

Four silhouettes came toward the front of the hotel in the dark. Trey listened to the clank of their spurs. The odds would be better than he figured, judging by the horses tied in front of the cantina. Only four of the men had come out to nose around.

"Let me handle it," Trey warned. "I'll do the talking, if that's all they want."

The four dark shapes swung toward the carriage. Trey could see their guns outlined against the pale caliche road behind them. One of the men was tall and broad-shouldered, wearing a wide-brim hat that was curled at the sides. He seemed to be walking just ahead of the others, a leader of sorts, Trey guessed.

Trey stepped away from the carriage wheel with his right hand dangling near the butt of his Colt. "What's for you gents?" he asked in a quiet voice.

All four men halted when they heard Trey.

"Just a little information," the tall one said. "Wanted to know which outfit you ride for. Never seen you in these parts before today."

"I work for Maria Valdez," Trey replied coldly, "if it's any of your affair. Which it ain't."

A silence passed; then the tall cowboy spoke. "Never heard of anybody named Maria Valdez 'round here. Is she the lady who rides in that fancy buggy?"

Trey nodded slowly. "She is the owner of the carriage, but once again, that's none of your affair. I'm merely bein' polite, answering your questions."

Trey heard a dry chuckle coming from one of the shadows, then a voice. "Might keep you alive a while

171

longer, stranger, bein' real polite to Tom."

Trey sighted toward the shadow and spoke. "I'd figured on living a long time," he said, allowing his voice to drop to almost a whisper. "Anybody who figures otherwise is liable to get a hole shot through him."

Another brief silence, and then a question from one of the other men. "You must think you're pretty good with that gun you're wearing, stranger. Are you as good as you say?"

Trey tensed the muscles in his right arm. "One way to find out, and that's to reach for your gun like you meant to do it in a hurry. If the lights go out inside your skullbone, you'll know I was just a shade faster than you." Trey took a deep breath. "Now, boys, I've grown weary of all this idle talk. State your business with me, or clear out."

The tall cowboy cleared his throat. "Wanted to know if you took a side in this cattle war," he said, with an edge creeping into his voice. "Wanted to know whose side you was on, you and the gent standin' behind you."

Trey waited a few seconds before he gave his answer. "I'm not taking a side," he said. "Just seein' the lady through to Santa Fe."

Trey's manner had taken some of the bravado out of the men. Even with a gullet full of whiskey, they weren't ready to challenge a man who stood up to them as Trey had done.

"We was just bein' careful," one of them said. "This country is full of Dolan's men. That Santa Fe ring has been hirin' gunfighters from all over the place to back Tom Catron's cattle contracts. When we seen that low-tied gunbelt, we got curious."

Trey wasn't about to lose his advantage now. "That kind of curiosity could get you killed," he said evenly. "Like I said, I'm seein' the lady to Santa Fe. Any man who tries to stop that carriage is gonna get

172

his blood spilled for his trouble. I never met this feller Dolan. Don't know Chisum either, but my gun ain't for hire in a range war. All I want is clear passage to Santa Fe for the occupants of this carriage. It's real simple."

The tall cowboy turned to the others. "Let's head back to the cantina, boys," he said. "I'm workin' up a powerful thirst with all this talk. Don't see no reason to bother these two gents any longer. They ain't Dolan men, so there's no need to get crossways."

Two more of the cowboys turned away, but one remained, a short fellow in a misshapen top hat with a crumpled crown. Trey's caution grew when the little cowboy did not turn away with the rest.

"I wouldn't hire on with Dolan if I was you," the cowboy said. His voice was soft, almost gentle, and there was no fear in it. He stared Trey in the eye boldly, like a man who wouldn't run away from trouble. "Dolan and his men are a bunch of thieves, stealin' cattle from honest ranchers. Big John Chisum is an honest man, but he's up against a gang of owlhoots who'll do anything for a price."

"It doesn't concern me," Trey said with a calm, level tone. "I want no part of it. When the lady is safe at her father's ranch, I aim to move on farther west."

The little gunman stared at Trey awhile longer, until one of his friends spoke.

"C'mon, Billy. Let's go get drunk an' leave these fellers alone."

The man called Billy turned slowly, still watching Trey; then he gave a shrug and walked away. Trey watched the man's back for a time, until all four men were headed back down the street for the cantina.

"That small one," Stiles began, sounding thoughtful. "He was the one to worry about. The rest of them lost their nerve, but not the one they called Billy."

Trey grunted and turned back to the carriage wheel. "You're a better judge of men than I gave you credit for, gambler. You were right, to figure Billy for the troublemaker. If I'd given him just half a chance, he'd have pulled his gun."

Stiles returned his pistol to his coat pocket and let out a long sigh. "That took courage, Trey," he said quietly, watching Trey's face, "not backing down from those four."

Trey shrugged off the gambler's remark, though he did not let it rest completely. "I never back down from anybody, gambler," he said. "If you get the chance to know me a little better, you'll know that backin' down just ain't my style."

Stiles was still staring at Trey when Trey settled against the carriage wheel.

"I can believe that about you," Stiles answered, "although it puzzles me . . . why a man like you isn't afraid of dying. It isn't simple bravery either. I've been watching you. I'd almost be willing to wager that you've given up on living, somehow. You don't seem to care if you live to see another sunrise."

Trey tilted his hat brim over his face and pulled his blanket under his chin. "Don't try to figure it out, Mr. Stiles," he said in a hoarse whisper, closing his eyes. "You'd never understand."

The gambler took a seat next to another wheel and wrapped himself in his blanket. "I understand giving up on the future," he said in a faraway voice. "At Andersonville, with men dying all around me, I knew what it meant not to worry about what tomorrow might bring."

Trey didn't answer the remark. In minutes, he was asleep.

Chapter Eighteen

At the echo of a distant gunshot, Trey's eyes flew open. In the same instant his right hand was clawing for his Colt. Tossing his blanket aside, he scanned the darkness quickly, trying to clear the sleep fog from his brain.

Where had the shot come from? He trusted his senses; there was no doubt about the gunshot. Remembering the gambler, he looked over to the spot where Stiles had been. A blanket lay in a crumpled heap beside one carriage wheel. The gambler was gone.

Trey's first instinct was to check beneath the seat for the money chest. He scrambled to his feet and reached under the leather cushion, with an ear cocked for the sound of another shot, to find its source.

The money was still hidden below the seat. So where was Stiles? And who was doing the shooting?

Then a dull realization entered Trey's thoughts. Stiles was a card player, and like the fool he was, he'd gone off to find a game where he could fatten his purse.

"The El Torito," Trey whispered. "The damn fool's gone down there to try his luck against those Chisum cowhands. They've probably killed him for dealing off the bottom of the deck. Serves him right, for sticking his nose where it don't belong."

Trey walked away from the carriage with his gun leveled, to see the front of the cantina. Lantern light spilled from the windows of the place across the empty caliche road. The seven saddled horses still stood quietly at the hitch rail, and for the moment, there was silence.

He debated the wisdom of heading down to the cantina, leaving the money unguarded. Stiles deserved whatever fate had befallen him at the hands of the drunken cowboys, if he'd been fool enough to go down there alone for a card game.

"Just that one shot," Trey muttered. No one else had come out on the street to investigate the noise. Was the gambler dead? Or had the lone shot come from another source?

Trey let out a whispering sigh and started toward the El Torito on the balls of his feet. He could take a look inside one of the cantina windows to learn what had happened to Stiles and then go back to sleep while someone mopped the gambler's blood off the floor. The damn fool had tried to run his crooked game surrounded by whiskey-tough cowhands carrying guns, and most likely paid for the mistake with his life.

Trey approached the hitch rail cautiously, covering his progress with the .44. He would be out of sight of the carriage and its valuable cargo when he went to the cantina window; thus Trey promised himself that he would only take a glimpse of what was inside.

He climbed to the boardwalk soundlessly and crept to a lamplit window. There, in the middle of the cantina, he saw Stiles, standing inside a circle of grim-faced cowhands with their guns pointed at the gambler's head.

"They haven't killed him yet," Trey whispered.

He ground his teeth together, knowing what he would do in spite of himself. It went against his grain when one man faced overwhelming forces, no matter what the reason. "I oughta kill him myself," he added, as he swung away from the window toward the door.

When he stepped around the door frame and shouldered through a pair of batwings, heads turned in the group around Stiles. Trey raised his Colt shoulder-high and spread his feet slightly apart.

"Put the guns down, boys," he said. "First man to move can count on a bullet." Trey cocked the .44 and waited, tensed for the moment when one of the men might turn a gun on him. He found the little cowboy in the top hat and aimed for him. "You'll die first," Trey promised in a voice like gritty sand.

The little cowboy grinned, revealing odd buck teeth in the top of his mouth. "We was just havin' a little fun," he said, in that same soft tone. "Your partner claimed the pot with a heart flush, but his wasn't the high hand. Charlie Bowdre held a straight, queen high. Charlie won the hand, fair an' square."

From the corner of his eye, Trey saw Stiles turn for the door. The look on the gambler's face was one of outright fear.

"I won the hand," Stiles said weakly. "I claim the eighteen dollars. It's rightfully mine, Trey."

Trey's cheeks hardened. For now, the Chisum cowhands were content to talk things out without gunplay. "You were a damn fool, Mr. Stiles, to buy into the game in the first place. I oughta let 'em fill you full of holes." Then Trey looked around the group and took a deep breath. "We've got no quarrel with you boys," he said. "You've had your fun. A flush beats a straight in any man's game; so let Stiles have his pot, and I'll take him out of here."

The cowhand named Billy lowered his pistol to his

side, still grinning. Slowly, one at a time, the other men holstered their guns and looked toward Trey.

"Havin' a little joke, mister," one cowboy said. "Hell, anybody knows that flush is high hand." He looked at the gambler. "Take your winnings." Then he looked back at Trey. "You can put that shootin' iron away. We wasn't aimin' to kill him. Just playin' a joke, 'cause he acted so all-fired smart with a deck of cards."

Trey dropped his pistol to his side, still wary of a sudden move. "Get your money," he said to the gambler. "And leave enough for table stakes in the next game. Then get outside. You've caused me enough aggravation for one night. Make it quick!"

Stiles reached across a table to his right and fisted a pile of coins that filled both hands. He pocketed most of the money, then counted out an ante for each of the seven cowboys, after casting an unhappy glance Trey's way. "Done," he said softly, as he started for the swinging doors. He saw the angry expression on Trey's face and looked away when he passed Trey to go out on the boardwalk.

Trey backed up until he felt the batwings behind him, then touched his hat brim in a lazy salute. "Enjoy the game, boys," he said, parting the doors as he departed into the darkness.

Stiles was waiting for him behind the tethered horses. Now Trey's anger was at a full boil.

"That's the dumbest goddamn move I ever saw a man make," Trey snarled when he reached the gambler's side. "You walked into a room full of drunks, thinkin' you could outsmart 'em. Are you blind, Mr. Stiles? Couldn't you see they were wearin' guns?"

Stiles spread his palms helplessly. "All I wanted was a friendly hand of poker," he said, hurrying to keep up with Trey's longer strides as they walked back to the carriage. "They tried to cheat me, Trey. It was an honest game, until they saw they couldn't win."

"I was right the first time I met you," Trey grumbled, stalking across a dark corner of the vacant lot. "You're a damn fool, Stiles. You haven't got enough sense to know when you're buying into trouble. In the morning, I want you to saddle your horse and get the hell away from me. If you ain't gone by first light, I'll kill you myself, to save anybody else the powder and lead."

"I'm sorry it happened, Trey," Stiles said quietly. "I needed to make some money. I'm almost out of food, and my horse needs a sack of grain. If the game had been honest, I'd have won enough to stake me halfway to California."

Trey grunted. "You came within a whisker of becoming a permanent resident of Las Vegas," he snapped. "You got the bad habit of getting guns stuck in your face."

Stiles shoved his hands in his pockets as they neared the carriage. "I was merely trying to make a living," he complained. "I dealt the hand fairly . . . you've got my word on that."

They arrived at the carriage, where Trey sat down beside the wheel and covered himself with his blanket.

"I don't want your word on anything, gambler," Trey growled, bringing the blanket up to his chin. "But I'll give you my word on another matter: if you get out of that bedroll one more time before dawn, I'll shoot you and leave you for the buzzards. Stay put until dawn, Mr. Stiles, and then I want you out of my sight forever! Is that understood?"

The gambler nodded silently, pulling a blanket around his thin shoulders, then removing his hat. A minute passed; then Stiles spoke softly, just as Trey was drifting off to sleep. "I'd like to stay with you until we reach Santa Fe. Another gun might come in

179

handy if you run across some of Dolan's men.''

Trey ignored the gambler's question right at first. "You've yet to prove you can shoot anything, Mr. Stiles," he said later. "That was a lucky shot you took at those Indians."

"I can shoot," the gambler replied. "Given the chance, I'll prove it."

At dawn, while the horses were being saddled, nothing more was said about last night's incident. Maria, Juan, and the boy came down from the hotel, and when Maria saw Trey, she smiled sweetly and came over to him. She was dressed in tight denims that outlined the curve of her hips, and a man's shirt, open at the neck, revealing an expanse of creamy skin which drew Trey's attention until she spoke.

"Good morning, Trey," she said, her eyes sparkling. "Did you sleep well?"

"Hardly at all," Trey replied glumly, glancing toward Stiles. "We had visitors last night, the Chisum cowhands. I persuaded them to leave us alone, and then this gambler goes over to the cantina to get in a card game with the bunch. Had to go over and get him out of a tight spot. Lately, he's been more trouble than he's worth."

Maria's face darkened. "He seems like a gentleman. Facing a long road to Santa Fe, I was glad to have him along."

Trey sighed and shrugged his powerful shoulders. "I reckon we can keep him with us 'til we get to your father's place. One more gun might discourage men with bad intentions."

Maria reached up to touch Trey's cheek with a fingertip. A broad smile widened her face. "Your beard is growing," she said.

"I aimed to shave it off before we left town," he answered. Now his face felt hot, under the woman's

180

lingering stare. "There's a bath house just down the street. Keep an eye on things while I'm gone."

Maria drew her hand away. "You have a handsome face, Trey," she said softly. "But you hardly ever smile."

To prove her wrong, he grinned down at her. "How's that?" he asked, feeling foolish.

Now it was Maria's turn to blush. Coloring deeply, she replied, "I like it very much." She turned away from him suddenly and went over to the carriage, just as Juan and Carlos returned leading the harness team.

Trey went to his saddlebags and removed a clean shirt and socks. As he started away from the carriage, he caught the gambler's eye. "I'm headed down for a bath," he said. "Keep an eye on things while I'm gone."

Stiles was standing beside his saddled gelding. Relief flooded his face. "I'll keep a close watch," he said.

Trey knew Stiles had been making preparations to leave on his own, as Trey had instructed the night before. Not a word had been said between them until now.

Remembering his razor and shaving soap, Trey returned to his gear and took out everything he needed. Then, with a vision of Maria's beautiful smile floating before him, he trudged off toward the bath house in a brighter mood.

At the back of a two-room adobe he paid a dime to a pudgy Mexican woman for a hot bath. He was alone in the tiny bath house and liked it that way. Soon, the woman brought steaming wooden pails of water. With a bar of scented soap, Trey settled back in a big cast-iron tub to soak off layers of trail grime. Now and then, he dozed contentedly, resting his head against the back of the tub while daydreaming about Maria. There was no doubt about it now; she felt an attraction. And there was no doubt that he felt the same way. He hadn't wanted it, this attraction between them. It had come about slowly, against his wishes. He had led a solitary existence for so many years that being alone seemed natural now.

He wondered if the feeling would pass. Or would it deepen, and complicate his life? Sharing his life with a woman did not fit with the plans he'd made. Since Marybeth and Billy had died, he had been a drifter with an empty soul whose only happiness came from being on the move from place to place. Maria could never replace Marybeth in Trey's heart. He told himself not to expect it, as he sat in the steamy tub, thinking things through.

"She doesn't really know me," he said aloud, passing the bar of soap over his skin. "She won't like what she finds, when she gets to know me better."

His doubts rang hollowly off the walls of the bath house, and he wondered if he was only trying to convince himself that a relationship with Maria would ultimately fail.

"I'm too set in my ways now," he whispered. "Been a bachelor too long to change."

Later, after a luxurious soak, he applied shaving soap to his chin and scraped the razor across his beard stubble, watching his reflection in a shard of mirror on a table beside the tub. As he shaved, he tried to put his feelings for Maria out of his mind.

"When we get to Santa Fe, I'll head west," he said. "Maybe north up to Colorado Territory, or wherever else I take the notion to travel."

He climbed out of the tub when the water cooled, to put on his clean shirt and comb through his hair. When he was satisfied with his appearance, he strapped on his gun and paused in front of the mirror again.

He grinned, more than anything else to see what a grin looked like on his clean-shaven face. "She

182

wanted to see a grin," he said softly, "so I'll give her one. Women! Why the hell would any woman care about seeing a man grin?"

He clumped out of the bath house, to cast a look down the road. His gaze lingered briefly at the hitch rail in front of the El Torito, where last night the Chisum cowboys had left their horses. The rail was empty now, and Trey decided the men had cleared out. Stiles had almost gotten Trey into a fracas from which the chances of surviving had looked mighty slim.

"The damn fool has got no sense," he grumbled, starting down the street in pale morning light. He sighed. "I reckon it took some guts to walk into that cantina to buy into the game. Guts, but not much good sense."

When he reached the carriage, the team was harnessed, and Trey's roan was tied to a rear wheel. Stiles was mounted on his sorrel, keeping an eye on the street, watching the few curious passersby who came along at this early hour.

Trey walked over to Maria, to accept a warm tortilla filled with chorizo sausage and cheese. "Thanks," he muttered; then he gave her a grin.

She smiled back at him. "We are ready, Trey," she said in a lilting, musical voice. Then she glanced back at the gambler. "Are you allowing him to ride with us?" she asked quietly, so Stiles couldn't hear.

"I reckon so," Trey answered. "He got my hackles up last night, but today I'm in a better mood. Another gun might be a help, if we run into more difficulty northwest of here."

Trey took a bite of the sausage tortilla and sauntered back to the gambler. "Stay back about a quarter mile and keep your eyes open," he said.

Stiles nodded. "I'm obliged, Trey," he said softly. "And I'm sorry about what happened last night."

Trey shrugged and wheeled for his horse. When

the cinch was pulled to tighten the saddle on the roan's back, the gelding backed its ears and gave Trey a swish of its tail.

"Take it easy, hoss," Trey mumbled, fitting a boot into a stirrup to mount. "Can't sit your back if the saddle's loose, so take that unhappy look out of your eye. Looks like you'd show some appreciation for those new shoes I paid for, instead of complaining first thing in the morning about that cinch."

When Trey was aboard, he noticed that Carlos was watching him from one side of the carriage. The expression on the boy's face was one of surprise.

"Do you always talk to your horse, señor?" Carlos asked. "And does it understand?"

Trey chuckled. "I talk to this roan now and then, but it's never shown any evidence of understanding a word I say. If I thought it understood, I'd likely talk to it all the time when I was off to myself."

Carlos took a step closer to the roan, searching Trey's face. "Perhaps you will not be by yourself anymore," he said softly, "if you decide to stay at my grandfather's *rancho*."

Trey shook his head quickly, glancing past the boy to see if Maria was listening. "I don't figure to stay. Maybe a day or two, to rest this horse."

Carlos held a finger to his lips, to tell Trey that he was about to reveal a secret. "*Tía* Maria says you will stay with us, señor. Just last night, I overheard her talking to Juan about it, when they thought I was asleep." Then Carlos lowered his eyes to the ground in front of him. "I hope you will stay, *señor*," he said very quietly.

"It ain't very likely, son," he replied.

Chapter Nineteen

The road climbed and fell sharply west of Las Vegas, winding around towering mountains, then across deep valleys thick with pine and undergrowth. Now and then, they passed lumbering freight wagons pulled by yokes of oxen. Some of the teamsters exchanged friendly waves with Trey and the occupants of the carriage. One wagon driver told Trey that he'd found the tracks of barefoot ponies crossing a flat a few miles to the west, but he related that the tracks were old.

The climb took them to much cooler air, forcing Trey into his great coat before noon. Puffy clouds scudded across the sky and, for a time, robbed the mountains of the sun's warmth. In places Trey found more of the white-barked trees growing in clusters, and he wondered what they were called. Small herds of deer grazed on high, grassy slopes above the trail. Trey became entranced by the beauty of the mountains. It seemed the farther west and north he traveled, the scenes became more remarkable, grander, on a scale larger than anything he had seen before.

"I suppose I could be happy here," he said to the horse.

The roan flicked its ears and continued up a

steepening climb to the top of a pass between two slopes. In places, the road had turned rocky, forcing the carriage to bump over fist-sized stones lying in the ruts.

At the top of the pass, Trey halted the roan to wait for the carriage to struggle up the road. Beyond, a wide valley stretched to the next steep climb. The trail ran arrow-straight across the valley floor, and when Trey examined it, suddenly his eye fell on a horse grazing at the edge of a stand of pines. Squinting, he also noticed that the horse bore a saddle, though it seemed to be grazing freely, trailing its reins.

"Could be trouble," he said, scanning the open meadows around the spot where he found the horse.

He waited for Juan to drive to the top of the pass; then he leaned out of the saddle and spoke. "There's a saddled horse down there, and something don't add up. Wait here, until you see my signal that all's clear."

Trey touched the roan's ribs with a spur and sent the gelding off at a lope down the descent into the valley without waiting for Juan to reply. Trey's senses told him that something was amiss near the wandering horse; he couldn't define just what it was that sent a warning into his brain, but it was there.

The roan galloped down the slope to the valley floor, where it lengthened its strides to a full run. Trey pulled his coat away from the butt of his pistol and got set for whatever lay in store.

"Maybe it's nothing," he told himself. "Could be the horse broke free during the night and wandered off." Down deep, he didn't put much stock in that notion. His nose for trouble had caught a subtle scent at the top of the pass.

He slowed the gelding when he drew near the bay horse. Trey rested his palm on his gun butt, watching the trees around him as he rode up to the bay. Long before Trey pulled back on his reins, he noticed a wet bloodstain on the saddle tied to the bay, and then more fresh blood on the grass below the horse where it had run down the stirrup leathers.

The roan bounded to a stop. The bay lifted its muzzle and nickered softly, walking over to touch noses with Trey's horse. Trey's eyes were on the bloodstains; he followed them slowly, halting his gaze when he saw a shape in the distance that did not belong on the valley floor.

He urged the roan toward the spot at a walk, drawing his Colt to make the approach, sweeping his surroundings with cautious looks until he rode up on the body of a man. Checking the trees around him again, Trey swung down when he was satisfied that no one was lurking in the shadows.

He found a young cowboy lying on his back, encircled by a pool of blood. A gaping hole below the cowboy's ribs oozed fresh blood onto the grass, glistening wetly in the sunlight. A second look told Trey that the boy was still breathing, though shallowly, a very slight rise and fall in his chest.

Trey knelt beside the wounded man. "Can you hear me?" he asked. The young cowboy's eyes were closed.

For a time, there was no response. Trey lifted one eyelid with a finger, discovering the glaze of pain he expected to find when he saw the eyeball. "Can you hear me?" he asked again.

A soft groan fluttered from the cowboy's lips. Pinkish foam was clotted around the man's mouth, evidence of a bullet through his lung. Then the cowboy coughed. Crow's feet webbed the corners of his eyes when a stab of pain went through him; then he relaxed, and a gurgling breath rattled in his throat.

"Damn," Trey muttered, knowing that nothing could be done to save the man's life.

The cowboy groaned again, and blinked once.

"Help me," he whispered, wagging his head back and forth.

"Not much I can do," Trey answered. "I've got some whiskey in my saddlebags. It'll help with the pain. Can you tell me who did this to you? Did you see who shot you?"

The boy gave Trey a faint nod. "Posse," he hissed, clenching his teeth. "Taggart . . . claimed . . . I stole . . ."

Suddenly the cowboy's eyes flew open. His arms and legs went stiff; his eyes bulged. A whimpering cry escaped his tightly closed lips, and his chest convulsed as his spine went rigid.

"Easy, son," Trey said softly. "It'll be over soon." He placed his hand on the boy's shoulder, certain that it was too late for the whiskey to do any good. The boy would be dead in a matter of a few minutes.

The dying man's feet began to twitch. He dug his boot heels into the grass. "Hurts," he cried. One hand found Trey's shirt sleeve, and his fingers clawed into the fabric, trembling with effort until they knotted in a viselike grip.

Trey looked away from the boy's face. It seemed a thousand times that he'd witnessed men die during the war. A powerless feeling had always overwhelmed him when he saw the sight, as it did now. There was nothing he could do to make the pain any less, or shorten the agony of it.

Off in the distance, Trey heard a running horse. When he looked over his shoulder, he saw Stiles galloping toward him. Then Trey glanced up at the ridge where the carriage sat, wishing the gambler had stayed to protect the occupants.

Stiles slowed his horse and jumped to the ground before the sorrel slid to a halt. Trey saw the pistol gleam in the gambler's fist as he trotted over.

"What happened?" Stiles asked, stumbling to a

188

halt near the body, his eyes wide with fear and concern when he saw the blood.

"Somebody shot him," Trey replied wearily, feeling the boy's grip tighten on his sleeve. "He couldn't tell me much. The bullet went through a lung, and he won't last much longer. He said something about a posse, and somebody named Taggart."

"A posse of Dolan's men," the gambler sighed. "Maybe that same bunch we had a run-in with below Las Vegas." Then Stiles took a quick look around. "Any sign of the men that did it?"

Trey shook his head. "Get back to the carriage and lead them down off that ridge. I'll stay with the boy 'til he goes. Ain't likely he knows I'm here, but my conscience won't abide with riding off until it's over. Keep your eyes open. Whoever did this to the boy can't be far, judging by how recent it appears. I'll be along when he stops breathing. Catch his horse. We'll take it to the next town. Maybe there's something in his saddlebags that'll tell us who he is." Trey glanced around him then. "I'll pile some rocks over him, so the wolves will have a harder time scattering his bones. Now get moving, Mr. Stiles. Don't leave them alone up on that ridge any longer than necessary."

Stiles turned for his horse. "It's that range war the newspaper editor told me about," he said over his shoulder. "Looks like it has claimed another victim." He mounted his horse and looked down at Trey. "This is proving to be mighty dangerous country, Trey. The woman is plenty worried about her father, and not without good reason, so it would seem. Where are those soldiers when they are needed?"

Trey tried to pry the cowboy's fingers off his shirt. "Like you said yesterday, the militia is taking a side with Dolan and Catron, so it ain't likely they'd do much about what happened here anyway."

"That's what the editor said," Stiles replied. "Those men at the cantina talked about it last night. One of them said it will be all-out war before the snow comes to the mountains. That one named Billy Antrim seemed to know a lot about it. He said they'll go gunning for Jimmy Dolan if there's any more killing."

The cowboy's body jerked involuntarily, and his eyes batted open, then shut. The wet sound had worsened in his throat.

"This shooting is liable to touch things off," Trey muttered, watching the dying man's face. "Get back to the carriage, Mr. Stiles. Those folks shouldn't be left alone."

The gambler turned his horse and struck a lope away from Trey. Trey listened to the cowboy's breathing above the thunder of the sorrel's hooves. Stiles rode over to the bay and tied its reins to his saddle horn; then he was off toward the ridge at a slower pace with the horse in tow.

Half a minute later, as the carriage rattled along the road behind Trey, the cowboy took a shuddering breath, and his chest stilled.

"It won't hurt any more now," Trey whispered around the tight feeling in his throat.

He got up and searched for stones to toss over the body, carrying as many as he could in the crook of an arm to form a shallow pile over the corpse. Once, he stuck a hand into the dead man's pockets and found only a small plug of chewing tobacco and a pocket knife with the initials "R.J." carved into the handle.

When the body was completely covered Trey stood back to examine the job, dusting off his hands. "Sorry, son," he said in the softest of voices, "but that's the price a man can pay when he straps on a six-gun. Some prices come higher than others. Yours was mighty high for a kid to pay."

He turned away from the grave and mounted his

roan tiredly, as though he had labored long and hard with the rocks. In truth, the weight had been heaviest for his heart to bear, seeing another young boy die needlessly, the way so many had while the war raged.

He caught up with the carriage in the middle of the valley and halted beside it. Maria's dark eyes were full of questions, as were Juan's.

"What happened back there?" she asked.

"Looks like some of Dolan's posse men killed a ranch hand," he replied. "Young feller. Before he died, he named Taggart as the man who shot him." Trey swallowed. "There wasn't time for the boy to say much more."

Maria cast a worried glance toward Juan. "We must hurry," she said, with urgency in her voice. "I fear for *mi papa*."

Juan shook the reins over the backs of the team and drove the carriage away at a trot. Trey swung a cautious look around them, waiting for Stiles.

The gambler rode up leading the bay and shook his head. "Not a thing to identify the dead man," he said, motioning toward the saddlebags, "just a change of clothes and a little coffeepot with a handful of beans."

Trey nodded silently and wheeled his horse. The road now ran due west, toward a range of bald peaks. He judged the time at two o'clock as he roweled the gelding to a lope away from the gambler.

When he galloped past the carriage, he glimpsed Maria's face in the shadow below the canopy. Her hands were pressed to her cheeks, as though she'd been crying. Without the words to comfort her, he spurred the roan away from the carriage to lead the way up the side of the mountain, thinking how good it would feel to have his arms around Maria then.

Later, he smiled inwardly. It no longer troubled him to have thoughts about the woman . . . about intimacy with her. His feelings had changed. He found himself actually looking forward to the next chance he had to wrap her in his arms.

He slowed his horse when he was a quarter mile out front, to focus his attention on the trail. In the back of his mind, he saw the young cowboy, lying in a pool of blood, the victim of a range dispute Trey knew almost nothing about.

"We're riding straight into a cross fire," he told himself, as he considered the risks. "It'll be a piece of luck if we make it to Santa Fe without shooting our way through."

Holding the roan to a jog trot, he started up the slope, past clumps of trees where a bushwhacker might have an easy time, waylaying unsuspecting travelers. It had begun to seem that both sides in the conflict were determined to find out where an outsider's sympathies lay. While it didn't make much sense that either faction would care where Maria Valdez stood in the affair, both the Dolan forces and Chisum's men had shown curiosity about her. And about Trey. It was the expensive carriage, he supposed; that represented wealth, and wealth meant power. And as tensions mounted between Dolan and Chisum, men were watching closely to see where the powerful forces would align.

"I'm staying out of it," he said, as a promise to himself. "If Maria's father is smart, so will he."

The road wound its way up the mountain. Trey scanned the surrounding countryside with all the caution he could muster. The men who had shot the young cowboy were somewhere in these mountains, and only a fool would ride headlong into a bunch of proven killers.

Near the top of the slope, the road turned and dropped sharply into another steep-walled valley. Trey squinted into a lowering sun and then quickly hauled back on his reins. At the far end of the valley, he saw a column of smoke rising lazily into the still air.

He studied the smoke for a time, guessing its source. "A campfire, most likely," he said. He could hear the carriage wheels bumping up the mountain behind him. "It'd be safer for me to ride down there and see who made that fire. It could be Dolan's posse. Or simple travelers, like us."

He waited for Juan, watching the smoke. Thick stands of trees prevented him from seeing its origin. When the carriage rolled to the top of the climb, Trey spoke to Juan.

"Hold up right here, until I wave you down the mountain," he said. Then he pointed at the column of smoke. "Somebody's got a fire down there, and until I know who it is, we'll play things real careful."

Maria was watching him from the back seat. "Could it be those men who killed the cowboy?" she asked.

Trey could only shrug. "We'll know soon enough. Stay here. I'll give a signal if the road is clear."

Touching the roan with a spur, he started down the trail into the valley. This time, his senses told him nothing about what lay in store. The fire could come from half a dozen innocent sources that did not pose a threat to his party. Still, after finding the dying cowboy, Trey would admit to being jumpy about things.

Chapter Twenty

His nerves calmed some when he saw the canvas wagon sheet in the distance. It was a small wagon, of the type many settlers used to haul their belongings westward toward more promising farmlands. Trey slowed his horse to approach the camp, still wary of trouble in spite of his discovery that the fire glowed near the wagon and not within the campsite of an armed gang.

When the sounds of his horse reached the camp, a woman in a long blue dress peered around the back of the wagon. Then a man in a suit coat and baggy trousers appeared beside her. A shotgun was balanced in his right fist. Trey gave the couple a friendly wave and rode toward them. As he came closer, he could plainly see the concern on their faces over a stranger riding up to their fire.

Trey halted his roan and touched his hat brim politely. "I don't want to worry you folks," he said. "Me and my party are just passing through. We saw your fire, and with all the difficulties in these parts, I rode over first to see where the smoke was coming from. Bein' careful."

The man and the woman were young, early twenties, he guessed. Although they both were still wary of him, he sensed their relief when he declared his purpose.

"There's been a lot of trouble," the man said, looking at his wife, then back to Trey. "Yesterday, a bunch of men stopped us an' started askin' questions. Me an' Clair are headed up to Oregon, an' we figured those men meant to rob us—"

The man was interrupted by the sounds of coughing, coming from inside the wagon. He glanced toward the wagon, but the woman was already hurrying to it, her features pinched with worry.

"Our daughter's sick," the man said. "She's got this terrible fever, and you can hear how bad she coughs."

Trey nodded once, watching the woman climb into the back of the wagon. "Sounds like the girl needs a doctor," he said.

The man shook his head in frustration. "We're tryin' to git to Santa Fe. It's the closest doctor, only Sara can't hardly stand to travel. When our wagon bounces, it starts her to coughing worse than ever."

Trey looked over his shoulder, to the ridge where the carriage was waiting for his signal. "I'll ask Maria if she knows what to do," he said. He reined his horse and trotted away from the camp, until he reached a place in the road where Juan could see him from the ridge. As soon as he waved his hand over his head, he saw the carriage start down the road toward him.

When he rode back to the wagon, he heard the child coughing endlessly. The girl's father was eyeing him suspiciously from a corner of the wagon bed, still cradling his shotgun as proof that he was not completely satisfied with Trey's story.

Trey sat his horse until the carriage arrived. Only then did he step down and walk up to Maria, feeling the man's eyes on his back until he spoke.

"There's a sick girl in that wagon," Trey began.

196

"Her parents are trying to reach Santa Fe to find a doctor, but they say the girl's coughing is so bad that she can't travel. I figured you might know a remedy for the cough, Maria. You can hear how bad it is."

Maria came quickly from her seat. When she stood on the ground, she turned to Juan. "Juan knows the *curandero* secrets," she said. "Come . . . have a look at the child. See if there is anything you can do for her."

Juan nodded and tied off the reins. Climbing down stiffly, he walked toward the wagon with Maria at his side. Trey aimed a look down their backtrail as the gambler rode up while Maria spoke to the woman.

"Trey tells me that your daughter is ill," she said. "Please let Juan take a look at her. Juan is a trusted friend, and he has bottles of powders and oils in our trunk. Perhaps Juan has something that will help your daughter."

"We're mighty grateful," the girl's mother said, moving to one side to admit Juan into the wagon bed.

"Sara's real sick," the girl's father added. "We'd be obliged if there's anything you can do for her."

Stiles rode up beside Trey while Juan disappeared into the back of the wagon. "What's the trouble?" he asked.

"A sick child," Trey replied, inclining his head toward the camp. "The old man is some sort of healer down in Mexico, according to what Maria said. Juan is taking a look."

The girl started coughing again. From the corner of his eye, Trey saw the gambler shake his head.

"Back east," Stiles began, "lots of folks believe that steam helps a cough. They boil a pot of water and breathe the steam. It seems to help."

Juan stuck his head out of the wagon and spoke to Maria in rapid Spanish. Maria whirled and hurried toward the back of the carriage to open the big trunk.

197

Trey listened to the girl's cough and thought about the delay. The sun was almost touching the peaks to the west, and soon it would be dark. Maria hurried from the carriage carrying a small leather pouch. She handed it to Juan and climbed inside.

Carlos jumped down from his seat, staring in the direction of the wagon bed. "Someone is very sick," he said softly. "Shall I unharness the team, Señor Trey?"

Trey shook his head. "Not yet," he answered, casting a look at their surroundings. "There's still a few hours of daylight left, and this ain't the best spot to defend if trouble shows up."

Carlos studied Trey's face. "You are always thinking like a soldier," he said. "I will try to remember to think like a soldier, too."

Trey was about to say more, when he saw Maria climb out of the wagon. She started toward Trey, concern mirrored in her eyes.

"The child is near death," she said softly, barely above a whisper. "I have offered to stay the night here, so Juan can perform his cure. But before I gave the promise, I came to ask you if you agreed. Juan fears that the child will die unless she receives his help."

Trey thumbed back his hat brim and nodded. "We can camp here until tomorrow morning, I reckon," he said. Then he looked around at the trees. "This isn't the place I'd have chosen, but it'll do."

Maria gave him a half smile; then she whirled for the wagon and trotted to it to speak to Juan in Spanish.

The girl's father sauntered over to Trey and the gambler, his shotgun now leaning against a wheel of his wagon. "Please join us, gents," he said. "Clair has a pot of coffee boilin' at the fire. I'm Tom Adams, and you're welcome to share what we have."

"I'm Trey Marsh, and this is Woodrow Stiles. We

198

carry our own provisions, but we're thankful for the offer. We'll make camp just the other side of your wagon and see to our horses while Juan is attending to your daughter."

Trey took Adams' handshake, looking at him closely for the first time. Adams was thick-muscled, with calloused hands that most likely belonged to a farmer. A rusted iron breaking plow was tied to one side of the wagon as evidence of Adams' profession.

Stiles was down off his horse when Trey turned around. "I can see to the team," Trey said, handing Stiles the reins to his roan, "if you'll hobble the horses."

"I will help with the team," Carlos said quickly, pulling his shoulders back to stand a little straighter.

Trey chuckled. "I'd almost forgotten that you can handle this team by yourself," he said. "Lead them over here and we'll take the harness off."

Carlos stood proudly, then went to the team and led them in Trey's footsteps toward an opening in the trees to one side of the road.

The coughing had only worsened during the first few hours of darkness. Trey sat beside their fire, palming a tin coffee cup for its warmth, while the child coughed in increasingly violent spasms in the back of the Adams' wagon. Earlier in the evening, he'd caught the scent of pungent salve on Juan's hands when the old man had come to the fire for coffee.

The gambler accepted the bottle of whiskey when Trey offered it, to add some to his coffee. "That little girl is getting worse," Stiles said.

Trey nodded. "Maria says the girl could die before morning," he said softly, thinking.

Carlos sat beside Trey, watching the flames. "Juan is a good *curandero*," Carlos whispered. "He will

199

save her life."

Trey let the subject drop. "I'll go take a look around," he said, tossing out the last of his coffee before he stood up. "All these campfires will be like a beacon if there's anyone around. I'll be back as soon as I'm satisfied that we're alone."

He walked away from the fire to circle the camp. Stars winked at him from a velvety black sky. Entering the trees, he went more cautiously. For a couple of hours it had worried him to be seated near a fire, silhouetted, an easy target. Moving about in the dark, he felt better. Old habits were hard to break, especially when the habits had helped to keep him alive.

The child's coughing echoed through the trees while he crept around the camp. If he were any judge of sickness, the girl would probably die. When he'd glanced in the back of the wagon just before dark, he'd found a frail child beneath a covering of worn blankets, her face sunken and paled by her illness. He didn't put much stock in the old man's Mexican cures, although he had no better solution, so far from a doctor.

Trey made a careful circle around their campsite and could find nothing amiss. The silence in the mountain valley was absolute, until an owl hooted somewhere in the trees during his return to the campfire. Walking past the Adams' wagon, he saw Maria standing alone at the edge of the circle of firelight. He moved toward her and spoke when he was in earshot.

"Sounds bad," he said, between fits of the girl's coughing.

Maria turned to him, her brow pinched. "Juan says the water is breaking free inside her lungs," Maria whispered. "It sounds worse, but he claims it must happen for the child to get well."

"I reckon he knows what he's doing." Trey sighed,

admiring the lines of Maria's face.

"He does," Maria said. "The coughing potion is made from roots and bark. My father says it is an ancient secret, known only to the *curanderos*. Juan tells me the child will live, and I believe him."

To avoid an argument, Trey changed the subject. "I checked the woods around our camp. Looks like we're alone. For now."

Maria shook her head; then the corners of her mouth lifted. "I am cold. If you put your arms around me, I would be warm."

He took a step closer to her and placed his palms atop her tiny shoulders. "Like this?" he asked, feeling his heartbeat quicken.

She snuggled against his chest and gazed up at him. "This is better," she whispered.

Trey took a quick glance around them, to see who might be a witness. They were alone. The gambler and Carlos were at the second fire, near the carriage and the horses. Tom Adams and his wife were inside the wagon with Juan, watching over the child.

Then Trey summoned his nerve and bent down to kiss Maria's lips, lightly at first, pulling back to see her reaction. And when she closed her eyes, he kissed her again, harder this time, allowing his lips to linger against her mouth.

A knot of hot sap popped in the fire, and Trey pulled back. Maria smiled and opened her eyes.

"I have a different feeling inside me when you kiss me," she said. "A strange feeling, a feeling I never had before."

Trey was seldom at a loss for words. But just now, staring down at Maria's beautiful face with her admission ringing in his ears, he struggled to find the right thing to say. "I reckon I get a funny feeling, too," he said. Then he laughed softly. "I suppose it could be this cool mountain air."

His remark brought a frown to Maria's brow,

though her eyes held amusement. "Why can't it be that feeling you told Carlos about?" she asked. "The feeling that comes between a man and a woman who are . . . falling in love with each other?"

Now his heart was beating rapidly. He knew he must choose his words carefully. "I suppose it could be," he said hoarsely. "Is that what you think it is?"

She mocked him with a look, a slight tilt of her face as she arched her eyebrows. "I have no experience with this feeling," she replied. "You are the first man who ever made me feel this way."

She was pushing him toward a statement that love was beginning between them. And though he recognized it, he was reluctant to make the admission openly. "You're a beautiful woman, Maria," he said. "Any man would be a fool not to feel special when he holds you in his arms."

She wouldn't let it drop at that. "You haven't said that you could love me, Trey. Could you?"

He caught his breath and thought about his answer. "I know it's possible. I've been alone for so long . . ."

She traced a finger across his lips, and her expression softened again. "Are you afraid of being in love with me?" she asked.

He swallowed hard when he heard the truth of it. "Maybe," he answered. "Maybe I'm afraid I'll make a fool of myself."

She stood on her tiptoes then, and kissed him. It was a deep kiss, and her hand closed around the front of his shirt. Her lips were soft and warm, and for a moment, Trey lost himself in the feel of her mouth, and the tingling sensation that raced down his arms. He tightened his embrace around her shoulders, and he heard her moan softly. Then, as if she thought better of her actions, she pulled her mouth away and stepped back, pushing him back with her palm.

"We both need time," she said, "to find out how we

feel about each other." She glanced past him, to the back of the wagon. "I must go now, to see if Juan needs my help."

She was off toward the wagon before Trey could say any more. He watched her walk away with a mixture of feelings. Her kiss had filled him with old desires for a woman, of the kind he'd felt when he'd held Marybeth in his arms.

"Damn," he whispered when Maria disappeared into the wagon bed. "I wish to hell I didn't rattle on like that when I'm around her. If I'd kept my mouth shut . . ."

He turned for the fire where Stiles and Carlos were sitting, oddly light-headed now. Pretty Maria Valdez was about to throw a kink into all his plans, the plans he'd made so long ago, to drift from place to place searching for just one man who was faster with a gun. All the blind rage he'd bottled up inside him after he'd laid his wife and son to rest was still there. Would that anger get in the way if he fell in love with Maria? Perhaps a better question than any other . . . was he capable of loving someone else now? How could he be sure?

He trudged up to the fire and picked up his whiskey. When a thirsty swallow went down his throat, he made up his mind to think about other things. If his affection for Maria grew stronger, he would deal with it then. He had a job to do first, seeing that the woman and her party made it safely to Santa Fe. After they arrived, he could examine his feelings. And hers. For now, it was enough to share her kiss now and then.

He picked up a blanket and spoke to the gambler. "I'll bed down somewhere close to the horses," he said. "No tellin' who's liable to try to slip up on us out here."

He stalked off into the trees with the bottle of whiskey, wondering if he'd be able to sleep.

*   *   *

Dawn brought a change to the little girl's condition. The salve Juan had spread over her chest had somehow worked a feat of magic, and the child felt better, coughing less. Around a breakfast fire, Juan accepted thanks from the Adams family, along with a plate of hot biscuits ladled with honey Clair Adams had prepared. Everyone enjoyed the meal, and the fact that the girl's condition had improved.

"Time we started," Trey said, when the food was eaten.

Tom Adams shook Juan's hand; then he wiped a tear from one of his cheeks. "I'll always be in your debt, sir," he said.

Trey left the others to saddle his horse. Many dangerous miles remained to be traveled before they reached Maria's ranch. Twenty dollars in gold was at stake, and it was time he got back to earning his money.

Chapter Twenty-One

Due west, into a mountain range Trey's map identified as the Sangres, the road climbed and fell with greater frequency. The ruts showed more sign of heavy travel now, the hoofprints of many shod horses and the tracks of iron-rimmed wheels. Before noon, they encountered the first of several big freight wagons laden with barrels of flour and kegs of nails. Drawn by lumbering yokes of oxen, the wagons were slow to negotiate the steeper climbs.

When the sun was directly overhead, Trey rode up on a wagon pulled by two yokes of slow-moving oxen. A grizzled freighter clad in buckskins walked beside the lead yoke. When he saw Trey he lifted a hand, pausing in the road as his oxen continued down the ruts.

He was looking past Trey, to the carriage, when Trey stopped the roan at the edge of the road.

"You ridin' shotgun fer gov'nor Wallace?" he asked, as he ran a gnarled hand across his beard.

Trey shook his head. "There's a woman in that buggy," Trey replied. "Never met the governor. I'm new around here."

"New?" The freighter's voice indicated surprise. "Then, you'll wanna be careful, mister, after you swing past that next mountain."

"How's that?" Trey asked, when it seemed the man did not intend to explain himself.

The freighter's glance went to Trey's gunbelt, then back to Trey's face. "There's a bunch of them Regulators over yonder," he said. "Camped close to the road in a thicket of aspens. You'll see the smoke when you cross that ridge."

"What are Regulators?" Trey asked.

The man grunted unhappily. "Damn nuisances, if you ask me. They get themselves deputized by a judge someplace. Claim they're out to stop the rustlin', only there's some who'll swear Regulators are doin' most of the rustlin' themselves. Agitators is what I call 'em. I'd swing wide of 'em if I was you."

Trey squinted at the western horizon. "We had a run-in with them before," he sighed, "if you're talking about Dolan's men."

The freighter shook his head. "Regulators are on Chisum's side, mister. Appears you already know a thing or two 'bout this cattle war."

Trey frowned. "We've been warned. The men we ran into had badges, and they said they worked for Dolan."

The man chuckled dryly. "Likely they do. Both sides are wearin' badges, claimin' to represent the law. Ain't neither side law-abidin'. Those badges are just an excuse to poke their noses into another man's affairs."

Trey touched his hat brim. "I'll keep my eyes open. Thanks for the warning." He sent the roan forward with the touch of his heels, puzzling over the bit of news.

Now it appeared both sides in the conflict held out to represent the law in the Territory, according to the freighter. They wondered how anyone could sort things out, when Chisum's Regulators and Dolan's posse men both wore badges and claimed official status. It wouldn't matter much if Trey and his party could avoid them. But the man had said Regulators were camped over the next mountain; thus it seemed unlikely that Maria's carriage would be allowed to pass without questions being asked.

Glancing back, he saw Juan hurrying the team past the wagon and oxen. A quarter mile back, Stiles trotted his sorrel down the ruts. Trey got set for whatever lay in store beyond the mountain, with his mind made up to avoid any shooting. If he could. Maria's safety was the most important thing, and the safety of her nephew and the old man. If lead started to fly, the occupants of the carriage would make easy targets.

It had begun to seem that traveling across New Mexico had been a poor choice of directions, back when Trey first decided to make the ride. But if he hadn't come when he did, he would not have met beautiful Maria. Since last night's brief intimacy, when she'd spoken of the feelings she was developing for Trey, he hadn't been able to think of much of anything else. Most of the night, seated against a tree guarding the horses, his thoughts had been filled with wonderful recollections of that moment. And even now, facing danger on the other side of the mountain, he could not shake the memory of her soft lips against his, or the nearness of her body when he held her in his arms.

Hadn't she also said to give things time? Did that mean she expected him to stay at her father's ranch for a while? Carlos had said he heard his aunt talking about it with Juan. He wondered if he might be riding into an entanglement that would keep him in New Mexico Territory for a long time to come.

Trey shook his head, to clear his thoughts. Resting his palm on the butt of his .44, he sent his horse up the winding road that would take him over the mountain.

*　　*　　*

He glimpsed the smoke from a campfire curling above a thicket of white-trunked trees; aspen trees, the freighter had called them. He halted the roan and waited for the carriage, deciding to ride alongside it until they were past the Regulator camp. When the team trotted over the crest of the slope, Trey swung over and kept his horse near one carriage wheel.

"There's a camp up there," he said. "The gent driving the oxen said they were Chisum's men. Keep your rifle handy, Juan, in case they try to give us any trouble."

The old man shook his head, reaching under the seat for his Sharps. Trey glanced back to Maria and saw the worry on her face. "Just bein' careful," he said, to reassure her. "Seems like everybody in the Territory wants to know our business on this road."

Maria nodded silently and put her arms around her nephew's shoulders. Carlos was staring out the front of the canopy at the column of smoke.

Trey heeled his mount out in front of the team and kept his eyes on the aspen grove. Outlined in the trees, he saw men and horses. Were these the men who had shot the cowboy he'd hastily buried? Was Taggart a Regulator? Or a Dolan man?

The sounds of the carriage brought men to the edge of the trees to watch them pass. Trey rode stiffly in the saddle, awaiting the first sign of difficulty. From the corner of his eye, he saw two men mount their horses back in the aspens.

"Here they come," he said under his breath. "Here come the questions about who we are, and where we're headed."

A pair of geldings galloped away from the thicket. Two men in flop-brimmed cowboy hats bore down on the carriage. One cowboy carried a rifle loosely across the pommel of his saddle. Looking past the

208

páir, Trey counted eight or nine more men half-hidden by the tree trunks.

The two men rode in front of Trey to block the road. One dark-skinned rider with Mexican features held up a hand to halt Trey.

Trey sawed back on his reins and heard the carriage rattle to a halt behind him. "What's the problem?" he asked sharply, as if irritated about the delay.

"Checking travelers," the Mexican said in a toneless voice, as though he had the authority to stop traffic and did not need to explain. He eyed Trey's gun, then the passengers in the buggy more carefully. He saw Maria, and spoke to her in Spanish. *"Quien es?"*

"La familia de Porfirio Valdez," Juan replied gruffly.

The Mexican cowboy bowed his head politely. *"Passe,"* he said, swinging his horse off the road.

As quickly as they had been stopped, they were sent on their way again at the mention of Porfirio Valdez. Trey roweled his horse past the two men, watching from the corner of his eye until they were away from the spot. When he turned back, he saw Stiles hurry his horse to the rear of the carriage without incident. The two Regulators sat their horses passively to watch the carriage roll away.

"Maria's father is an important man in these parts," Trey concluded. "Chisum's men knew who he was, and they let us pass."

Half a mile from the aspen grove, Trey looked back again. The men were gone now.

Trey reasoned that the Regulators knew Maria's father was aligned with John Chisum, or leaning that way. Otherwise, Trey's party would not have been given passage so freely. If Porfirio Valdez had taken a side with Chisum in the range war, then the Valdez ranch could expect problems from Dolan and

Catron, if it had not happened already. It helped explain why Maria was so anxious to get back to her father. If Porfirio was truly neutral in the matter, there would be little to worry about.

"Another complication," Trey told himself, looking past the roan's ears at the next climb in the trail. "Maria and her father will be drawn into the conflict if they have sympathy for Chisum's position. And that means trouble with Dolan's posse men, and most likely gunplay. Maria knows about her father's leanings, and the trouble it could bring to the ranch."

The roan started up a rocky grade. On both sides of the road, the Sangres jutted into a sky full of puffy clouds. The clouds often blocked out the sun, adding to the chill in the air. Trey hunkered down inside his coat collar, then reached into his saddlebags for the bottle of whiskey.

They made camp in a ravine south of the trail as dark shadowed the Sangres. Juan built a small fire and put coffee on while Trey, Carlos, and the gambler attended to the horses. When they were out of earshot of those at the fire, Stiles sidled over to Trey and spoke softly.

"Those men looked like they meant to give us a hard time back there, Trey," he said. "What did you say to them?"

"It wasn't what I said," Trey answered. "When they asked who Maria was, they recognized her father's name and let us pass."

Stiles frowned. "Her father must be an important figure in territorial politics," he said thoughtfully.

"All rich men are important, Mr. Stiles. Money is power, most any place you find it."

"That's certainly true," the gambler replied, casting a look over his shoulder at the fire. "But this also means that the other side knows who he is . . .

210

Maria's father, I mean."

Trey nodded. He had contemplated the same thing. "By the map, we're about two days from Santa Fe." He sighed. "We'll be damn lucky to get there without running across some Dolan men."

Stiles was scowling now. "And perhaps they won't bluff so easily as they did the last time," he added.

Trey turned to the gambler, with a set to his mouth before he spoke. "I wasn't bluffing, Mr. Stiles. I never run a bluff. If a one of them had made a move toward his gun, I'd have killed him, and as many of the others as I could. Don't ever figure that I'm bluffing, gambler. I'm not a card player."

The tone of Trey's voice was enough of a rebuke to end the discussion. Stiles turned for the fire and walked away.

Trey heard Carlos come up behind him.

"I have a very important matter to discuss with you, señor," the boy said. "I waited until we were alone."

Trey found himself grinning over the serious look on the boy's face. "What is this important matter?" he asked.

Carlos squared his shoulders. "It is *Tia* Maria. She has spoken with me in confidence today. About you."

Trey wagged his head. "If it was said in confidence, then you shouldn't tell it," he replied.

Carlos looked Trey in the eye. "But it has to do with the plans you have made, señor," he continued. "You must change your plans at once!"

Trey was genuinely puzzled. "Why's that?" he asked.

The boy swallowed and looked at the fire, then back to Trey. "You said you planned to leave us at my grandfather's *rancho,* after only a day or two of rest. But when you learn about what *Tia* Maria told me, you will make plans to stay with us. Of that I am sure!"

"Just what did Maria tell you?" he asked softly.

Carlos lowered his voice. "She says that she has fallen in love with you. You make her heart feel happy, in a way that it never has before. Surely, señor, knowing this, you will stay and marry *Tia* Maria?"

Trey hesitated. "She told you that?"

"Yes, Señor Trey. She whispered in my ear, so that Juan would not hear her. Now you must change your plans and stay with us."

Trey let out a sigh. "It ain't quite that easy, son. There are lots of other things to consider."

Carlos pinched his brow. "What other things?"

"It's hard to explain," Trey said. "Maybe when you're a little older, you'll understand. A man and a woman have to talk about lots of things before they become husband and wife."

Then Carlos took a step closer to Trey, and there was a plea in his voice when he spoke. "Please talk to her, then. Talk about those things, so you can stay with us forever."

Trey chuckled softly. "Forever's a long time. And there's lots of things we'd have to talk about. But I'm glad you told me how she feels about me. I'll talk to her sometime, when we're alone."

Carlos smiled now. "Tonight would be a good time. After Juan and Señor Stiles are asleep," he said boldly.

Trey almost laughed out loud. "There'll be plenty of time for that," he said, looking toward the fire. "Let's go get something to eat. I'm about half-starved."

Carlos fell in beside Trey as they started back for the circle of firelight. "Do you love her also?" he asked, in a voice barely above a whisper.

Trey thought about his answer carefully. "Maybe," he said. "I reckon you could say she makes my heart happy, too. Could be we're both startin' to feel the

212

same way about each other. I'll talk to her, first chance we get."

Carlos was beaming when Trey glimpsed his face in the light from the fire.

"I will go to sleep very early, señor," the boy whispered, "so you will have the chance tonight!"

He was alone guarding the horses, nursing his bottle of whiskey, when he heard soft footsteps coming toward him in the dark. He turned around and found Maria huddled inside a bulky woolen coat to keep out the night chill. Before she reached him, he caught the scent of her.

"Everyone is asleep," she said softly. She came very close and stared into his eyes. "I couldn't fall asleep. Perhaps it is the cold in these mountains."

He placed the bottle beside a tree trunk and then took her in his arms. "Maybe this'll warm you up some," he said, thinking how foolish his remark sounded, for she understood his motives.

"Yes," she whispered, smiling. "That is better."

He thumbed back his hat brim and kissed her gently, lightly brushing his lips against hers. "I've wanted to do that all day," he said, when he took his mouth away.

She pressed her palms against his cheeks. "So have I," she sighed; then she kissed him back, adding pressure, opening her lips slightly. A gentle breath flared her tiny nostrils. Then she pulled back and searched his face. "I think I'm falling in love with you, Trey Marsh. I've never been in love before, but I get this silly feeling in the pit of my stomach when I'm near you. What do you think?"

He answered her question with a deep, lingering kiss, allowing his thoughts to be carried away by the pleasure of it.

213

Chapter Twenty-Two

It happened while Trey was investigating the length of a rocky pass. He had ridden between walls of stone on either side of the trail for about half a mile, galloping the roan far ahead of the carriage to be sure of safe passage through a tight spot. Suddenly, he heard a distant gunshot behind him, and the sound brought an involuntary jerk on his horse's reins when his muscles went taut.

He wheeled the gelding around and drummed his spurs into the roan's sides. The echo of hoofbeats clattered off the cliffs as he hurried his horse back toward the carriage. Just one shot had been fired, and in the following silence, Trey's worries grew. Why had the gun sounded? And why were there no more? For three days there had been no Apache tracks. They were a day's travel from Santa Fe, and he had guessed that they were close enough to the territorial capital to avoid any Indian troubles.

He saw the group of horsemen circled around the carriage when he rounded a bend in the pass. The carriage was halted at the mouth of the narrow canyon. Quickly, he counted better than a half dozen men blocking the road. The sight sent Trey clawing for his .44 as the roan galloped headlong down the length of the pass.

Faces turned among the riders when they heard the sounds of his approach. One of them whirled his mount and drew a gun.

The distance closed quickly, until Trey was in range for his Colt. But he worried that a misplaced shot might strike a passenger in the carriage; thus he held his fire, watching the man who faced him with a six-gun. Who would fire the first shot?

When Trey was a hundred yards from the trouble spot, he caught a glimpse of the gambler. Stiles was racing his horse toward the carriage at full speed. Sunlight glinted off the barrel of his revolver.

Several of the riders turned to confront Stiles, swinging away from the carriage to halt the gambler's charge. With their forces split now, the men seemed less certain, glancing to each other as though awaiting instructions. Trey felt immediate relief when he could see that no one inside the carriage was hurt. Had the lone gunshot been fired in the air to halt the buggy?

At fifty yards Trey slowed his horse, lifting his .44 so that it was in plain sight of the men. Trey knew the first shot that was fired would start a blood bath, and with Maria, Carlos, and Juan caught in between.

Twenty yards from the carriage, where the range would be deadly if any shooting started, Trey hauled back on his reins and brought the roan to a sliding stop. Searching the faces of the men, alert for a sudden move by any of them, his mouth twisted to a snarl. "Let the carriage pass!" he shouted, waving his gun barrel menacingly at the group. "You've got no right to stop peaceful citizens on a public road!"

A hard-faced cowboy on a big dun gelding turned his horse to address Trey. He was holding a six-gun at his side, half-hidden near his leg. "I've got a legal right," the man said evenly. He opened the lapel of his long duster coat to show Trey a gleaming badge.

Trey saw the gambler bring his sorrel to a

bounding halt a few yards behind the carriage. Stiles was looking over at Trey with a question on his face.

"You'd better have a good reason," Trey said, listening to his horse blow beneath him, badly winded from its run. "We've broken no laws."

The cowboy gave Trey a crooked smile. "I'll be the judge of that," he said. "You'll get yourself killed if you interfere with us. I asked the pretty lady in the fancy buggy a question, and until she gives me an answer, this contraption stays right where it sits."

Trey's eyelids slitted. "I'm a hard man to kill," he replied, fighting to bridle his temper. "Let the carriage pass. The woman has done nothing wrong."

Now Trey found more guns trained on him. Two men were covering Stiles.

"I don't take orders from some saddle tramp," the cowboy said hoarsely, after the grin left his face. "Holster that gun and keep your nose out of official business or I'll haul you to the Santa Fe jail. Or to an undertaker's parlor, if you try to use that gun."

Maria spoke then, ending the standoff briefly. "It's all right, Trey," she said, leaning out from underneath the canopy. "I'll answer the question. I am Maria Valdez, daughter of Porfirio Valdez. Our ranch is northwest of Santa Fe, at Agua Frio springs. We are returning home."

Now the hard-faced leader of the group was staring at Maria. "So you're ol' Porfirio's daughter?" he asked. "Your pa hadn't oughta refused Jimmy's offer to buy his calves. I reckon Porfirio's havin' some regrets that he didn't sell. Heard somebody shot him a few weeks back. Heard it was accidental." Then the cowboy laughed.

"My father has been shot?" Maria cried.

The cowboy shrugged. "That's the word I got. Didn't kill him, so I heard. Maybe it taught him a lesson."

Maria turned quickly to Juan. "We must hurry!"

217

she cried, as tears welled in her eyes.

Rage boiled inside Trey's chest, though he knew he could not risk a gun battle when Maria and the boy might be caught in the middle. "Let them pass," Trey snapped, fixing the leader of the group with a stare. "When the woman and the child are out of danger, we can settle this."

"Let's take him to jail, Frank," another cowboy said, waving his pistol in Trey's direction. "I'll put the irons on him."

Frank appeared to be conducting a debate with himself while he watched Trey. He still carried his gun beside his right leg. "Just how do you aim for us to settle it?" he asked.

Trey's jaw clamped, then relaxed. "Any way you want it," he answered softly. "Whatever suits you. But first, the carriage goes on its way, unless you make it a habit to make a name for yourself against women and kids."

Frank's face darkened. "You've got a big mouth, don't you?" he asked.

"I can back it up," Trey replied. "Let the carriage roll through and I'll show you I'm a man of my word."

"Please no!" Maria shouted, her voice thick with anguish. "We must reach my father quickly. Please, Trey! We must hurry!"

Frank wore a lopsided grin. "Better listen to the lady," he said, "or we'll be fittin' you for a pine box. Soon as you holster that gun and tell your friend back there to do likewise, we'll let the buggy go."

Trey struggled to control himself. One well-placed bullet would quickly wipe the smile off Frank's leering face. But the danger was too great that flying lead might strike Maria, or Carlos. He decided the confrontation with Frank could wait for another time. Slowly, Trey lowered his Colt and fitted it back in its holster. "Put that gun away, Mr. Stiles," he

218

said, as though the words had a bitter taste.

Frank's leer widened. "Now you're bein' smart," he said. "We'd have killed you if you'd done things otherwise. I oughta listen to Buck and haul your ass to jail. But I'll let it slide this time, on account of this pretty Mexican woman has gotta see about her pa's gunshot wound." He turned to Maria. "Can't have it said that Frank Taggart ain't got a heart when it comes to pretty women."

Trey's blood ran cold. This was Taggart. In his mind's eye, Trey saw the young cowboy lying in a patch of bloodstained grass, whispering Taggart's name. More than ever now, Trey wanted to put a bullet between Frank Taggart's eyes, yet he couldn't. Not until Maria was safely out of the way at her father's ranch with Carlos.

"Let the buggy through," Frank said, pulling his horse out of the roadway, but with his gaze still fixed on Trey. "This feller with the big mouth has decided to show some sense."

Several of the others chuckled as they reined their horses away from the carriage. Juan slapped his reins over the rumps of the team and hurried the carriage past Trey into the mouth of the rocky pass.

Trey motioned for Stiles to ride through, but he held his horse a few yards from Frank Taggart and his deputies until Stiles and the buggy were were well into the canyon.

Then a slow smile crossed Trey's face. "We'll meet again, Taggart, you and me," he said, sounding downright casual about it. "And when we do, things will go differently. I'll look you up in Santa Fe, after the woman and child are at her father's ranch. Then we can square this little misunderstanding. You've got my word that we'll see each other again. I buried a young cowboy back down the road a few days, and he said he owed you for the hole in his belly. So I'll square that debt, too, when I come."

Trey wheeled his mount away just as Taggart's expression had begun to change. Taggart's eyes were pinpoints when Trey spurred the roan into a lunging gallop that took him quickly into the pass, out of good pistol range.

Then Trey's hands knotted into fists. "I'm gonna kill that son of a bitch," he promised himself, feeling the roan lengthen its strides to catch up with the carriage. "I'm gonna kill him slow, if I can, so he'll know what he done to that boy."

At Maria's insistence, they traveled in the dark. Trey tried to comfort her when they rested the harness team, but no words could bring an end to her soft crying.

"He said your father was wounded," Trey said once, when they watered the horses at a stream. "Maybe it isn't bad. Maybe he's under a doctor's care."

Maria looked up at Trey with tear-filled eyes. "He needs my help, Trey," she sobbed. "I only pray I'm not too late."

Pushing the horses beyond their limits, they risked the dangers of traveling at night, stopping more frequently for rest as the hour approached midnight. According to Juan, they might reach the ranch just after dawn if they could continue without difficulty to Santa Fe.

Trey rode out front, closer to the carriage than before, sipping whiskey while huddled inside his coat to stay warm. Now and then the gambler would gallop to the front for whiskey, and to exchange a few words with Trey.

"I should have stayed closer to the carriage," he said, taking the bottle from Trey. "When they fired that warning shot, I came as fast as I could, but I'd gotten down to put on my heavy coat because the air

220

was so cold. That Taggart is an arrogant fellow. A badge does strange things to some men."

Trey grunted, remembering the exchange with Taggart and his men. "Appears every man in the Territory wears some kind of tin star," he said, fisting the neck of the bottle when Stiles handed it back. "I'd have killed Taggart, if it hadn't been for the woman and the boy being so close."

Stiles chuckled without intending any humor. "You made it plain you weren't afraid of him. I can't quite figure you out, Trey. You are an intelligent man, as your colonel's rank would indicate, yet you look death in the eye and never blink. If you'd behaved the same way during the war, you wouldn't be here now. There would be a grave with your name on its somewhere in Virginia, or Tennessee. Something changed you."

Trey took a long swallow of whiskey. When the burn subsided, he said, "My name's on a grave in Galveston. It reads William Treyble Marsh Junior. Right beside it, my soul is buried with a woman named Marybeth Marsh. When I found out they were dead, a part of me died with them. Haven't cared about a damn thing since. Now, I've explained it, so stop asking me questions about why I do things. I'm ready to die, Mr. Stiles. I've been ready since the summer of sixty-five."

The gambler looked across at Trey, holding his horse beside the roan as they proceeded up a rocky climb in the dark. "Some men take their own lives," he said quietly. "Hundreds of them did at Andersonville."

The direction of the conversation had begun to irritate Trey, though he had been the one to reveal a secret part of his past to Stiles. "I didn't have the courage," Trey admitted, as a wave of old pain made him wince inwardly. "I suppose it's the only thing left that I'm afraid of. Now get back to your position, gambler. I've already told you more than I've told anyone else, so be satisfied with it. That's all you'll ever get out of me."

Trey urged his horse away from Stiles, wanting to be alone now with his thoughts. But as he rode through the night, he saw the weed-choked graves floating before his eyes, and remembered the terrible pain of it. Over the years he had tried to shut the memory out, but it always returned to haunt him.

"I could never be a husband to Maria," he whispered, gazing up at the stars. "There'd always be that memory. It could never be the same as it was with Marybeth."

He closed his eyes briefly when the painful recollections became stronger. Billy Marsh would have been about the same age as little Carlos now . . . if he had lived . . . if those goddamn Yankees hadn't burned Galveston to the ground.

Later, he uncorked the whiskey again and drank deeply. As the roan crossed a starlit ridge, he heard a coyote howl on a slope high above the trail. The sound made him think about how much he had become like the coyote, living out a solitary existence away from everyone else, seeking a mate who could not answer his lonesome call.

He drank until the bottle was empty, climbing the silent Sangres with a similarly empty heart.

Chapter Twenty-Three

Santa Fe at sunrise presented both a welcome and beautiful sight. Hundreds of adobe structures caught golden sunlight across hillsides and valleys. Red clay tile roofs covered the larger adobes, adding a splash of color. And even at this early hour, a pall of dust arose from wagon traffic along a heavily traveled road leading west. Juan said it was a route for freight wagons moving into Arizona Territory where numerous cavalry posts battled the Apaches to keep roads open to California and Oregon.

Trey stayed close to the carriage as Juan hurried the team through Santa Fe. An hour past dawn found the city still half-asleep, stores still closed, the plazas empty. Only the huge freight wagons seemed to ignore the hour. Spans of mules and yokes of oxen pulled creaking loads of goods past silent, shuttered store windows, choking the streets with their dust.

Juan pressed the team around strings of wagons, slapping his reins over the lathered bays. Trey admired the old churches and opulent homes nestled behind thick adobe walls and locked iron gates. Most of the pedestrians Trey saw were of Mexican descent. At one of the plazas, a group of Indians clad in brightly colored blankets and headbands were gathered around a smoldering fire. They were not

Apaches, by their dress, nor were they carrying any weapons. Some rested atop bundles of lamb's wool that were piled at the edge of the road around the plaza.

Juan kept the team in a long trot, following a road leading to the northwest that climbed a hilltop out of Santa Fe. Now and then Trey glanced below the canopy. Maria's face looked drawn. A long night without sleep had taken its toll on her. Trey could feel the stiffness from so many hours spent in the saddle, and his belly rumbled from hunger.

As they began the climb out of Santa Fe, Stiles galloped his horse up to Trey and leaned out of the saddle to be heard.

"I'll be staying in town, Trey," he said. Then he grinned. "I've got enough of a stake to buy into a game or two. Time I started making a living." He extended a hand to shake with Trey. "Good luck, Colonel Marsh. This is where we part company."

With their horses trotting shoulder to shoulder, they shook hands.

"Good luck to you, Mr. Stiles," Trey said. In a strange way, he was sorry to see the gambler depart. "I'll admit I was wrong about you, gambler," he added. "You've got more guts than I gave you credit for. I've fought alongside some brave men in my time, but I don't reckon any of them showed any more courage than you did along this road. I'll call you a friend, Woodrow. You've got backbone."

Stiles acknowledged the compliment with a tip of his hat; then he reined back to have a word with Maria and Juan. Trey could hear him above the rattle of the harness and the bang of the carriage wheels.

"I'll be saying goodbye," he said, lifting his hat again politely when he addressed Maria. "I hope your father is doing well."

"Stop the carriage," Maria commanded.

Juan pulled back on the reins and halted the team.

Trey saw Maria reach below the carriage seat. He was frankly puzzled by the delay, until he saw Maria jump down from the buggy to hand the gambler a golden coin.

"Here is a small token of payment for your assistance," she said, looking up at Stiles while he examined the coin. "You risked your life to help us, and I wanted you to know that we are grateful."

The gambler's face was flushed. "I wasn't expecting any payment, ma'am," he said softly. He glanced toward Trey. "I joined the fight for our mutual defense. However, since my pockets are all but empty, I'll accept your generous offer." He stuck the coin in a pocket of his coat, then touched his hat brim and swung his sorrel back in the direction of town. A few yards from the carriage, he turned back and waved.

Maria hurried back to her seat below the canopy. "*Andele!*" she cried.

Juan clucked to the team and shook the reins over them. The carriage jolted forward, continuing up a grade to the top of a hill at the outskirts of the city.

Trey fell in behind the carriage, remembering the gambler and the surprise on his face when he glimpsed the gold coin. Had Stiles known there was a fortune in gold below the carriage seat, he might have behaved very differently. Trey understood men's greed, and just then he was thankful that the gambler hadn't known about the gold. It was better to remember Stiles fondly for the risks he'd taken, without knowing whether the gold could have turned a gambler into a thief.

The narrow road they followed now twisted and turned, climbing rocky hillsides, then down into shallow ravines. Traveling west and slightly north, they soon entered forests of pine and oak. Then, hidden in the trees until they were very close, they came to broad, grassy meadows thick with lush grazing. Later, at one of the meadows, they found a herd of longhorn cows.

Trey squinted to see the brand on the cows' flanks. A Bar V had been burned into the sides of the animals, and Trey guessed it was the Valdez brand. He urged the roan up beside the carriage and spoke loud enough to be heard above the wheels. "Are these your longhorns?" he asked.

Maria nodded, and it was then that he noticed she was crying. He gave her a sympathetic wave and pulled the roan away. Maria didn't want conversation now, not until she knew her father's fate.

They were roughly two hours away from Santa Fe when Juan swung the team north on a seldom-traveled caliche lane running between stands of pine. The sweet scent of the pines filled Trey's nostrils as he followed along behind the carriage. The lane crossed a flat meadow, then disappeared into more trees for a gradual climb up a hillside.

At the top of the hill, with the vista of tall mountains all around, Trey saw a broad valley. The valley floor had been cleared of trees. To the southwest, a neatly tended cornfield stretched to the end of the valley. In the middle of the valley was a sprawling adobe house . . . low-roofed, surrounded by a low adobe wall reminding Trey of a fortress. Outside the wall sat several smaller adobe huts, and to the north of the house, a barn and pole corrals had been built along the edge of a small stream. A windmill fanned its wooden blades between the corrals.

"Damn, what a beautiful place," Trey whispered, keeping his roan at a trot behind the carriage. "Porfirio Valdez has got one hell of a spread here."

Juan whipped the harness horses to a run down the lane toward the house. A black dog ran out from an opening in the adobe wall, barking a series of angry yelps. Then a pair of cotton-clad men wearing big straw sombreros appeared from the hallway of the barn, and Trey saw sunlight glint off the rifles they carried.

"They're expecting trouble," he said under his breath. For Maria's sake more than anything else, Trey hoped that Porfirio was not badly hurt. Or dead from his gunshot wound.

Now the carriage raced for the gate in the adobe wall, dust flying skyward from its wheels. Trey sent his horse to a lope and followed Juan through the opening, to a sun-baked stretch of caliche hardpan in front of the house.

Trey examined the big house before he slowed the roan. It was a rambling affair, with a red tile roof. Huge wood beams jutted through the tops of the adobe walls for roof supports. Small windows were closed by wooden shutters. Big clay pots sat on a long wooden porch across the front of the house, shaded by a thatched roof of dried limbs. The ranch house showed evidence of care. Though the yard inside the fence had no grass, it was neatly attended.

The carriage rattled to a halt, and almost before the wheels had stopped turning, Maria had jumped from her seat and was running up the front porch steps, with little Carlos close at her heels.

Trey saw a swarthy Mexican woman open the front door to admit Maria before Maria reached the entrance. Trey kept an eye on the two Mexicans hurrying toward the house carrying rifles.

Juan climbed down slowly from the carriage, standing stiffly for a moment, until the pair of ranch hands rounded the gate into the yard. Trey heard Juan instruct the men with the care of the harness team, talking in Spanish. Then Juan turned to Trey.

"Give them your horse, señor," he said, sounding tired when he said it. "These vaqueros will give it the best of feed and a clean stall. Bring your belongings to the house. There is good brandy in the kitchen."

He grinned. "I think we deserve a drink."

Trey stepped down and handed the reins to a young Mexican boy who stood expectantly at the roan's shoulder. The boy bowed and waited for Trey to pull his bedroll, saddlebags, and rifle boot off the roan before leading it away toward the barn.

Trey carried his gear to the front porch while Juan lifted the money chest from its hiding place and disappeared inside the house. The plump Mexican woman spoke quietly to Juan as he went in. Trey did not understand what was said, but he guessed it had to do with Porfirio's condition. The woman's face was grave when she spoke, and Trey judged things had not gone well while Maria was away.

"Come in, señor," the woman said, smiling now.

Trey carried his saddlebags and rifle into a cool, dark hallway. A polished wood floor stretched toward dark corners of the house. A fire burned in a stone fireplace at the back of a large front room. Plush leather chairs sat in front of the fireplace. Trey walked to one of the chairs and settled down contentedly, pulling off his hat. He let out a sigh. The night-long ride had left him weak. Hunger and lack of sleep battled each other inside his head.

He heard voices coming from the back of the house. Admiring the neat appointments around the room, the expensive furniture and wall decorations, he almost missed hearing Juan walk into the room with a pair of glasses and a decanter of brandy.

"How's Maria's father?" Trey asked, as Juan poured into the glasses.

Juan scowled. "He is very sick. Very weak from his injury, however the doctor who comes from Santa Fe says he will pull through, given time." Then Juan lowered his voice. "There have been more difficulties with the men who work for Catron. Some came a few days ago. They made threats, telling Paulito and Arturo that Señor Valdez must sell his calves to Tom

228

Catron before the first frost. Paulito said the men came with many guns."

"How is Maria taking it?" Trey asked.

Juan shook his head. "She is crying, of course," he sighed.

"At least her father won't die," Trey whispered, both to himself and to Juan. He took a sip of brandy, then another, savoring the sweet taste.

"There will be much trouble here in the days to come," Juan said quietly, studying Trey's face. "Catron's men will come back, and Señor Valdez will refuse to sell his cows to them, as long as there is breath in his lungs. He is a very proud man, *mi patrón*. He will not bow down to the men from Santa Fe."

Trey considered Maria's predicament. Alone, running the ranch with three Mexican vaqueros, she would stand little chance of handling the difficulties she would be facing from men like Frank Taggart and the gunslicks in Dolan's employ. "Maybe I'll stay around for a few days," Trey said, thinking out loud. "My horse could use a rest, and so could I."

Juan's leathery face parted in a grin. "It will make Maria very happy if you stay," he said. "And you promised Carlos a lesson with your pistol. He will be happy, too, if you stay."

"It wouldn't be for very long," Trey protested. "Just a few days, until me and the horse are rested up."

Juan's grin only broadened. "I understand, señor," he said softly; then he added more brandy to Trey's glass.

They were given a meal of beefsteak, fried beans, and warm tortillas beside bowls of hot salsa. Maria came to the table late, and by her eyes, Trey knew she had been crying. She took a chair at the big wooden table off the kitchen, a chair beside Trey's.

"How is your father?" Trey asked, though he already knew the answer, asking out of duty and politeness.

Maria closed her eyes briefly. "He is very weak. I told him about our journey . . . all the difficulties. And I told him about you. After supper, my father would like to meet you. He is resting now, so he will be stronger when he talks to you. My father has . . . a proposition he wishes to offer you, Trey. I hope you will listen."

Trey cut into a delicious piece of steak. "I'll listen to what he has to say."

He felt Carlos watching him.

"I hope you can stay for a while," the boy said. "You promised to show me about the *pistola*."

Trey nodded. "I haven't forgotten," he replied, being careful to chew his food with his mouth closed. "Maybe tomorrow, after we've all had some sleep."

Maria turned to him. "Rosa has prepared our guest bedroom for you," she said, merely toying with her food as she talked, without appetite now. "It is small, but the bed is quite comfortable."

Trey chuckled softly. "Tired as I am, I could sleep on a pile of rocks."

The woman Maria called Rosa came into the room carrying small bowls. She placed one in front of Trey, and then the others.

"What is this?" Trey asked, eyeing a caramel syrup floating atop a yellow substance.

"It is called *flan*," Carlos said quickly. "It is sweet custard made from eggs and sugar. You will like it!"

Now it was Maria's turn to laugh. She looked at Carlos lovingly and patted his hand; then she turned to Trey. "We are so very glad that we found you at Fort Sumner," she said, smiling at him, looking more beautiful than ever. "I told my father that we would have surely lost our lives had it not been for you, Trey. My father wishes to express his gratitude for what you have done. And to talk about another matter."

Trey stuck a spoon into his bowl of custard. "I'll listen," he replied. "I'm not in any real hurry to go."

Their eyes met suddenly when Trey looked up. Something moved gently inside him, a stirring. Perhaps it was his heart.

Chapter Twenty-Four

Porfirio Valdez watched Trey from his pillow. Dark black eyes appraised Trey carefully, as though they could see Trey's innermost thoughts. The old man's cheeks were sunken and pale, and his breathing was shallow, irregular. A lantern globe glowed softly on a bedside table, painting shadows on the adobe walls around the big four-poster bed. The bedroom was at the back of the house. Porfirio had asked that he and Trey be left alone. Outside, beyond a dark window, stars brightened a night sky. For a time, the old man said nothing, making his study of Trey's face by lamplight.

"I am most grateful to you, Señor Marsh, for bringing my daughter and my grandson safely to me," he said. His voice was hollow, hoarse, a gravelly sound. "My family is my most precious possession. This land, this ranch, it means nothing by comparison. Do you understand the value of a family?"

Trey nodded once. "I did . . . a long time ago. My wife and son were killed during the war. I have no family now, but I understand that there is nothing more precious."

Porfirio closed his eyes, as if a stab of pain came and went; then he looked up at Trey. "Maria told me that she has explained what is happening between

Tom Catron and John Chisum," he began in a rasping tone. "You have seen some of it for yourself, I understand."

"We ran across men from both sides," Trey replied. "They all claim to represent the law. It was Catron's men who shot you . . . ?"

The old man hesitated before he answered. "I was wounded from ambush. I heard the shot, and felt the pain in my chest. After that, I remember nothing at all. Paulito found me where I had fallen off my horse."

"You refused to sell your calves to this Dolan, the man who ramrods things for Catron." Trey sighed. "Don't take a very smart gent to figure things out."

Porfirio stared at the canopy above his head. "The cattle contracts are making men rich. The government pays, without ever seeing the beef," he said quietly. "Thomas Catron and his followers are crooked men who cheat the government with the beef they sell. But they must have cattle to fill the contracts. It is a very bad situation. Honest ranchers are being forced to sell to Catron. If they refuse and seek the open market for better prices, Dolan and his men provide a fateful accident. Governor Wallace has no understanding of things here. There are some who say he chooses to turn his back to it."

"It has come down to whoever can hire the most paid guns," Trey suggested. "It becomes the law of the gun."

"Yes," the old man whispered. Then he looked at Trey. "My daughter tells me you are very good with a gun, Señor Marsh. She told me that you are a fearless man, and a deadly shot." He looked down, to Trey's gunbelt. "Is your gun for hire?" he asked.

Trey took a deep breath. "That depends. I won't go gunning for a cause I don't believe in, or shoot a man who isn't my equal with a weapon. I had a bellyful of killing during the war. I watched too many men die.

But neither will I allow some gunslick to ride roughshod over innocent folks, or take advantage of people who can't defend themselves. I've done my share of killing when men went up against me, but I wouldn't call myself a gunfighter. I won't follow orders another man gives me when it comes to using a gun. I've got a conscience, and I won't go against my principles, if that's what you're asking."

Porfirio shook his head. "That is not what I asked of you, Señor Marsh. I asked if your gun was for hire. I wish to employ someone who will defend my family, and my ranch. The lives of my family, and my vaqueros, must be spared."

Trey hooked his thumbs in his gunbelt. "I'd listen to that kind of proposition," he answered.

The old man struggled up on his elbows, shaking from the strain of it, his face knitted with pain. He reached over to the table beside the bed and picked up a small leather pouch; then he lay back against his pillow and offered the pouch to Trey. "Here is five hundred dollars in gold, Señor Marsh. All you must do to earn it is to protect my family and the people who work for me. No questions will be asked of you about how the job is done. You must stay until the snows come in December. Then you will be free to leave, and the money is yours."

Trey stared at the pouch. Five hundred dollars was a fortune, a life's work for most men. "I hadn't planned to stay that long," he said. "I'm something of a drifter. I get the urge to move on."

"Only until December," the old man said, growing weaker after the effort to rise from his pillow. "After the snows, I will make other arrangements for my family's safety."

Trey made a turn for the bedroom door. "I'll think it over," he replied. "In the meantime, don't worry about Maria or the boy. If any of Dolan's bunch shows up around here, they'll have more trouble

235

than they bargained for." He walked to the door and gripped the doorknob.

"My daughter," Porfirio whispered. "There is something in her eyes when she speaks your name. Be gentle with her, Señor Marsh, for she is all I have left. Her, and the boy."

He was up before dawn, prowling the ranch yard with a cup of coffee Rosa had prepared. As the sun grayed the eastern sky, he walked to the barn to inspect the stall where his roan had been stabled. He found the horse nibbling fresh clover hay, and he could see the brush strokes in the horse's coat where someone had given it a rubdown. The roan nickered softly and flared its nostrils to catch Trey's scent when he came to the stall. Trey rubbed the animal's nose, pleased with the care it had been shown.

Rays of sunlight beamed over the mountains to the east, driving away the night chill. Lanterns flickered behind windows in some of the huts outside the wall. Trey swept the valley with a slow, lingering look. He wondered if he could be happy here. Or would the urge to move on come as it always had when he stayed in one place too long.

He heard footsteps coming from the house and saw Maria walking toward him, huddled in her coat, shoulders rounded against the cold.

"Good morning, Trey," she said brightly, when she met him halfway from the stable. "Rosa said you were outside." She studied his face. "Have you thought about my father's proposition?"

"I've been thinking on it," he replied, staring into her eyes. "He wants me to stay until December. That's a long time for me to be in one place, but I reckon I'll give it a try. He made me a very generous offer. It'd be hard to refuse."

Maria frowned slightly. "I had hoped you would

agree to stay for other reasons," she said. "I suppose I hoped you would stay because of your feelings for me."

Trey tossed out the last of his coffee; then he took Maria in his arms. "I do have feelings for you," he said quietly. "I haven't felt this way about a woman in a long time. Since . . ."

"I understand," she whispered. "Please stay with us until December. Then you can decide if there can be more between us."

He lowered his face and kissed her gently, worrying that one of the ranch hands might see them embrace. Maria returned his kiss, and then she smiled at him. "Breakfast is ready. And Carlos is already dressed and waiting at the kitchen table for his first lesson with a gun."

Trey shook his head, grinning. "We'll go behind the barn where the shooting won't disturb your father. Tell your father that I agree to his offer. I'll stay 'til the first of December. Maybe longer . . . if things work out."

Maria took his hand and led him toward the house.

Carlos gripped the Colt with both hands and tried to steady it while Trey knelt beside him to give instructions.

"Let the sight rest on that stump, then squeeze the trigger very gently. The gun will kick a little, but don't let it frighten you. You'll get used to it."

The boy's face was a mask of determination. His finger closed; then there was a mighty roar that knocked him back on his heels. The muzzle of the .44 lifted sharply. Carlos blinked, and shook his head sadly. "I missed the tree," he said. "The *pistola*, it kicks like a mule!"

"Cock the hammer and try again," Trey said. "This time, pull the trigger very slowly, keeping the sight on the stump."

Carlos raised the heavy gun again and thumbed back the hammer; then he steadied his hands and nudged the trigger as Trey instructed. The Colt blasted, jolting the boy back a half step; then a smile creased his brown cheeks. "I hit the tree!" he exclaimed. A chunk of bark was missing from the pine stump, leaving a white scar.

"Better," Trey said, clapping Carlos on the shoulder. "Now try again." He glanced over his shoulder, sensing that someone was watching. He saw Maria standing behind the corner of a pole corral to witness the shooting practice.

Carlos cocked the gun and aimed carefully, spreading his legs slightly apart to prepare for the kick. The Colt roared and spat flame. The bullet nicked the side of the stump and sent bark flying to one side. "I hit it again!" he cried. "Only this time, it was not a tree. It was a Yaqui warrior!"

The vaquero named Paulito pointed to a mountaintop. He had shown Trey the boundaries of the ranch, and they had been in their saddles most of the day. "Beyond that mountain is the Matthews Ranch," he said. "The cattle bear a Slash M brand on the left shoulder. Señor Valdez owns twenty sections of land. Some of it is very rocky, with little grass. But in the valleys, the grass is good."

"I've seen enough," Trey said, reining the chestnut gelding he had saddled for the day. The roan needed rest. It had been a long, hard ride up from Tascosa, and the animal had earned a few days without a rider on its back.

Paulito led the way across a grassy meadow. A small herd of fat longhorns with calves at their flanks scattered when the riders approached. The Valdez cattle Trey had seen were large-framed and thick-bodied. They carried more beef than the average longhorn and showed the result of good breeding and ample fodder. On the far side of the meadow, the two men started down a slender trail through a pine forest. Paulito's pinto gelding knew the way back to the ranch without assistance from its rider.

When they reached the valley, they rode around the edge of the corn field. Trey spotted a rider on a big black gelding coming toward them, and he recognized Maria at once. She hurried her horse to a lope and met them halfway down the length of the field.

"Now you have seen our ranch," she said proudly. "Let me show you one more place, a very special place during the summer. You can go back now, Paulito. I will show Señor Marsh the springs."

Paulito waved and rode off at a trot. Maria smiled at Trey, as though she had been part of a conspiracy.

"I wanted to be alone with you," she said. "Come. Follow me and I will show you the beautiful springs."

She rode off at a gallop before Trey could answer. He swung the chestnut and hurried along in her tracks. Southwest of the corn field, Maria turned into a tree-choked ravine, down a faint game trail almost overgrown with grass and low bushes. For half a mile, the trail wound around tall pines and undergrowth, when suddenly the pathway ended at a sparkling pool of water beneath a falls spilling from a rock ledge above the pool. Brilliant wildflowers grew on the banks of the spring pond, reds and yellows, and a tiny white flower with a golden center.

Maria dropped from the back of her horse; then she turned to Trey. "Isn't it beautiful?" she asked.

He got down slowly, admiring the natural beauty of the spot, listening to the musical sounds of the waterfall upon the surface of the pool. "It's about the prettiest place I ever saw," he said, tying the chestnut's reins to a low pine limb. He walked to the edge of the pool and found clear water. Colorful stones on the bottom caught sunlight, deepening the hues of red and blue and pale green. A fish darted away from Trey's shadow; then he felt Maria's hand in the crook of his arm.

She was looking up at him when he turned.

"I wanted you to see this place," she said. "I wanted to be the one to show it to you. I come here alone, when I need to think about things. It is a special place for me."

He was stricken by her beauty then, standing in warm sunlight, her hair flowing over her shoulders, framing her remarkable face, the soft lines and smooth skin. He placed his palms against her cheeks and bent down to kiss her full on the mouth, and the kiss was harder than he had intended.

Maria moaned softly and pressed her body against his. Her arms wound, snakelike, around his neck, her fingers curled into his untrimmed hair. Her embrace tightened, and her lips parted even more as her arms pulled his mouth against hers.

He let his hands drop to her waist. He pulled her to his chest and felt her breasts through the fabric of his shirt. Maria's tiny nostrils flared as her breathing came more rapidly. For a time her arms held him fiercely. It was as if a dam had broken somewhere inside her and now her emotions were beyond her control.

Then suddenly, she drew back and closed her eyes. "I must behave like a lady," she said softly. "I don't know what came over me just now. I'm sorry, Trey."

He did not answer her, but took her hand, leading her to a grassy spot on the bank above the spring pond. He knelt slowly and pulled her down beside him without saying a word. He took off his hat and tossed it to one side, then lay back on the soft grass and pulled her down beside him. She offered no protest when he wrapped his arms around her and kissed her again, gently at first, then much harder, tightening his grip around her shoulders.

The sounds of the waterfall drowned out Maria's soft moans as Trey's right hand moved slowly from her shoulder to her waist, then down the curve of her thigh. Somewhere in a treetop above the spring, a lark gave its lyrical call to the soft summer wind.

Chapter Twenty-Five

Five peaceful days at the Valdez Ranch had given Trey enough time to experience the beginnings of a feeling that he belonged there. Riding the pastures, often with Maria at his side, he also felt the bond between them growing. They shared secret moments together whenever they could find them, though it became increasingly difficult as Carlos became more attached to Trey, always begging for more schooling with a firearm.

Late in the morning, on a quiet day while Trey showed the boy how to fire Juan's Sharps rifle, Trey looked up toward the lane into the valley when he heard the hoofbeats of a running horse. A sorrel galloped toward the ranch house. Even from a distance, Trey knew the rider. It would be an unexpected pleasure to have a visit from Woodrow Stiles.

Trey carried the rifle through the barn, then toward the gate in the adobe wall where Stiles was headed. Watching the gambler ride up, Trey's brow furrowed. Stiles was hurrying his horse more than necessary. Was the gambler in trouble again? Seeking Trey's help out of another fix?

Stiles jerked his lathered gelding to a halt near the opening in the wall, and by the look on the gambler's face Trey knew there was trouble.

"You're in a mighty big hurry," Trey said, before Stiles jumped to the ground.

"Some of Dolan's men are headed this way," Stiles began, glancing over his shoulder. "Frank Taggart and three or four more are coming out to give Porfirio Valdez one last chance to sell his calves to Tom Catron. I overheard them talking a couple of hours ago at the Ace of Diamonds Saloon. They went to saddle their horses, and I came as quickly as I could to warn you."

Trey swung a look toward the house, remembering a pair of shotguns kept in a cabinet near the fireplace. A shotgun would help even things if the men wanted a fight at close range. "Thanks for the warning," Trey replied. "That horse of yours is winded. Take it to the barn. One of the vaqueros will see to its care. I don't reckon Maria would mind lending you a fresh horse for the ride back to town."

Stiles opened his coat, to show Trey a cross-pull holster and a heavy Colt .44 with polished wood grips. "I thought I'd stay to lend you a hand, Trey," he said, half grinning. "I won a bigger revolver in a poker game the other night. I figure I owe you, for the times you helped me out of a tight spot."

"I'll handle it myself," Trey said. "I'm obliged for the offer, but this isn't your fight; so stay out of it."

But Stiles wagged his head side to side. "I'm staying," he said flatly. "I'll stay out of things . . . unless somebody goes for a gun."

Trey sighed. "Suit yourself, Mr. Stiles," he said. "Take that horse down to the barn. I'll grab a shotgun and tell Maria what you heard in Santa Fe. It ain't likely to be a peaceful discussion when they show up."

Trey hurried to the front door and let himself in. He took one of the shotguns from the cabinet, and pocketed a handful of shells. Then he heard footsteps coming from the back of the house.

Maria came into the front room. "I heard someone come in," she said, scowling when she saw the shotgun in Trey's hands. "Is something wrong?"

"Maybe," Trey replied. "Some of Dolan's men are headed out here with a last demand that your father sell his calves to Catron. I want you to get Carlos inside, and tell Paulito and Arturo to stay out of sight." Then he smiled down at her. "And that includes you, Maria. I want you out of the way if any shooting starts."

"Oh, Trey!" she cried, throwing her arms around his neck. "I knew something like this had to happen. Please be careful."

He placed one palm against the small of her back and whispered in her ear. "I'm alive because I'm always careful. Now get Carlos inside, and you stay with him. Don't come out, no matter what happens."

She was crying when he pulled her arms from his neck. He kissed a tear from her cheek, then whirled and trotted out the front door. Glancing to the rim of the valley, he found the lane empty. For now. He broke open the double-barrel twelve gauge and thumbed two shells into the openings. When the gun snapped closed, he rested it beside the gate in the wall and drew his .44 to check the loads, working the muscles in his cheeks unconsciously as his temper started to rise. Frank Taggart and his men would not hand down any ultimatums at the Valdez Ranch today, he promised himself. There would be blood on the ground before that happened.

He heard Stiles hurry from the barn, his boots clumping over the caliche. Trey made up his mind to keep the gambler out of the fight. Stiles had shown him a favor, riding out to give the warning that Taggart was coming, and that was enough of a risk for a man who had no involvement in the controversy.

245

Stiles was out of breath when he reached Trey.

"Come inside," Trey said, motioning the gambler toward the front door. "If you insist on helping, then wait near the door, to make damn sure none of Dolan's men get inside where they could harm Maria or her family. If something happens to me, make sure nobody gets inside the house. You'll be doing me a favor."

Stiles followed Trey to the porch. "If any shooting starts, I can back you up from here," the gambler said.

Trey ignored the gambler's promise and showed him through the doorway. "Stay here, and keep out of sight," he said. "I can handle most anything they throw at me."

Stiles put a hand on Trey's shoulder, forcing Trey to pause before he went back outside. "There's too many of them for one man to handle by himself, Trey," he said quietly.

Trey met the gambler's stare with one of his own. "Kinda depends on who the man is," he said coldly. "They've never tangled with me before, and if they do, I can promise them they'll regret it."

Trey walked out and sighted the rim again. Back of the rim, he could see a cloud of dust arising from the lane. "Ride in, Mr. Taggart," Trey whispered, clenching his teeth. "I'm about to teach you some goddamn manners your mama forgot to show you."

He walked to the gate and stood within easy reach of the shotgun, to await the arrival of the Dolan men. Powerful muscles bunched, then relaxed, in his arms and shoulders. Flexing the fingers on his right hand, he prepared as best he could for the moment when some fool decided to go for a gun against him. The mood Trey found himself in now, it would be a fatal mistake.

Five horsemen trotted over the valley rim and started down the lane toward the house. Trey's mouth went dry as he spread his feet slightly apart, dangling his hand near the butt of his .44. A mad excitement swelled up in his chest long before the riders neared the adobe wall. By the time Trey recognized Taggart riding at the front of his men, Trey's anger had risen to a full boil, a slight tremor entering his fingertips as he waited for Frank Taggart to make his threat against the Valdez Ranch.

The five men halted their horses a few yards from the opening and waited for the dust to settle around them. Trey's stare was fixed on Taggart's face, figuring how it would go when the gunplay erupted, as Trey knew it would. He would see to it himself.

"I do believe you're that feller with the smart mouth," Taggart began; then he glanced sideways, to his men. "This is the feller who made all them smart remarks, about how him an' me would settle things sometime." Taggart turned back to Trey, then chuckled. "Now'd be as good a time as any," he added, putting menace in his voice.

Trey forced a slow grin, drawing his lips back across gritted teeth. "Suits the hell outta me, Taggart. You're a goddamn coward who needs four friends to back his play. But I don't give a damn how many men you bring with you. Mainly because I'm gonna kill you first, if you go for a gun. State your business here, and then get the hell off this ranch or I'll hang you up by your boot heels and let your friends watch you dangle."

Taggart's eyelids hooded. "You're a fool, cowboy, whoever you are," he said. "The feller to my right is Buck Jones, an' he can kill you a'fore you can blink. Right next to Buck is Billy Barlow, an' he ain't no slouch with a gun either. If I give the order, my men will gun you down, and that'll be the end of you."

Trey eyed the man named Buck Jones, just a quick glance. Jones carried an ivory-handled gun low on his leg. Barlow's gun was tied high around his waist, and Trey knew he would be much too slow. A quiet moment passed; then Trey spoke. "I warned you once, Taggart, and I never warn a man twice. State your business and then get the hell off this ranch."

Taggart stiffened. "Tell ol' Porfirio this is his last chance to sell his cattle. Otherwise, he ain't gonna have any cattle to sell."

Trey shook his head back and forth. "Tell Tom Catron and Jimmy Dolan that the Valdez calves ain't for sale. Not to the likes of them. And if anything happens to cattle around this ranch, or if any of them come up missing, I'm coming to Santa Fe to look you up personally, Taggart. I'll kill you, and that's a promise."

Now Taggart's cheeks turned hard. Cords of muscle stood out in his neck. "You're a damn fool, cowboy," he said. "You're askin' to be sent to a grave."

Trey tensed the fingers of his right hand, for he sensed that the time had come. "Clear out, Taggart," he said hoarsely. "You got the answer to your question, now ride!"

Taggart cast a sideways glance at Buck Jones; then he gave a slight nod of his head. Jones' bearded face parted in an evil grin as his hand started toward his pistol.

Trey pulled and fired in one fluid motion, stepping back a half step as the .44 exploded in his fist. The bullet struck Jones in the throat and jerked him backward before his gun cleared leather, toppling him over the rump of his frightened horse. The roar of Trey's gun had just begun to die when Trey aimed for a man to the left of Taggart and fired again. The slug made a cracking noise when it slammed into the man's ribs and went through his chest, then out his back in a shower of crimson rain.

Horses bolted away from the adobe wall, whickering, trying to flee the bang of Trey's gun. Riders clawed for their saddle horns in the confusion, struggling to stay aboard churning, swirling mounts. It was all the time Trey needed.

Trey aimed for Frank Taggart; then he hesitated, for his sights fell on Taggart's back. Taggart was spurring his horse away from the wall as hard as he could, trying to make his escape from the melee. Trey wouldn't shoot Taggart in the back; he swung his Colt to a cowboy aboard a rearing bay horse, for a gun flashed sunlight in the cowboy's hand.

Trey fired, and the gun slammed into his palm, spitting out its life-stopping load. The cowboy gave a sharp cry and pitched sideways out of his saddle. Trey watched the gunman land hard on the barren caliche . . . the gun clattering to the ground beside him. Galloping hooves muffled the gunman's groan; then his arms and legs went still.

Two men spurred furiously away from the house: Taggart and the man he called Billy Barlow. Remaining in a battle-ready crouch, Trey swung his gun barrel over the fallen men cautiously, until his sights came to rest on Buck Jones.

Jones sat up with his hands clasped around his bleeding throat. Blood spilled between his fingers down his shirtfront, pooling in his lap. Jones' eyes were walled white with pain. The other two gunmen lay still, the way all men did when death took them.

Trey walked over to Buck Jones, leveling his gun in Jones' face. "You were too damn slow," Trey said, feeling his anger begin to subside when he glimpsed Taggart and Barlow racing up the lane out of the valley.

Jones coughed. Blood squirted from the hole in his neck when he expelled air from his lungs. Then his eyes focused on Trey, and the look was pure hatred.

"You're finished," Trey said quietly. He walked over to Jones' pistol and stuck it in his belt.

Stiles came trotting out to the fence with his gun

drawn. He looked down at Buck Jones, then the pair of dead men. "I saw what happened," the gambler said, looking at Trey then. "Jesus. I never saw a man so fast at the draw. Back when I told those posse men and the soldiers about you, I was merely having a little fun with them. I had no idea that I was telling them the truth about you."

Trey holstered his Colt and glanced in the direction of the barn. "The truth about me is real simple, Mr. Stiles," he said, speaking in a faraway voice. "I'm not a gunfighter, but I won't let another man push me, or push any of my friends. There are three men lying near you who would attest to that fact, if they could. I have one more bit of unfinished business with those men from Santa Fe. A message I aim to deliver to Thomas Catron. I'd be obliged if you'd stay here while I make the ride to town. I won't be gone long."

Worry darkened the gambler's eyes. "You can't just walk in Catron's office and threaten him," Stiles said.

Trey's features darkened. "Who says I can't?" he asked, starting for the barn.

The lawyer's plush offices and his waiting room for clients were furnished with expensive chairs, where three men in business suits sat, smoking cigars. Mahogany tables bore a layer of fresh wax. Trey walked through the door into the waiting room, a door that read, "Thomas Catron, Attorney At Law." Trey walked up to the desk of an appointment secretary and spoke in a low voice. "Which office is Tom Catron's?"

She pointed to a heavy oak door. "That one," she replied, "but you can't go in. He's with a client."

Trey turned away from her desk and walked to the door she had indicated. He opened it and walked into a room lined with bookshelves, to a large desk where a dark-skinned man with fleshy cheeks sat, his jowls puckered by a white paper shirt collar.

"You can't come in here like this," Catron said, scowling with annoyance. "Can't you see I'm busy?"

A slender man in a vested suit sat across from Catron's desk, hands folded atop a leather briefcase.

"Like hell I can't," Trey whispered, lowering his face until his nose almost touched Catron's. Then Trey drew his Colt .44 and stuck the barrel of the gun into Catron's open mouth. Trey cocked the hammer gently. The click was an ominous sound in the silence of the office. "I'm going to give you some advice," Trey said evenly, his lips drawn back as he spoke. "Tell your men to stay away from the ranch of Porfirio Valdez. Tell Dolan and Taggart. Make sure they understand that if anyone shows up at the Valdez Ranch with a threat about selling his calves to you, I'll kill both of them, and then I'm coming to Santa Fe to kill you. Make no mistake about my intentions, Catron. I'll splatter your brains all over this office wall if just one more gunman shows up at that ranch."

Catron's eyes bulged. He tried to speak, but the gun muzzle distorted his words. But Trey only nudged the weapon deeper into Catron's mouth.

"I just killed three of your hired guns," Trey hissed. "A man Taggart called Buck Jones, and two more. I'd have killed them all, only they rode away like a pack of yellow cowards. Listen to me closely, Catron, because I never warn a man but once. If you send anybody else to the Valdez Ranch, I'm coming after you."

Slowly, Trey withdrew the gun from Catron's lips. Catron swallowed. Beads of sweat had formed quickly on his forehead in spite of the coolness in the room.

"I understand," Catron said softly. "Porfirio can

sell his cattle to whoever he wants."

Trey gave Catron a quick nod. "You're bein' sensible, Catron," he said, dropping his gun back in its holster. He turned for the office door, then stopped. "I hope you are a man of your word," Trey added softly. "Because I goddamn sure am, and the proof will be headed back to Santa Fe tomorrow morning, so the three of them can be fitted for coffins."

He stalked out of the office, then out to his horse, with his mind made up to stop at a store along the way so that he could buy a bottle of good whiskey.

Chapter Twenty-Six

Riding through the pines, protected from wind-driven sleet and spits of tiny snowflakes, they came to the edge of the spring pool and swung down from their saddles. Above the top of the ravine, a raw wind howled, sweeping sheets of snow and ice over the falls. It was the first snowstorm of winter. And the first day of the month of December.

Trey loosened the cinch on his roan, taking note of the gelding's thickening winter coat of hair. Maria's black had begun to put on long hair, too. She pulled the latigo strap and let her saddle cinch hang loosely under her horse's belly.

Trey pulled off his gloves and walked down to the edge of the pond. A thin layer of ice had already formed around the edges of the spring. Last night's bitter cold had begun its work.

Maria came up beside him and stood for a time, looking at the pool, then the falls. A smile crossed her face; then she turned to Trey and touched his cheek. "It is so quiet here," she said. Only the sounds of falling water interrupted the silence around them.

Trey looked up at the falls. "That storm will dump a pile of snow down here before morning," he said. "Looks like this blue norther will be a bad one.

Probably won't be able to come back here until the spring thaw."

Maria shook her head. She looked at Trey. "Will you be here when the snows melt?" she asked.

He stared across the pool a moment, considering his options. "I've thought about it a lot," he said. "Wondering what I oughta do this winter."

She showed worry on her face. "What have you decided?" she asked.

He took a deep breath. "The trouble is over here at the ranch," he began. "Catron and his men won't be bothering you any longer. I hear they've got their hands full with those Regulators down around Lincoln. Stiles told me that a boy named Billy Bonney has gone to work for Chisum, stealing cattle back from Dolan. Folks down there call him Billy the Kid. I figure the warning I gave Tom Catron will keep him from rustling cattle from your herd." Trey turned to Maria then. "So, I'm not really needed around here."

Maria shook her head. "But you are needed, Trey. I need you, and so does Carlos."

Trey chuckled. "That's different," he replied.

Maria came closer to him, nestling her face against his chest with her arms around his waist. "I had hoped you would stay," she said.

"I might," he said later, after a silence. "You've got to understand one thing about me, Maria. I've been alone for so long now that I'm not sure I can live any other way. I suppose I've grown accustomed to my solitary existence. I may not be able to make a change."

Her arms tightened around him. "I love you, Trey. Even if you decide to leave, I will still love you."

He lifted her chin with a fingertip, so that her eyes were on his. "That's the most difficult part for me," he whispered. "I love you, but I wonder if I'm cut out to be . . ."

"A husband?" She asked the question with a smile. "My husband, and perhaps even a father to Carlos?"

"I reckon that's it," he said. "I gave up on all that, after Marybeth and Billy died."

Maria's eyes closed. "I can't replace the wife you lost. Nor can Carlos replace your son. But we both love you, if that makes any difference."

"It does," he sighed, thinking. "I'd be a fool to ride away from a beautiful woman who loves me. And the boy needs a father, although I'm not the right man for the job."

She snuggled her face against his chest again. Her arms held him close to her. Above the falls, the wind gusted, and the rattle of sleet pattered on the stone cliffs. "I have never loved another man," she said. "I can only judge by the way I feel about you. I want you to stay."

He gazed down at her then. "If it didn't work out . . . if I got the old urge to move on, it would only make things worse."

"Perhaps," she whispered, above the howl of the wind. "I would never want to give you up."

He had given a lot of thought to his circumstances over the past few weeks. "Maybe I'll stay until spring," he said quietly, staring past the spring pool. "If things work out between us this winter, I could make up my mind after it thaws."

Her face was beaming when she looked at him. "I love you, Trey Marsh," she said. "If that makes a difference, you'll stay." She stood on her tiptoes to kiss him. Her lips were wonderfully warm when her mouth covered his.

Later, he glanced up at the swirling snow and told himself that being with Maria was what he really wanted. Old habits were hard to break, but when he held this beautiful woman in his arms, he knew the urge to ride toward another horizon was a part of his past.